TO THE REPUBLIC: BOOK ONE

FRACTURED NATION

A NOVEL

KURT WINANS

OPEN WINDOW

Livonia, Michigan

Cover design, interior book design,
and eBook design by Blue Harvest Creative
www.blueharvestcreative.com

Published by Open Window
an imprint of BHC Press

Library of Congress Control Number:
2016909956

ISBN-13: 978-1-946006-54-7
ISBN-10: 1-946006-54-8

Visit the author at:
www.kurtwinans.com &
www.bhcpress.com

ALSO BY KURT WINANS

THE NEW WORLD

Pilgrimage
(Book One)

Second Moon
(Book Two)

Evolution Shift
(Book Three)

TRAVEL BOOKS

College Football's American Road Trip

ACKNOWLEDGMENTS

Our American society and the government structure under which we reside receive my first thankful acknowledgement, as it would be foolish of me to not recognize how important both aspects were to the creation of this work. In terms of grand scale we live in a country on the global map that permits its citizens, under most circumstances, to voice their opinion and have open discussion about what we individually deem to be problems or challenges within our ranks. We as that society are not perfect, nor should we be so arrogant as to believe otherwise, but we are allowed to write books that may bring some of those imperfections into question without fear of repercussion such as being tortured or sent to the gallows for doing so.

The countless members of our armed forces, both past and current, deserve recognition for their assistance as well. They continue to provide a blanket of security which helps to maintain our way of life, and I have the upmost respect for each and every one of those brave men and women that serve our nation. To that end, I owe a special thanks to a friend of mine. He has asked me to list him simply as Richard H., U.S. Army 1982-2006, Combat operations. Through many discussions, he helped me to properly list certain military terms such as equipment or weapon identification that I mention within the body of this work.

Finally, I would like to thank my wife Cathy. As per the norm, she has stood by me during the entire pursuit of this most recent endeavor. Cathy showed patience during the sometimes frustrating moments, and joyful support during the many triumphant hours. I could not have done this without her.

And now, it's time to get on with the show.

Kurt

FRACTURED
NATION

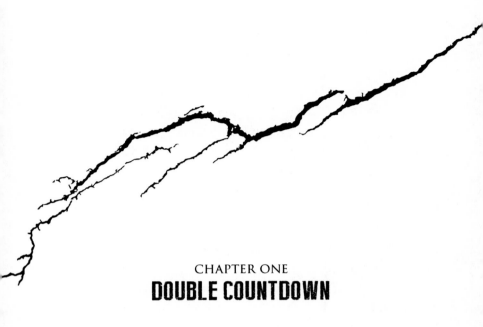

CHAPTER ONE
DOUBLE COUNTDOWN

With a prime viewing position successfully staked out several hours before, the group of five men tightened their protective circle around little Savanah as the massive crowd pressed inward. Each of those six souls were now only minutes away from earning their reward for having braved the cold snowy night, and the ever mounting level of craziness that currently surrounded them.

Glancing down at Savanah, a smart and inquisitive soon to be eight year old blonde, Samuel H. Tillman asked, "How are you doing sugar?"

With bright green eyes and an infectious smile she looked up from under the brim of her new cowboy hat to reply, "I'm fine grandpa."

Then her father, Kyle Tillman, placed his hands on Savanah's shoulders and asked, "Are you still warm enough honey?"

"Yes daddy, but I can't see anything with all these people around."

"Don't worry about that Savanah. Your grandfather promised that you could sit on his shoulders to see the big event, and he never goes back on a promise."

A short time later, with the snowfall finally beginning to lighten up, Samuel pulled the burn phone from the right pocket of his heavy winter coat to check the time. It read eleven forty-eight, so he turned to the oldest of his five grandchildren, who had just days before celebrated his momentous twenty first birthday, and said, "It's almost time Jason. Will you lift your sister up onto my shoulders please?"

"Yes sir, just tell me when you're ready."

Then Samuel looked at the two staff security personnel he had brought along from Texas and said, "We will do this in a simple box pattern around me while Savanah is up on my shoulders, and I want the two of you behind us. Kyle and Jason will cover the two forward positions."

A simple nod of comprehension from each man provided confirmation that Samuel's directives would be adhered to. Then with a tip of his favorite well-worn cowboy hat he smiled down toward the youngest of his grandchildren.

Savanah looked up at her hero and asked, "Is it almost time grandpa?"

"Yes it is young lady, and if you will do me the honor, Jason will help you climb onto my shoulders so that you can see everything."

After an approving nod, she was lifted high into the air by her oldest brother, as Samuel flexed the knees of his six foot three inch frame a bit to receive her. Then Jason took his position as the forward left sentinel and braced to hold his ground. As if Mother Nature had then responded to a collective plea, the snow stopped falling just a few minutes before midnight and the final countdown began. Thousands of other citizens joined in with Savanah as she counted backwards from ten with enthusiasm, and then the illuminated ball dropped signifying that the Eastern Time zone of the United States had just begun the year of 2026.

With confetti then swirling around her head and in the sky above, Savanah laughed joyously. After several minutes she reached down for the giant gloved hand that firmly grasped her right ankle and exclaimed, "You were right grandpa, this is really fun!"

Samuel, a strong and still physically fit man of sixty-six, replied, "Well I'm glad that you like it sugar, and you can stay up there on my shoulders for as long as you like."

The massive crowd remained in a joyful feverish pitch as they celebrated the dawn of a new year, and wouldn't begin to show noticeable signs of thinning for nearly another hour. During that time Savanah never stopped smiling, so her grandfather knew in his heart that he had done the right thing. She had now witnessed the Times Square New Year's Eve event in New York City, and depending on what the future brought forth, it may have been her only opportunity to do so. While maintaining their protective box formation around Samuel and his granddaughter, the group slowly moved through the crowd toward the Premier Hotel on west 44th. Although it was only steps away from their staked out viewing position, the time had advanced to nearly one thirty before they stood in front of the lobby entrance. Once they had moved inside to the safety of that lobby, Jason lifted his sister from their grandfather's shoulders and placed her gently on the ground with a smile and a high five.

A moment later the elderly family nanny and cook, Ms. Holloway, moved toward them. She had been around the family long enough to have helped Samuel and Victoria raise their three sons, Kyle, Mason, and Chance, followed by each of the five grandchildren that had come along since. In recent times Ms. Holloway had taken extra care to ensure little Savanah's safety, as she now understood that her own advancing age and declining health would prevent her from attending to the needs of the next Tillman generation. Having done a masterful job with her numerous duties throughout the decades, and exhibiting unwavering loyalty toward the Tillman family in the process, the insightful woman deserved and received the upmost respect from every member of that family and those who were employed by them.

After wishing Savanah a happy new year, and then extending the same courtesy to her employer and the other four gentlemen, Ms. Holloway prepared to whisk Savanah away to the sanctity of their suite. Already socialized by her nanny in the graces of how a southern lady should behave when parting company, Savanah provided a verbal thank you to each of her five gentlemen escorts. Then she gave her grandfather, father, and oldest brother a hug and a kiss on the cheek before departing for a long blissful sleep.

Seconds after watching the ladies enter the elevator, Samuel turned toward the members of his most loyal inner circle and said, "I would also like to thank each of you for helping to make this evening a reality for Savanah, and I believe that it's time for the five of us to have a drink. We need to celebrate the undertaking of this New Year."

His eldest son Kyle, a man of forty one who mirrored his father's height and physique, replied, "I think that's a great idea sir."

Pulling a flask from the breast pocket of his coat, Samuel handed it to his grandson and said, "It would be foolish of me to believe that this will be your first drink of whisky Jason, but it's the first opportunity that your father and I have had to share one with you since you reached the legal age."

Never wanting to be dishonest with his grandfather, Jason replied, "Thank you sir, and you are correct, this is not my first whisky. However, this whisky will have more significant meaning for me than any that I have had in the past. I have looked forward to sharing a drink with you and dad for a long time, and now here we are. What should we drink to?"

"That's a good question Jason. Perhaps we should all contribute a thought to that as you pass my flask around the circle. Don't be shy gentlemen, if you want to drink to something specific, please feel free to speak your mind."

As the flask reached the conclusion of the second rotation, Samuel passed it once again to his grandson. Then he said, "You can finish the last of that Jason, but only if you can provide one final toast."

Reaching for the flask Jason replied, "That seems fair enough sir. I suggest that we toast to the success of the overall plan."

The intent was well received by his four companions, as they collectively agreed that the goal to which he spoke was of paramount importance. Now approaching two o'clock in the morning on the east coast, Samuel pulled the burn phone from his coat pocket again and dialed one of the few numbers that it contained. Speaking softly he said, "This is number two. I'm in the apple with a few of the other players and Savanah, but I plan to be home in less than a week. I hope that when the dawn of the year we have all been waiting for reached you, a festive celebration began at your location. Now we can all commence with our own lengthy countdown towards a brighter future. Are you and the members of your team still on schedule, and fully prepared to move forward?"

CHAPTER TWO
A WORM IN THE APPLE

After enjoying the majority of his winter break for the holidays with the entire family in Texas, and then the final few days of the time off in Manhattan with a lesser portion of them, Jason returned to the rigors of his present calling. On Saturday January third 2026 he bid a temporary farewell to Savanah, and her escorting entourage, while they all stood on the departure curb at La Guardia airport. Then having seen them all move inside to begin the tedious process for their commercial flight to Dallas Texas, and Samuel's separate flight to Denver Colorado, Jason climbed into a taxi that had just unloaded a few other holiday travelers.

As with previous journeys the taxi ride was slow but adventurous, so Jason was relieved to not be at the wheel. When the taxi eventually did make its way through the frustrating level of traffic back into central Manhattan, the driver dropped his faceless fare off at the directed location of Grand Central Terminal. With advance ticket already in hand due to the courtesy of his grandfather, Jason surveyed the massive departure screen to learn of the appropriate boarding platform. His train bound for the United States Military Academy at West Point and points beyond would depart in less than an hour, so he made a visit to the gift shop and picked up some snacks for the journey. What he didn't realize as he subsequently made his way toward the boarding platform was that he had been singled out as a vulnerable target.

While standing in patient solitude on the platform before it was time to board, Jason studied the movements and habits of others who were destined to ride on the same train with him to various stops along the line. Then his reactive speed was suddenly put to the test, as he heard a thunderous voice from behind him. In what had become an instinctive habit of extreme socialization, or academy brainwashing as some would refer to it, Jason snapped to attention when an unfamiliar voice inquired, "Cadet, what do you have in your hand?"

Within an instant of snapping to, Jason replied with the compulsory "Sir", followed by the explanation of, "Just some food for the train ride sir." Then he waited for identification and instruction from the mystery voice. As neither came his way throughout an extended pause, he realized that there had been a definitive break in a well-established and time honored protocol. Jason began to wonder what was happening, but the question, and his posture, was then put to ease when a local New Yorker came into view from behind with a playful smile on his face.

Jason believed that the overweight, unshaven, and sloppily dressed man appearing to be in his mid-forties could not have been affiliated with the military in any way. That suspicion was instantly verified when he heard, "Sorry about that buddy, but it's just too easy with you cadets. My name is Nick Spano, and I'm from Highland Falls. I have been pulling that particular gag, and several others, on West Point cadets whenever the opportunity presents itself for about twenty years now. I still remember the first kid in your current position. He was in his plebe year, and his voice had the drawl of somewhere in the south. I'll never forget his name either as it was quite bizarre, I mean who names their son Chance? Well anyway, most of the time when I pull this gag the result has been just like his and yours. You all blindly snap to attention without even knowing the reason why you are doing it."

Thinking inwardly that while the antics of Mr. Spano were just one more example of why there had been a need to initiate the overall plan, they also didn't warrant an extreme reaction such as a martial arts takedown at the present time. With that in mind Jason's response to the man's statement began somewhat measured and jovial, but he was prepared to alter that approach if need be. He didn't want to provide the civilian with any level of respect for his lack of ingenuity, or to further enable his quirky habit by referring to him as sir. With a now fully relaxed posture, Jason replied, "It's alright Mr. Spano, but the gag is a bit overdone don't you think? I mean, you don't actually believe that you are the only person to use that trick on cadets throughout the past twenty years, do you?"

Having been somewhat taken aback by the candid response of the cadet, Nick Spano began a reply of, "Well I…"

Jason didn't give him the opportunity to advance any further and verbally cut him off at the knees. With a slightly escalated tone he snapped, "Save it mister, your explanation would be meaningless to me! As for cadets coming to attention without knowing the reason why, you're incorrect. We all come to attention as a show of respect for those who have earned it. You can rest assured however, that you would have never received such a response from me if you had approached from where I could have seen you as opposed to creeping up on my blind side."

With that the smile went away from the intrusive man's face, and he replied, "Well, look what we have here. That's the first time that I can remember any cadet defiantly talking back to me and being tough minded enough to defend their actions. You must think that you are something special kid."

"No Mr. Spano, I don't think that I'm special. I will however stand up for my actions and those of other cadets without reservation. I doubt that you have the slightest idea of what is required of a cadet at the academy, or anywhere else for that matter, on a daily basis. From the looks of you Mr. Spano, you couldn't survive a single day within the confines of our rigorous schedule either physically or mentally. Now you certainly don't have to respect me, but it could be foolish on your part to disrespect me!"

Feeling rather insulted, the man instinctively tensed his right arm to strike. Then he glanced around to see that several other civilians had taken an interest in the escalating discussion. Sensing that this was not the proper time or place for a physical altercation, he relaxed his arm and said "That sounded like a threat you little punk, and when we meet again, I will take great joy in pummeling you as we discuss it."

Then the man moved further on down the platform, and Jason retreated a few paces in the opposite direction to create additional distance between them. Even with that, he kept an eye on the actions of Mr. Spano out of fear for any repercussion that might result from their candid exchange.

Having witnessed the entire event, and sensing the tension that lingered, another West Point cadet who had followed the civilian at a safe distance onto the platform then moved toward Jason. Speaking softly he said, "Don't worry about that guy; he did the same thing to me a few minutes ago under the big departure screen."

Glancing to his right Jason saw the uniform of a fellow cadet and replied, "I'm sorry to hear that. People like that man have no respect for those in the military, or what we as cadets have to endure on a daily basis. He should be put in his place by someone who has more authority than me."

"I agree with your assessment, but it's doubtful that will ever happen."

Now paying less attention to the heavyset man further down the platform, and more upon his fellow cadet, Jason noticed that he wore both the first class insignia of a senior cadet and the five bar "railroad tracks" on his collar of a Battalion Commander. The cadet was one of the highest ranking members of the corps, so after snapping to attention once again, Jason said, "Sorry sir, I didn't realize..."

"Relax cadet. We haven't reported back to duty at the academy yet, so let's just leave rank out of this entire situation. Besides, there's no need to apologize for anything."

"You aren't going to report me for my actions of a few minutes ago with that civilian?"

"Reporting cadets for every little infraction is not my style of leadership. Besides, even if I were the type to report you, in my opinion there was no infraction. If anything you should receive praise. You did a good job of momentarily curbing that civilian's behavior without allowing the situation to escalate beyond control."

"Thank you for understanding my position. I hope that there will come a day when people like that civilian won't be missed."

"So do I, but unfortunately that time is not yet upon us. Perhaps it will be someday, but for now you did the right thing to say your peace and let it go."

What the senior cadet didn't realize was that Jason hadn't really let it go. Although Jason's internal wheels were still churning over the altercation, and the comments made about an incident of roughly twenty years ago, his demeanor had satisfied the Battalion Commander that everything was fine. Then he capped off the impression of passiveness when he calmly replied, "You're right, nothing will happen today."

A short time later a boarding announcement was made, so the contingent of passengers made their way onto the train and Jason once again bid farewell to Manhattan. Without any doubt the city had provided, and perhaps always would, an endless stream of excitement, but for him the apple was in decay. As such, the teaming and mostly disorganized activity that seemed to never end could only be endured for a few days at a time. Now he could stretch out and relax for a little while in relative comfort without being pushed or bumped into by people with some vital agenda or by those who simply weren't paying attention to where they were going.

As the train pulled away to begin what would become a northerly trek on the western side of the Hudson River toward the United States Military Academy, Jason reflected on how much he preferred a boat ride to West Point on the Hudson instead. In many cases during the warmer months of the year, he had enjoyed such a ride to unwind from the craziness of the apple in the relative solitude of an outside deck location. It was indeed something that could not be attained by taking the train to West Point, and he had spoken with several other cadets who had done the same. Unfortunately even if such a ride were possible during the time of this particular January endeavor, the current temperature in the upper thirties and the accompanying heavy stinging rain would have made an outer deck location far less attractive.

Seated facing his new acquaintance who had invited him to partake in a relaxed conversation, Jason felt that the company of a fellow cadet provided a welcome change to the solitude without becoming intrusive. Throughout the journey the two cadets carried on a discussion covering many topics, and the seeds of what could be a lasting friendship took hold. Jason became well informed as to the background and philosophical beliefs of his new friend simply by sitting back and listening with limited interruption. That strategy had also enabled him to reveal only limited amounts of information regarding his own upbringing or the Tillman family. Jason learned that the Battalion Commanders name was Kevin Flores, and that he hailed from a place called Oro Valley just north of Tucson Arizona. His grandparents had come into the United States from Mexico during their youth, and were proud that they had followed the established protocol to become legalized American citizens. While his parents and other portions of the family resided in Arizona, he also had aunts, uncles, and cousins' who had willfully returned to live in Mexico. Kevin also revealed that he had spent much of his limited free time before attending West Point exploring various mountainous terrains in the American southwest, and was well versed in how to survive in desert climates. Based on that, he expressed a desire after his graduation to be posted at a duty station in a hot and arid location. Kevin's main course of study was focused on reconnaissance with an intended future in the area of air traffic control, as he believed those skills could be of practical use for a career after retiring from military service.

At the conclusion of the train ride, the cadets prepared to disembark with the other passengers. Some were civilian personnel employed by the academy, while others, such as the prankster Mr. Spano, were civilians who lived or worked in the town of Highland Falls just south of the academies Thayer Gate. Jason focused on the actions of the heavyset prankster, and watched the man labor as he walked solo into the distance. More information would need to be gathered to determine if Nick Spano was important enough to bother with, and Jason decided that he would set those wheels in motion shortly after returning to his barracks.

Back on the academy grounds as the two cadets moved to the west from the train station and the Hudson, there would need to be a return to the associated protocol of life at West Point. Now midway through his junior year as a second class cadet, and with the most challenging aspects of academy life seemingly already behind him, Jason wanted nothing but smooth sailing during the upcoming term. Snapping to attention in the event of curious onlookers, he said to his new friend Kevin, "Thank you for the conversation on the way up from Manhattan. If your schedule permits, then perhaps we can find a way to continue our discussions at some point in the future."

Understanding the need for such protocol and that they were sure to run into each other from time to time, as well as being impressed by the way his subordinate cadet had controlled a potentially violent situation, the reply was quick. "Thank you as well. I think that would be a good idea."

With that Jason nodded and waited for the upperclassman to depart. A moment later he headed toward the barracks where he would report in for duty nearly an entire day ahead of the required time for doing so. Later that evening, he took a stroll up the hill toward the academy chapel and Lusk reservoir just beyond. After ensuring that he was alone in the wooded area, Jason pulled the burn phone that his grandfather had given him earlier that day from his pocket. Then while looking across the reservoir toward the empty, dark, and snowbound Michie Stadium, he hit speed dial for the only number that it contained.

A woman's voice on the other end said, "This is number twenty three, is everything alright?"

"Hello number twenty three. This is Jason, and yes, all is well."

"Then why are you contacting me at this time? Your next scheduled report isn't due for several weeks."

"I understand that ma'am, but I have a possible recruit and two requests that could merit immediate consideration."

"I see. Then please proceed."

"Thank you. First, there is another cadet who could become useful with the overall plan as a recruit. He's a first classman of high cadet rank named Kevin Flores, and his hometown is Oro Valley near Tucson Arizona. Preliminary information based on a lengthy interview looks good, but we will need a detailed investigation of him and his family before a determination can be made."

"Understood, and I'll put somebody on it right away."

"Thank you."

"What about the requests?"

"They are related, and may prove to be nothing, but my instinct tells me that they need to be looked into."

"Understood, what do you need?"

"First, could your team gather some information on a man named Nick Spano? He's a civilian that's roughly forty-five years of age who is living and potentially working in Highland Falls New York. He boasts of harassment toward cadets throughout the past twenty years, and I would like to have him repaid for those efforts."

"Understood. Do you feel that the information on this civilian should be treated as a high priority?"

"No, but I would like to be briefed on your findings if possible."

"That's not a problem. And the second request?"

"Can your team research how many plebe cadets named Chance where at West Point during the 2006 - 2007 academic year?"

"That's a strange request, but sure. I'll have the answer before your next contact."

"Thank you, and should that contact still be on the predetermined date?"

"Yes it should. Don't use your burn phone again before then if possible, and contact me on the first day of February."

"I understand and confirm the first day of February."

With that Jason placed the phone in a small zip lock bag, buried it near the exposed root of a tree, and returned to his barracks.

CHAPTER THREE

DENVER, COLORADO

Samuel Tillman exited the underground train servicing the various terminals of the Denver International Airport, and then shuffled along with the mass of other airline passengers. While still buried within a herding formation, he then rode the escalator up toward the main concourse level. Fifteen minutes later Samuel had retrieved his luggage, walked to the predetermined curbside rendezvous point, and waited for his middle son Mason and nineteen year old grandson Beau to arrive. Those two had flown from Texas into the smaller Centennial Airport at greater Denver's southern edge aboard the Tillman family Gulfstream G280 jet earlier in the day. That had been done so Beau, now midway through his second year at the Air Force Academy in nearby Colorado Springs, could report back for duty sometime before Sunday evening.

As Mason pulled up to the curbside in a rental car that had been secured for a few days, Samuel glanced at his watch to verify the punctuality of his descendants. Then as Beau exited the front seat to help his grandfather with the luggage, he smiled and said, "Welcome to Denver sir. How was your time in the apple?"

Returning the smile of his second oldest grandchild, Samuel replied, "It was very nice thank you, and your cousin Savanah seemed to really enjoy herself."

"I'm glad to hear that sir. What about Jason?"

"He was very helpful during our time there as one would expect, but deep down Jason really dislikes Manhattan. It was obvious at the airport this morning that he couldn't wait to get out of there and back to West Point."

"Yes sir, he mentioned to me during the holiday break that he is over the apple."

"That's true enough Beau, but you should understand why. Both of you grew up in a relaxed environment with plenty of open space around you, and you still have a certain feel for that here in Colorado. Unfortunately Jason doesn't share that same luxury, as New York, generally speaking, is much more frenetic. But fortunately for Jason, his requirements there are nearly complete. Now his focus lies more on West Point, and the minimal future exposure to the apple will surely make him happy. Now, how was the New Year's eve celebration back home?"

"It was nice sir, but we all missed having part of the family there."

"Well that's good to hear, and we should all be together at the ranch next year. If our plan comes to fruition, then we will have a New Year's celebration beyond compare."

With Samuels luggage safely stowed in the trunk, the three generations of Tillman men drove away from the congestion of Denver's international airport. After enjoying a day filled with discussion of life at the Air Force Academy, a few nice meals, and events that included a hockey game between the Colorado Avalanche and the Dallas Stars, they retired to their hotel.

On Sunday morning, they awoke to discover that a storm had covered the surrounding area with a fresh blanket of snow, and a more significant amount was due later that afternoon. Although his Texas upbringing had not prepared him for the somewhat slippery conditions, Mason drove them south towards Colorado Springs to the best of his ability. The journey of slightly more than fifty miles along the snow covered interstate - 25 toward the Air Force Academy gave them plenty of time to chat about the overall plan, and how Beau could be an instrumental part in the success of that plan if Colorado did indeed come into play.

As they approached the northern gate to the academy grounds, a sentry motioned for them to slow. With no sticker on the window to identify that those within could be officers, faculty, or civilian employees, he motioned for the driver to stop and lower his window. Looking inside and seeing a cadet in the back seat, the sentry said to Mason, "Good morning sir."

Mason replied in kind, "Good morning to you as well."

"What is the purpose of your visit today sir?"

With a motion of his thumb back over his right shoulder, he said, "I'm returning my son from the holiday break so he can report for duty."

Then looking over toward Samuel, the sentry asked, "And who are you sir?"

Samuel looked at the sentry with a smile of pride and said, "I'm the cadet's grandfather."

After standing upright for a brief instant to signal another sentry, he peered back into the vehicle and said, "I understand gentlemen. Would you please pull over to the right and stop next to the sentry with his arm raised. A bus will be along shortly to return the cadet to his barracks."

Without looking toward the second sentry, Mason replied, "I understand, and thank you."

"You're welcome sir, have a nice day."

Once parked at the designated drop off zone, Samuel reached into a pocket of his coat to retrieve a new burn phone. Then he turned slightly so that he could see his grandson, and said, "Here's a new burn phone for you Beau. It's just like the one that I gave your cousin Jason yesterday morning, and I will tell you what I told him. I would like you to stick with the protocol that we discussed yesterday by hiding this in a safe place. Gather whatever intelligence that you think could be useful and commit it to memory. Then use this phone to contact number twenty three with your report on the first day of February. She will give you instructions as to what may be required of you, and when further contact will take place. Try not to use this phone at any time other than when number twenty three has instructed you to do so, but if you have some information that could require immediate attention, then don't hesitate to make contact with her."

Reaching for the burn phone, Beau replied, "I understand sir, and I won't let you down."

"Your father and I, along with the rest of the family, all know that Beau. You are a bright young man, and this won't detract from what you are attempting to accomplish here. Please stay focused on your studies to become a future pilot, while maintaining a low profile throughout the remainder of your second year."

A moment later the academy bus arrived as promised, and Beau stepped out to unload his gear from the trunk. As he shook the hand of both his father and grandfather, Beau said, "Thanks for dropping me off, and for everything that we did together yesterday and today."

Then Mason replied, "Good to have you with us Beau. Take care and I'll see you this coming summer."

As Beau confidently strode away from the car, Samuel said, "Alright Mason, let's get on the interstate and head north toward Denver. We have a lot of work to do back home, so we need to get to our plane before the next storm hits."

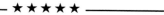

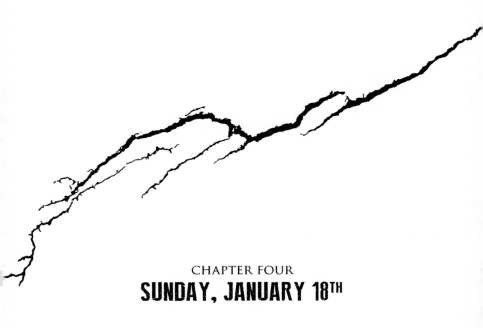

CHAPTER FOUR
SUNDAY, JANUARY 18ᵀᴴ

Savanah smiled with glee as her grandmother Victoria set the cake in front of her. The entire family of grandparents, parents, her older brother Blake, Uncle Mason and Aunt Courtney, her cousin Jennifer, and of course, Ms. Holloway had all just sung her a happy birthday. The only ones who were missing from the event were her oldest brother Jason and her cousin Beau, but Savanah understood that they were both away at school. Although her entire birthday weekend had been fun filled, this was the crowning moment. What made the day even better was that she could stay up late on this Sunday night, as the following day was a school and national holiday in honor of Dr. Martin Luther King's birthday.

After blowing out the eight candles and taking a good look at the cake, Savanah began to laugh. It must have been Blake's idea for the decoration, as her thirteen year old brother was always looking for ways to be creative with numbers. Aside from the candles, there was a big eight in the middle. Both of those made sense for her eighth birthday, but she didn't initially understand the rest of his message. Then she asked him, "Hey Blake, why did you have Ms. Holloway put some ones and eights all over the cake?"

The bright young man hoping to someday follow their parents' and grandparents' footsteps by attending Texas A&M then replied, "Because today is a special day of three ones and three eights. You were born on 1/18/18 and today you are eight. You will have other birthdays that have only ones and eights, like when you become eleven or eighteen, but today is the only time that you will have three of each!"

Running the numbers through her head, and realizing that her brother was correct, Savanah smiled and said, "Hey that's pretty neat. Thanks for thinking of that Blake."

"You're welcome Savanah, and happy birthday."

Samuel was seated comfortably in his favorite chair, with a smile nearly as large as that of his youngest grandchild while he gazed upon the majority of the Tillman family. He was proud to have built them such a marvelous home with plenty of room in the various wings for each faction of the family, and the massive central family room that they all currently occupied was his most favorite spot in the mansion. None of it had come without hard work and a savvy sense of business however, as Samuel had amassed a huge fortune via early oil, cattle, and real estate investments. Then after the dawn of a new century, he and Victoria had parlayed a large portion of their fortune with a move toward the even more lucrative information technology sector that had blossomed and prospered in Austin. Always searching for added diversification, Samuel had also invested heavily in the transportation sector of commerce with trucking, rail, and shipping companies that were now at his command. Those interests, although currently of huge benefit, would become even more so to him and the family during the course of the most recent endeavor and well beyond.

As for the family, Samuel loved each and every one of them for their respective strengths or shortcomings, but most notably for how they peacefully and respectfully interacted with one another. What Blake had done for his little sister's birthday cake was a prime example, and he hoped that the young family numbers whiz had been correct at claiming that Savanah would someday celebrate an eighteenth birthday. While sipping from his coffee and attempting to force the bad thoughts of her health from his mind, Samuel noticed something a little odd. As his wife Victoria was helping Savanah cut the cake, their youngest surviving son Mason stood and moved toward Ms. Holloway. After seeing him whisper into her ear, the elderly woman nodded as if receiving instruction from a superior and took his previous seat close to Courtney. On the surface it would have appeared to be a gentlemanly gesture, but although they were subtle, Courtney showed visible signs of her displeasure in the act.

Later that evening, when many of the family had retired to their respective wings of the mansion, Samuel strolled into the kitchen area to find his wife and Ms. Holloway enjoying a quiet cup of coffee. After receiving an invitation to join them, and pouring his own cup, Samuel said, "I want to thank you for your efforts this weekend Ms. Holloway. As usual everything was excellent, and it was abundantly clear to anyone paying attention that Savanah had a really good time."

"Thank you Mr. Tillman, she is a sweetheart of a young lady."

"She is indeed, and please don't tell any of the others that Savanah is my favorite."

With a wink of her eye and a slight wry smile, Ms. Holloway replied, "I'm very sorry Mr. Tillman, but I'm afraid that I couldn't hear what you just said."

With a nod of approval, Samuel returned her smile and said, "That's excellent dear lady, excellent. Now I need to ask you something, and I apologize if this is uncomfortable or too intrusive. Did Mason disrespect you in any way earlier this evening?"

With a curious look upon her face, she replied, "No Mr. Tillman, why do you ask?"

"Well it looked to me as if he demanded that you take his seat next to Courtney, and if that was the case, then his behavior was improper."

"I understand Mr. Tillman, but that was not how I interpreted his actions. He was rather insistent that I sit next to Courtney on the couch, but I would not have called it a demand."

"So you didn't mind taking his seat?"

"No. I would have preferred to remain standing in the event that Mrs. Tillman or Savanah needed help with passing around pieces of the cake, but I certainly didn't mind sitting next to Courtney."

"Alright, thank you Ms. Holloway. If you're sure, then we will leave it at that."

CHAPTER FIVE
PRESIDENT`S WEEKEND

As part of the envisioned yearlong celebration to commemorate America's two hundred fiftieth year of existence, the mid-February weekend honoring the birthdays of former presidents Abraham Lincoln and George Washington marked another in the intended series of planned events throughout 2026. Although it was true that New Year's Eve had kicked off the year with a grander than usual party, the mid-January birthday of civil rights leader Dr. Martin Luther King Jr. had subsequently become the first in the progression of celebratory milestones.

All three men, each in their own way, had been instrumental figures in American history, and their respective birthdays had become obvious choices when identifying key dates for celebrations throughout the year. Unfortunately the modern society of America was for the most part oblivious as to the accomplishments of each man. Like many of the three day holiday weekends throughout the year, most citizens had no clue as to the true meaning of why the day was being celebrated. With regard to the scope of Dr. King's accomplishments, he had showed tremendous courage and conviction while pursuing and bringing forth necessary changes in the mindset of American society that he hoped would provide equal treatment for all of her citizens. Washington was more commonly known as the father of the country by having been the most notable general in defeating the oppressive British forces during the revolutionary war, and then being elected as the first president of a newly formed nation. Lincoln, like Washington, had also served as the chief executive, but his legacy was based on being the man who held the nation together during the years when a bloody civil war seemed destined to tear it apart. Unfortunately only days after a peace accord had been reached that would preserve the union and enable the nation to once again move forward from that civil war, an assassin's bullet ended Lincoln's life. He, along with Dr. King and several other notable figures throughout American history, had their lives taken from them as a byproduct of their conviction in what they believed to be the correct course of action for the nation. It was only fitting that such men be recognized in perpetuity as those who committed the ultimate sacrifice in quest of a stronger and healthier nation, and Samuel was pissed off that leaders with such moral character had become nearly extinct in America.

For the mid-February celebration milestone, the powers that be within cities and towns all across the nation had brought forth an increased effort with regard to parades, fireworks shows and the surrounding festivities. In many of the southern or less mountainous regions of the country, winter was already beginning to loosen its grip, so the carrying out of such plans became less difficult for the organizers and participants. The collective mindset was to use the event as another step in the buildup and rehearsal process for the grand July fourth celebrations, and then continue with the same increased level of pomp throughout the various holidays of the fall season.

While watching the Washington D.C. fireworks show on the giant holographic wall screen in the comfort of their family room, Samuel said to no one in particular, "There's no way that our current

President, the one before him, or the one before that, would have had the intestinal fortitude or abilities to accomplish what either Washington or Lincoln did while ascending toward, or residing as, the leader of this country. Hell, for that matter I could go back into our history even further. The last person elected to the oval office who had actual frontline military experience resembling that of Washington, or a handful of our other former Presidents, was Bush senior and he left office nearly thirty-five years ago."

Emerging from the kitchen with a tray containing several cups, items that one might add to their coffee, and some cookies, his wife Victoria replied, "That's true enough dear. Unfortunately we don't appear to have any viable candidates for the presidency in the near future from either party who will alter that now well established pattern."

"You're absolutely right, and that lack of true understanding lessons the strength of our chief executive."

Then with a slight quiver in her tone, Victoria added, "I believe that a man or woman in that position should know what the frontlines are actually like before they so easily send others off to battle."

Sensing the discomfort in his wife, Samuel attempted to shift the subject slightly to relieve her strain as Ms. Holloway entered the room with a large pot of strong hot coffee for the group. After she placed it in the usual location, Samuel stated to the collective, "Well, Harwell has nearly three years left in his first term. Perhaps someone with a spine from either party will emerge as a serious candidate before he comes up for re-election in 2028, but in the meantime, Harwell's lack of both a backbone and quick decision making ability could serve us well."

Now seated within a few feet of her husband, Victoria fought back her emotions of the moment before and thanked Ms. Holloway for her help while offering her ageing confidant a seat. As Victoria commenced with her coffee ritual, she was quite pleased to see her second son Mason stand to surrender the seat next to his wife Courtney for Ms. Holloway. Then Samuel knew that his wife was back in form when she seized the opportunity to rib him and their oldest son Kyle with, "Well at least there is still one gentleman among you."

With that Kyle stood and, referring to the coffee cups, asked, "Can I help you pass those around mom?"

"That's an excellent idea, thank you Kyle."

Soon after Kyle delivered a cup to Ms. Holloway, Mason's wife Courtney, and then his own wife Ashley, Samuel asked, "Mason, have you secured a location for the training facility?"

"Yes sir I have. After scouting several possibilities, I have found a location that will be suitable for the various aspects of our needs."

"That sounds good Mason. Tell us more about it."

"It's on a large piece of nearly flat land in a remote southwest portion of the state, so no one will bother our personnel while they use it and the nearby mountain for high altitude training. We will also be able to carve out a small airstrip, and then construct the necessary support facilities with relative ease. Very few people would ever notice, or care, that work is being done."

"We can? That's fantastic. But how did you get permission to do that?"

"Well I haven't yet, but I'm sure that the owner will be agreeable."

"You know that assumptions can be dangerous Mason, especially one of this magnitude. How can you guarantee that the owners will comply with our needs?"

"Because the land was available for purchase, so I took the liberty of doing just that on behalf of the family. Technically, you and mom now own the flat piece of land that I speak of and the easement to it from the distant highway. You are the ones who need to give us permission to build the airstrip and establish a suitable cover for it."

Surprised by the decisive maneuver of his middle son, Samuel reached for the coffee that was being offered to him and replied, "Alright Mason, that's very good. Now tell us about the cover."

"I thought that we could set up our cover as a skydiving school, and that would explain to anyone who was curious as to why so many parachutes would be seen in the area on a regular basis. If they came to investigate, then the large rectangular shaped clearing that had been established within walking distance of the facility could be explained as the intended landing zone."

Looking around the family room to see if anyone had any thoughts on the matter to share, Samuel took a sip of his coffee and broke the silence with, "That is excellent news Mason, well done. I'm proud of you for taking the initiative with regards to the land for the airstrip, and I like the idea of the skydiving school. You should proceed with doing what is necessary to establish that cover and moving forward, but use a name for the facility that won't easily be traced back to the family."

★ ★ ★ ★ ★

CHAPTER SIX
SUNDAY, MARCH 8TH

Strolling into a popular Waffle House located within a highway junction town of Conroe Texas, Samuel noticed three familiar faces waiting for him in the corner booth. After requesting a cup of coffee from the waitress at the counter, he moved toward his friends and sat down. Then he said in a soft tone, "Good morning gentlemen, it's nice to see you again."

Seated immediately to Samuel's right, the most senior of the men replied, "It's nice to see you again as well number two, but why the urgent meeting?"

"I received some positive news yesterday afternoon that needs to be shared with all of you, and I wanted to provide you with as much time as possible to act upon it."

"Alright number two, what do you have?"

"The executives at various networks have agreed that as part of America's continuing yearlong celebration, each of our three possible target locations will have a live television feed during the pregame festivities and the contest itself. Of greater significance, at least from

36

our perspective, is the decision that those festivities would have more of an impact if they were to transpire on television simultaneously. Thanks to their thought process on the matter, we can now plan to move on all three sites."

"That's amazing number two. It has unfolded in exactly the same manner as you predicted, but how could you have possibly known that would happen?"

"Because I helped to plant a seed of potential profit that I knew could not be ignored by the network executives."

The man furthest into the corner of the booth then inquired, "How did you do that?"

After receiving and thanking the waitress for delivering his cup of coffee, Samuel waited for her to depart and replied, "We have had a friend working within one of the networks for several years now, and he has kept me abreast of opportunities that could be exploited. He had noticed a few years ago that although it didn't occur every season, from time to time each of the three locations would host a contest on the same calendar day. As luck would have it, two of the locations were going to host on our preferred day this coming fall. Then using that information to our collective advantage, I urged him to pursue the matter further. When he felt the time was right, he suggested to a superior that this coming fall could present a wonderful opportunity for a live television event."

"That's all it took?"

"Well, that and a little time. You know how the corporate world works, especially in the entertainment business. Someone suggests an idea, and if a superior likes that idea then they run with it and subsequently claim the credit for its conception. In this particular case our inside man pitched his idea to a known greedy corporate climber who possessed both the ability and ambition to contact the administrative offices of each institution. Just like that, the wheels were set in motion. Only one of the locations needed to make a slight alteration to their schedule in order for all three to host simultaneously, and their opponent for that day was eager to oblige when they learned they would in turn receive public recognition for assisting in the process. It was simple really. All they needed to do was flip the respective seasons when each institution would host during the scheduled home and home series."

The last of Samuel's three friends at the table joined the discussion by adding, "That's a clever way to get them to agree."

"Thank you, but our inside man at the network is the one who pitched the idea. He was quite correct when he voiced to me that the one thing that can always be counted on in our current culture is vanity. By offering publicly known credit toward them, the institution who has now become the visitor on that day set events in motion that have played beautifully into our hands."

"That explains the common day for hosting, but what about the start time."

"Once again vanity came into play. Although each of the three locations showed an eagerness to be one aspect of the festivities, none of them wanted the vulnerability of being shown up by either of the others as a consequence of having performed first. The idea of a simultaneous starting time was floated and subsequently agreed upon, so here we are."

"Very nicely done number two. So what time is everything set for?"

"The contest in the mountain zone will begin at one o'clock their time. That will coincide with a three o'clock start for the two locations in the eastern time zone."

The man in the corner stated, "That's a late start in the east for that time of year."

Glancing in his direction, Samuel replied, "True enough, but that could become an advantage during the evacuation process. The daylight savings time that just began this morning will have ended two weeks before the event to create a time change. Combine that with the shorter daylight hours of less than six weeks away from the winter solstice, especially that far north of this location, and the sun will have sunk to a lower position with regards to the western horizon. For the two locations in the east, that could be a hugely significant factor. In terms of attempting to escape the area, the approaching darkness should help each respective group."

The man contemplated what had been presented, gave an approving nod, and then added, "Your right number two, we can benefit from that."

With that Samuel took a sip of his coffee, and changed the subject slightly by stating, "Now then gentlemen, let's discuss what will need to be done in order to hit all three targets effectively. I realize that you have all done a tremendous job with your efforts to remain on schedule, but now we must identify and recruit additional personnel if we are to maximize the impact."

The senior man took the lead once again by asking, "Are you speaking of additional ground personnel?"

Answering to the group collectively, Samuel replied, "Although more of them will surely be needed, that aspect of the operation will continue to be handled by another faction. In your case, please maintain the focus only upon the air personnel. You will need to identify and recruit a total of forty-two individuals with the necessary skill set for the jumps."

"Forty-two, that's a significant escalation in personnel. Why the big change?"

"It seems that the networks have a patriotic idea for their television coverage that will require fourteen parachutes at each location. Although that will cause alterations to our original thoughts, it also provides us with a greater opportunity."

"Alright number two. At the moment we only have the twelve that you initially requested, but we shall do our best to locate an additional thirty."

"Thank you gentlemen, I know that you will. And please, all of you must understand that this is imperative to the overall plan. We have the necessary site for the training facility selected, and machinery is in transit. Your initial twelve recruits and the selected pilots for their training will be sent there shortly to begin construction. What I must be concerned with at the present time, is if the three of you need help in locating the thirty additional recruits. If you believe that you do, then I need to know that right now as opposed to a few weeks or months from now."

After glancing at each other for a few seconds, followed by a collective gentle side to side movement of their heads for verification, the reply was resolute. "There's no need for any additional help number two, we can contact number seven again and tap into the same gene pool that we recruited the current group from. There are many more who could be candidates, so we won't let you down."

With an affirming nod of his own, Samuel replied, "Alright gentlemen. Based on your results in the past, I believe in all three of you and thank you for your extended effort. Please keep me posted on your progress though, as proper documentation will need to be fabricated for each of the additional recruits."

"As you wish number two."

After having another few sips of his coffee, Samuel took three twenty dollar bills from his wallet and placed them in the center of the table before adding, "I appreciate you all coming on such short notice to this out of the way place. Now please allow me to take care of breakfast today gentlemen, and have something hearty before you all get back to work."

"Thanks number two. And since you brought it up, why did you choose this place?"

"There are lots of customers who come through one of these restaurants every day, and as long as you don't drastically over or under tip the waitress, no one will remember our group as anything other than a set of normal customers."

"I understand number two, and don't worry, we will be forgettable."

"Good, and please also keep this in mind. It's the opinion of number one that really matters with regard to your job performance. Although you may never know the identity of that person, I strongly suggest that you succeed with your newly given task."

"Yes number two, we understand."

Then as he stood from the table to depart, Samuel replied, "Good. Now I need to get over to College Station. I have to plant another seed of potential profit with the university administration."

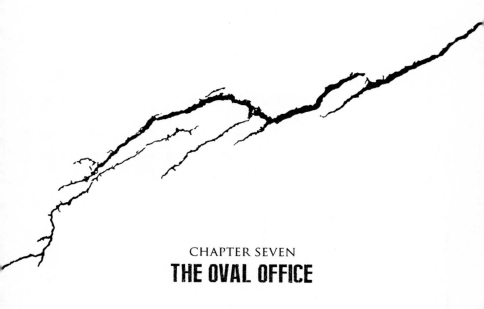

CHAPTER SEVEN
THE OVAL OFFICE

Greeting her boss as he entered the oval office, the President's personal secretary said, "Good morning sir, did you sleep well?"

"Yes I did thank you. How are you feeling today Mrs. Dawson?"

"Very well sir, thank you. Before we go over your schedule for the day, I have just received a phone call from the office of the Commandant at the Naval Academy."

While glancing at the files that had been laid upon his desk, President Jordan Harwell inquired, "Yes, and what does she and Annapolis want from me this morning?"

"It seems they are extending an invitation to you sir."

"Well that's nice I suppose, but what for?"

"Yes sir. They are asking you to attend a football game."

Now looking toward his secretary of many years, the President asked, "A football game?"

"Yes sir."

President Harwell understood that the woman currently serving as the commandant of the Naval Academy, who had extended said invitation, was never what one would classify as a sports enthusiast. With that knowledge he sarcastically questioned, "A football game? The Admiral does know that March twelfth is actually in the heart of basketball season doesn't she?"

"Yes sir, I'm sure that she does. Well perhaps not the basketball aspect, but she's assuredly familiar with the current date. I think that the Admiral probably just wanted to beat the others to it."

As Christopher Westin entered the oval from his own office, he heard his boss ask Mrs. Dawson, "Beat the others to it? I'm afraid that I don't know what you are talking about. Could you please elaborate for me?"

"Yes sir. It's concerning the celebration planned at each of the service academies this coming fall. They have all agreed to host a football game with a simultaneous kickoff on the Saturday following Veterans day in mid-November, and I'm sure that each of them will invite you to attend as the Commander and Chief."

Turning to his old friend and current White House Chief of Staff, the President asked, "Did you know about this Chris?"

"Yes sir. Apparently the academies arrived at the decision a few days ago. I just heard about their collective agreement last evening, and I was planning on bringing the matter to your attention today. I agree with the assessment of Mrs. Dawson. Each of the commandants will probably want you to attend their game, and by calling so early this morning, the Admiral has just proven that she believes the same."

"Yes, so it would appear."

"Unfortunately you can only choose one of the academies, and that will most probably upset each of the other two."

After a few seconds of silent thought, the President responded, "Well that's true, but there could be an easy way to eliminate the problem."

"What's that sir?"

"If I do receive an invitation from all three, I will simply decline all of them. I can send the representative of each military branch from the Joint Chiefs in my place."

"Decline them sir? But the event is scheduled for a few days after Veterans Day. As the Commander and Chief of all military forces, you should make a public appearance on that day."

"I agree whole heartedly Chris, but I have a better idea as to where that public appearance should be. I will need Mrs. Dawson to check on something first to see if it's possible, and if so, then we will move forward."

Stepping closer to her boss, Patricia Dawson asked, "What can I do to help sir?"

"Please look up the football schedule of my alma mater for the upcoming season, and if they are hosting a game on that Saturday, then that is where I will make a public appearance."

CHAPTER EIGHT
SUNDAY, MARCH 29ᵀᴴ

Staring at a six by eight foot map of Delaware, Maryland, and Virginia that had just been laid out before them on the office table, Samuel Tillman said to the group of six surrounding it, "Alright everyone. That was good work on the other eastern site, but now that we have finalized our intended plans there, we must turn our attention to the Maryland location. Before we begin though, it should be noted that we don't have an inside source who could provide us with additional up to the last minute intelligence reports. Also of concern is that the intended target is on a separate piece of land from the main body. For those reasons, I personally believe that the Maryland site could be more challenging for us than the New York location with regard to the necessary logistics."

Directly across the table from Samuel, one of his six most trusted members of the organization said, "I agree with your assessment number two."

"Thank you. Now the good news is that the Maryland location will be easier to figure out than the Colorado location. That unfortunately will be a nightmare for us to plan, so we will put that off until we have these logistics ironed out."

Another of those who were surrounding the table then asked, "With regard to Maryland, do you have specific thoughts on how we should proceed, or are you open to suggestion?"

"As with our discussions regarding either of the other two sites, this is an open forum."

"Since that is the case, I would like to propose an escape route to the east."

After a quick glance back toward the map, Samuel replied, "That is certainly one possibility, but please tell me why they should go east?"

"Well number two, I believe that they could obtain total surprise by doing so. With limited highway or road options to the east, no one would expect our team to travel in that direction."

Looking around the table at each of the other five, Samuel asked, "Does anyone have a thought in reply to this suggestion?"

Pointing with his finger at a specific spot on the map, the man immediately to Samuel's left replied, "With all respect to our friend, I don't believe that would be our best option. After escaping from the attack zone, our team would need to access highway-50 and travel eastward for roughly eight or nine miles before coming to a toll plaza for the bridge crossing over the Chesapeake Bay. That could present several problems, which could lead to the capture of both the ground and air personnel."

The man who had suggested the idea of an eastward escape route had taken no personal offence to the rebuttal, but he did ask, "Could you elaborate on the potential problems that you see?"

Looking across at the man, he replied, "Well first off the bridge could have had a recent accident or heavy weekend traffic heading toward eastern Maryland or Delaware. If so, then that could hinder the escape efforts of our personnel. For that matter, there could be a long line of cars at the toll plaza itself, or if the authorities have acted more quickly than we anticipate, the bridge could be closed due to the recent attack. If either of those scenarios were to transpire, then our team would be gridlocked in the traffic with no hope of escape."

Having listened closely, Samuel intervened by stating, "You make a valid argument, as that bridge is an obvious choke point. Let's assume however that our team does make it across the Chesapeake via the highway-50 bridge, how do you see things unfolding from there?"

"Well number two, it could get worse for them. Unless we set up a plan to evacuate our personnel from some remote location via either the water or air, they would be stuck on a rather large peninsula. There are very limited options for passenger ferries, and some of those would be closed for the winter by mid-November. The only bridge option other than what they had just traversed would be the one heading south toward Norfolk Virginia at the mouth of the Chesapeake. It's roughly one-hundred ninety miles from Annapolis through Salisbury Maryland and on to Kiptopeke Virginia at the north entrance point, with the three bridge spans and two tunnels of the structure measuring another twenty. That's a long way to travel on the peninsula toward a lengthy bridge escape route from it during what we must envision as being a high alert situation initiated by the federal government. I feel that as a result of the attack, a bridge of such strategic importance near the largest Navy base on the eastern seaboard will most assuredly be closely monitored. It could even be closed to automobile traffic by the time that our team arrives. If so, then that would leave only one viable route off of the peninsula by vehicle as backtracking to a position near Wilmington Delaware would be required. Unfortunately that option is well north of where they would have initially come across from Annapolis, so precious hours could be spent while attempting to reach it."

Samuel had listened closely to the breakdown of the challenges that the escaping ground forces could possibly encounter, and had made up his mind because of them. Then while staring with pleasure at his well-prepared friend and planner who had just enlightened the group, he stated, "It's obvious that you have put some advance thought into this scenario."

"Yes number two I have. Our friend is correct, as there would be an element of surprise. Unfortunately that surprise would probably not work in our favor. Therefore the way I see it, a planned escape to the east would be a mistake on our part."

Once again looking around the table for input, Samuel asked, "Can we all agree, based on the information provided by our friend, that we should pursue a course of action other than an escape route to the east?"

A collective mummer of voices could be heard, and the positive nodding of heads from every member of the group could be seen. Then the man who had proposed the idea said, "I agree as well. We should look into other alternatives."

Samuel nodded and said, "Alright, let's see what options are available to the west."

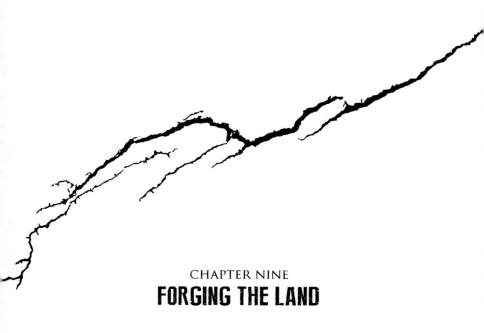

CHAPTER NINE

FORGING THE LAND

As Samuel and his group of attack planners were completing a three day session of tussling about over the best way to approach the challenges of their eastern targets, a group of six recruits flew into the training facility via a twin engine propeller aircraft to be greeted with a rather rough and abrupt landing. They followed the initial twelve recruited jumpers who had come in via bus two weeks earlier to begin work on various aspects of the training facility, and the added manpower was welcomed with open arms. Having arrived ten days after it was learned by number two that all three targets could indeed be attempted, the initial twelve had roughed out a partial airstrip and raised a portion of the tent village. Like those men, the newest group of recruits would be housed in tents and become fully immersed in the camping lifestyle. That would also apply for the twenty-four more that had yet to be secured as recruits, as the intent was to toughen each man up mentally while they also became more physically fit. This was planned with a belief that as the dusty confines of the temporary canvas village became increasingly crowded; there would be added motivation to complete construction of the more modern facilities.

As the plane bounced roughly while also slowing quickly on the short landing strip, one of the recruits said aloud, "I guess the first order of business will be to complete the runway."

His recruiter, who had been a participant in the clandestine meeting with Samuel at the Conroe Waffle House, replied to the entire group, "Sorry about the rough landing, and you are absolutely correct. We have to lengthen the runway another several hundred feet, while simultaneously smoothing out what has already, and will be, carved out of the landscape. Unfortunately when we get a spring rainstorm coming through as was the case yesterday; it can wash away part of what has been built. Once we address the runway issues, we will construct a hangar facility to house the planes and corresponding equipment. That facility will also contain a few large rooms that will house several bunks for sleeping, and a small dining area. The final aspect of construction will be the easiest to complete, as we will clear and outline a landing zone for the jumps with painted rocks that can be easily recognizable from a few thousand feet above. Of course every aspect of what I have mentioned will become simpler for us as our numbers continue to grow."

Another recruit asked, "What will we be using to accomplish all of that?"

"We have a dozer that was used to cut the path for the dirt road in from the highway. That bus over there literally came in the day after the final portion of that road was cut with the first twelve members of your teams, along with the tools and supplies they would need for setting up the tent village. Then the dozer was used to carve out what runway currently exists, and we will continue to have it roll back and forth to compact and smooth out the surface as we clear more brush. That's where all of you come in. You will be assisting the others, as the shrubs and rocks in the area that will become the extended runway will mostly be removed by hand."

After a nod of understanding, another recruit said eagerly, "All right, it sounds like we have a plan in place. Let's stow our gear and get to work."

A week later, on the day after Easter Sunday, another batch of six recruits arrived to a much smoother landing. As the plane came to a stop more than one hundred yards from the tent village, it was impossible for those within to ignore the flatbed truck carrying a load of trusses and stacks of lumber parked close by. With the runway nearing completion, materials had been sent in so that work could begin on the hanger facility. At least for the present moment the schedule had been maintained per the hopes of Mason and number two, so the intended cover of a skydiving school would soon be operational.

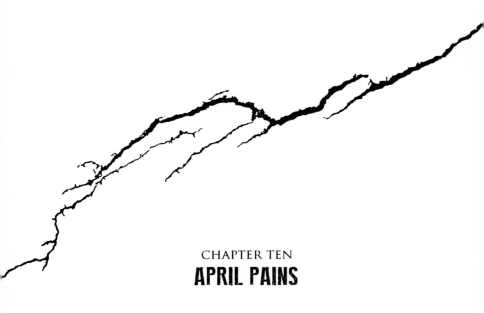

CHAPTER TEN
APRIL PAINS

Seated next to his son Mason, Samuel looked out the window of the Tillman family jet as the plane began final approach. This day, April fifteenth, was his least favorite day of the year, as the federal government mandated tax day continued to search for ways to take a bite out of his hard earned fortune. He and Victoria had been crafty with their finances throughout the years, and with help from some well-educated tax specialists, the federal intrusion had become less of a burden in recent years. Still, the day itself burned at his insides for how the government had required so much of the people, while providing so little tangible evidence of their proper stewardship of the funds that had been garnished from a huge collective of citizens. That perceived mismanagement, accurate or not, was one of several reasons that Samuel, along with many dedicated others, were embarking upon their current quest.

Gazing upon the city that was hemmed by both mountainous terrain and the flat regions through which the Rio Grande River flowed, Samuel realized that several years had passed since his last visit to the El Paso area. In honesty, he couldn't recall why he had last been to the western tip of his birth state, but the intent of his return was to serve multiple purposes. There was a planned face to face meeting with his old friend number thirty one so that future logistics and any intelligence that he and his team had gathered with regard to Fort Bliss could be discussed. That meeting, and subsequent conversations, would take precedence over all other things. Although the massive military base that stretched far into neighboring New Mexico was not significant throughout the early phases of the overall plan, its location would be of strategic importance during the later stages. Samuel and Mason would spend a few days in the area with number thirty one as their guide, and in so doing, learn all that they could about the region for future reference. When confident in the completion of that task, they would visit the land that Mason had purchased for the training facility on behalf of the family in early February.

Feeling a slight bump as their Gulfstream G280 jet touched down, Samuel turned to his son and said, "So you have flown out this way on a few occasions during the past couple of months to meet with number thirty one and visit the training facility. What are your impressions of him and his abilities?"

"You have introduced me to hundreds of people throughout my life dad, and some have been less than genuine, but number thirty one isn't like that. During my limited exposure to him, he appears to be a good man with solid decision making skills and a conviction toward our ultimate goal."

"I'm glad to hear that Mason, because you may be working with him for some time. I have known number thirty one for many years, and I was glad that he was willing to take on the responsibility of being the lead in the El Paso area. If we succeed with all our hopes, then this area of Texas will become extremely important in the future. Our cause will need good people out here, and what you learn from him could be beneficial for that future."

After coming to a stop on the tarmac, the flight attendant opened the door and unfolded the exit stairs. With Mason leading the way, she smiled with a wink and while placing her hand on his arm said, "Have a good time in El Paso Mason."

With a return smile and tone of voice as he moved past her that went well beyond that of a normal courtesy, he replied, "Thank you. I hope you enjoy your time here as well."

Only a few strides behind, Samuel had noticed the flirtation. But he reserved all comment until he and his son were down the stairs and well clear of the aircraft. What he had seen suddenly made him uneasy about Mason visiting the area via the family jet with such frequency. Then while using a subtlety of body language that could not have been detected by their flight attendant from behind at any distance, Samuel said, "Mason, I want you to continue walking at the pace that I set and keep looking straight ahead as I say this. Do you understand?"

Following the instruction, Mason maintained a forward gaze and replied, "Yes sir."

"Good. Now you are my son and I will always love you, but know this. Your mother would be one of several people who would kill you."

After a few seconds of silence, Mason responded, "Kill me for what dad?"

"Don't patronize me by playing dumb Mason. I saw the look that you and our flight attendant gave each other and the way that she stroked your arm. I first noticed a similar, although less obvious, flirtation during our flight home from Denver just after the New Year began. At the time I thought it was innocent enough, or perhaps just my imagination, so I dismissed it. Then I noticed a few times back home when you seized an opportunity to offer others a seat you had occupied next to your wife. There is some tension between you and Courtney to be sure, and coupled with what I just witnessed, you have given me the impression that I was incorrect in my assessment of early January. I now believe that there may be something going on between you and Domonique, and you need to end it before you lose control. Affairs taint everything that surrounds them Mason and the reach of one can go far beyond what most people would believe. If you have been, or are conspiring to be, with that woman, it could jeopardize everything."

"But dad, I haven't…"

Cutting him off quickly, Samuel added, "Deny it if you will Mason, but please listen to me closely. I'm aware that she is an attractive woman who is a little younger than your wife, but this would go way beyond the stupidity of cheating on Courtney and betraying the trust of her and your two children. Domonique has been in the family employ for several years, and has caught the eye of many business associates, both male and female, who have flown with me. In that regard you are not alone in lusting after her, as that list of people has also included your older brother at some point in the past. She has, in her own way, been a valuable and worthwhile tool for this family by flirting with certain individuals that helped close business deals, and even your mother is supportive of keeping Domonique on staff for that very reason. But Mason, all of that changes when it comes to you or Kyle, because we are talking about trust. As a flight attendant Domonique has done excellent work, but has also most assuredly overheard some delicate discussions while serving in her current job capacity. Even though she has been fully vetted by our security staff both before she was hired and during her employ, we don't want to ever provide her with a reason to become disloyal. If you become romantically involved with Domonique and then casually cast her aside, that could lead to a larger problem of attempted blackmail of our family. If such an event were to unfold, then that is when I would be joining the line of those who would kill you for your infidelity."

Realizing that his father's tone and message dictated total seriousness, Mason replied, "I swear to you dad, I have not been with Domonique."

"But you want to?"

"Well sure dad, the thought had crossed my mind. I mean just look at her. What man in his right mind wouldn't want to be with her?"

"Please don't be an idiot Mason, as that question simply answers itself. Any man in his right mind, especially one who has a family and responsibilities of a scope that go well beyond them, wouldn't want to be with her!"

Feeling rather embarrassed at forty years of age for having been called out and scolded by his father, Mason cautiously replied, "I understand sir."

Driving the point home, Samuel was quick to add, "I certainly hope that you do Mason, as there are a few different ways that this can be handled. The best scenario for everyone is that you get a grip on reality and stop flirting with her. That would mean that things could return to the way they were during past years, and I wouldn't need to worry about how Domonique would look at Courtney or your mother when they were using the plane. You don't have to be rude, but if she continues to flirt then tell her to stop. If she doesn't, then inform Domonique that I would like to speak with her about the terms of her employment contract and the lack of professionalism that she is displaying toward my son. A more aggressive approach would be to have you fly to and from El Paso and other destinations commercially as you oversee your particular aspect of the overall plan. If you're not using our family plane, then you and Domonique wouldn't have contact with one another and the problem could be solved. A third option unfortunately isn't as kind, and I would regret needing to go in that direction because she deserves better than what would be a ruthless solution."

"What do you mean by a ruthless solution?"

"I think you know exactly what I'm saying Mason, but I will spell it out for you. Domonique would need to be fired, and based on what I have said about her knowledge of previous discussions on the plane, that would mean that she would also need to disappear."

"Disappear? That seems rather harsh don't you think?"

"Perhaps it is, but not when you fully consider all that is at stake."

After several seconds of reflective thought, Mason said, "Well, I suppose that's true."

"I want you to think clearly Mason, as there's absolutely no supposing about this! Now for the moment it's up to you how we will proceed, and you need to focus on the big picture to help you determine the proper course of action. Please don't create a situation that would cause Courtney, your mother, or your children, to entertain the possibility of you being with Domonique. There should be no doubt on your part that such a romance would be short lived, because I will not hesitate to order a sanction on our flight attendant if necessary. Am I being clearly understood?"

With a gulp of disbelief, Mason replied, "Yes sir, I understand."

"Good. Now I see number thirty one standing just inside the glass doors. Let's keep this conversation between the two of us, and return our focus to the business at hand."

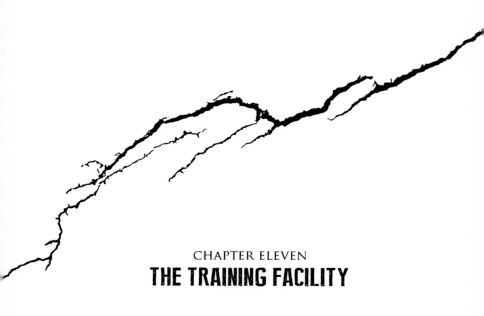

CHAPTER ELEVEN
THE TRAINING FACILITY

T hree days after landing in El Paso for the necessary meetings and scouting with number thirty one, Samuel felt that it was time for him to have a look at the training facility. Although the airstrip had been completed at the site to handle the needs of the jumpers from twin engine propeller aircraft, its length of compacted dirt runway simply wasn't suitable for the Gulfstream G280 jet to land and takeoff. At the advice of his longtime pilot, and having learned that Mason had done the same during both the purchase of the land and the construction of the airstrip, Samuel agreed to use the Pecos County Airport in Fort Stockton as an alternative for landing. Mason had also informed his father that the family owned a vehicle parked at the airport, which would make the ninety minute trip from Fort Stockton comfortable.

Just south of the small town of Alpine Texas, along the desolate highway-118 that led toward Big Bend National Park, Samuel and Mason neared their intended destination. With now less than three miles to go, Mason turned the suburban onto a dirt road heading east. In the distance, rising slightly over six thousand feet above sea level, they could see Bird Mountain. That would be used for high altitude training of the ground and air personnel for several months leading up to the time of their mission, and as a result of scampering about the mountain while forging trails, they would all be in the peak of physical health.

After a somewhat bouncy ride into the area of the facility, Samuel climbed out of the vehicle to see some familiar faces. The three men who had met with him at the Waffle House in Conroe where all standing next to what would soon be a completed hanger facility. While approaching the vehicle, one of them said, "Well hello number two, I didn't expect to see you here."

As the other two were only a few strides behind, Samuel replied, "Hello gentlemen. How are all of you doing this fine day?"

Motioning back over his shoulder, the first of the three said, "We are right on schedule. With help from number seven, the balance of the needed forty-two men will be brought in before the first of May. Everyone has been working well together, and as you can see, the airstrip is in good shape and the hangar facility is almost completed. We anticipate no problems with having the cover of a skydiving school fully operational before Memorial Day weekend."

"That's excellent news gentlemen, and the landing zone?"

"We have a crew working on that as well. Per your specifications, they have already cleared away the brush and smoothed out a large rectangular zone. Then they completed the inner lines of that rectangle measuring three hundred sixty feet by one hundred sixty feet with rocks of various sizes and painted them bright white. As of right now, they are working on the next rectangle that will be six feet outside of the first. When that is complete, they will move to the largest another fifty feet outside of the second."

"How long should that take?"

"Only a few days number two. We now have nearly our full complement of manpower, and those who are assigned to that aspect of the project are gathering the necessary rocks as we speak"

"Excellent, and have you contacted number twenty three to discuss documentation for the recruits?"

"Yes we have, and per your instructions each of the men were photographed before being sent here. Although it will take some time to complete, she will have her team begin the work on the necessary false identities for all of them."

"That's very well done gentlemen, well done indeed. Now, is there any possibility of my son and I having a look at the facility from above?"

"Certainly number two. Just say the word and I'll get one of the pilots to take you up."

"Thank you, and consider that word to be given."

CHAPTER TWELVE
MONDAY, MAY 4ᵀᴴ

G athered around the large office table as they had done several weeks prior, Samuel and the group of attack planners began another taxing session. Staring at a six by eight foot map of Colorado and the fringes of her neighboring states, they faced a daunting task. It was unrealistic to believe that the attacking force striking at the mountain zone site could achieve their goal in the same fashion that had been planned out for the two eastern locations. Additionally, a completely different escape plan would need to be conjured up by the collective brain trust, and in so doing, the need for any support from the ground personnel would undoubtedly be altered as well.

Fortunately Samuel had been working on each aspect of that problem for several weeks, and he believed that he had at least some of the answers that they collectively sought. He opened the meeting by saying, "I would like to remind all of you that this will be an open forum for suggestion as usual, and as the time for us to solve this issue is rapidly ticking away, I recommend that none of you hold back with your opinions."

The man who had exposed and detailed the downside implications of an easterly escape from the Maryland site then said, "Do you have something to lead us off with number two?"

"Yes I do. Per our previous discussions when we ironed out all the attack plans for New York and Maryland, and based on our collective inability to do the same with Colorado, I sanctioned manpower and financial resources into the area to explore possible solutions to our problem. That action has led to the identification of an exploitable situation and a few exchange points which could serve our purposes, but they will require a skill set that we have not yet tapped into."

"What are you getting at number two?"

"Well, per your passing mention of it as a possibility in eastern Maryland or Delaware if we had chosen such a directional escape; I suggest that we incorporate our own air support for the Colorado location."

"That's an interesting thought, but I wasn't really serious with that suggestion."

"That may be, and of course air support won't be needed in Maryland, but I believe that it will be necessary in Colorado."

"And that's where the exploitable situation and exchange points come in?"

"Yes indeed."

"Alright number two; it sounds as if you have a promising start in mind. Fill us in on your thoughts, and perhaps we can all build upon them."

"At this point I only have a small piece of the puzzle worked out. What I propose will be bold and daring to a degree well beyond that which will be required at the other two locations, but that is exactly why I believe it will work."

CHAPTER THIRTEEN

FRIDAY, MAY 15TH

B ased on the numerous discussions that had lasted for more than a week with his team of attack planners, and having finalized those intended logistics for the Colorado location, Samuel climbed aboard the family jet for a flight to Laredo. Once there, he hailed a taxi for the short ride to the border and walked across the bridge into Mexico. Waiting for him at a pre-determined restaurant in Nuevo Laredo was a jovial man of near fifty who greeted Samuel with a smile. Their meeting had been set up via a man in Oro Valley Arizona that Samuel had never met, but the intelligence gathered on the family background since January was comprehensive and showed that they had a tendency to recognize opportunity when it was presented.

Spotting the identifiable insignia that Samuel was told would be worn by his contact, he moved toward the man leaning against the bar. Then with extended hand he said, "It's nice to meet you sir, and may I offer my congratulations to you and your family for Kevin's upcoming graduation from West Point?"

Speaking nearly perfect English, the man replied, "Thank you very much. It's sometimes hard for me and my wife to believe that his time there is nearly complete. We will join my brother and his wife at the commencement in about two weeks, and it will be a proud moment for all of us. I also understand that my nephew and your grandson Jason have become good friends while at West Point."

"That's my understanding as well, and I hope that the friendship between our two families that Kevin and Jason have established will continue for years to come."

From the neighboring table a seated woman with her back to them added, "What a lovely sentiment. We feel the same way, and perhaps what we accomplish today will help to solidify both of our families' mutual desire."

Samuel turned toward the woman, removed his favorite cowboy hat, and said, "Mrs. Flores I presume? I'm glad that you both could make the trip from Monterrey."

Rising to face him, she replied, "That is correct Mr. Tillman, and it was no trouble at all. We often do business here in Nuevo Laredo, so that is why we suggested this location to my husband's brother in Arizona. Now then, how may my husband and I help you?"

"I would like to purchase an old helicopter that can be refurbished for transportation needs, and my understanding is that you could help me with that quest."

"That is correct. We do have access to a surplus of old helicopters of various models in the Monterrey area that have been retired from Mexican military service. Do you have an idea of what type you are looking for that will suit your purposes?"

"Yes ma'am I do. I'm looking for a model that was of Soviet design used by dozens of countries in the world throughout the past several decades. It's a MIL MI-8 HIP-C."

Mr. Flores took the lead once again and announced, "That's a fairly large bird Mr. Tillman, and depending on the model, it could be used for many purposes. I believe that you may already be aware of what such a helicopter is capable of carrying with regard to payload, as your knowledge of the model number and country of origin implies some research. Therefore it's reasonable to assume your understanding that the HIP-C is primarily a transport version as opposed to others that possess more lethal characteristics."

"Yes Mr. Flores. Thank you for pointing out the distinction, but I'm interested in something for the transport of personnel only."

"Very well then Mr. Tillman. I do know of two such birds that could be made available for purchase, and depending on how comfortable you make the passenger cabin during the restoration process, she could comfortably seat as many as fifteen."

Although more than willing to do business with the Flores family and their associates, Samuel remained cautious as to revealing the true intent of the helicopter. He replied, "Thank you Mr. Flores. That model is the size that I had in mind, but as it will be used to shuttle some of my business associates to places without a landing strip in comfort, the seating will be for no more than eight or ten."

CHAPTER FOURTEEN
MEMORIAL DAY WEEKEND

Slightly more than one hundred miles before the Madura would arrive at its destination port of Galveston Texas, a one hundred twenty foot fishing trawler eased its way into a position along the starboard side. Departing from her home port of Mersin on the southern coast of Turkey in the eastern reaches of the Mediterranean Sea, the massive container ship had needed more than a week to make its way into the Atlantic Ocean via the Strait of Gibraltar and then complete the crossing toward North America and into the Gulf of Mexico. After passing to the south of the Bahamas and Florida keys, she set a direct course toward Galveston. Now with the intended journey nearly complete, the Madura had slowed significantly as she closed on her port of call. Within one of her hundreds of shipping containers were several dozen crates that would require attention before reaching port and a potential United States customs inspection. Therefore, the crates had already been prepared for their transfer from the Madura onto the approaching fishing trawler.

With the smaller vessel matching the speed and course of the container ship, the captain of the trawler made a minor steering adjustment to port in order to edge his craft closer. As he did so, a large cargo net began to lower from above. Within seconds of touching down on the aft deck, his crew began to unload all of the crates. Then when the process had been successfully repeated twice more during the next ten minutes, the transfer was complete.

As the trawler increased speed and began to gently peel away to the starboard for a more northerly heading, her captain looked at his radar screen. Turning to the man who had come aboard early the previous morning in Galveston, he said, "Well Kyle, there's still nothing on the screen except for the Madura. It looks like we're in the clear."

His guest then replied, "While I will agree that things have gone smoothly up to this point, our task is far from complete. We still need to meet up with each of the other fishing boats at the established coordinates to offload our recent acquisition, and that must be done before we run into any Coast Guard patrols."

"Well according to the schedule that you provided, the first of the smaller fishing boats should rally up with us in about fifteen minutes. Will that make you feel better?"

"Of course, but my mood will only fully brighten when each of the six rendezvous are safely completed. I intend no disrespect to you or your vessel captain, but I won't rest easy until I have departed with the last of the smaller fishing boats. The shipment that we now carry is of vital importance to the overall plan, and it was not easy to acquire back in Eastern Europe. So I, along with number two, would hate to have any portion of this cargo wasted. Neither of us wants any of the crates dumped into the ocean to avoid a Coast Guard seizure, but that is what we must do if necessary."

Ninety five minutes later, Kyle Tillman climbed onboard the last of the six boats that had arrived in fifteen minute intervals. After the crates assigned to that boat had been stowed below, he fired off a salute to the captain of the trawler. Then as they prepared to part ways, he said, "Captain, I thank you for your assistance with this matter. I shall report to number two that you and your crew did a tremendous job with the transfer of cargo from the Madura, and the subsequent transition onto each of the smaller fishing boats."

Returning the salute in a sloppy fashion with the hand that now held a large envelope stuffed with cash, the captain replied, "Glad that the services of my boat and crew could be of help to the cause Kyle. Feel free to contact me again if the need arises."

With that Kyle nodded and the thirty-five foot fishing boat pulled away. A short time later they could see the coastline of southwest Louisiana, and if all went well, they would be able to unload the crates into an awaiting van within the hour.

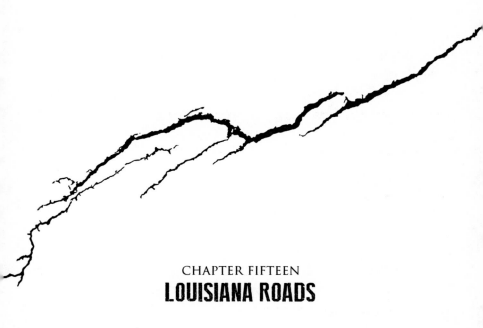

CHAPTER FIFTEEN

LOUISIANA ROADS

H aving met up with the fishing boats at the three remote south-west Louisiana locations of Johnson's Bayou, Holly Beach, and Cameron, five large vans made their way deeper into the state by moving north along various portions of highway-27. Although the hand selected driving pairs within the sparsely appointed vehicles didn't know it, they were all being carefully scrutinized while performing a trial run that would serve as their so called final exam. If they completed their current task without any problems, then each of the women would become part of the larger group of ground personnel that would be deployed in the fall.

After Kyle arrived at Johnson's Bayou on the last of the fishing boats, he helped the men on the dock load the crates into the awaiting van while the driver waited patiently. Then he gave them each some cash for their effort, and climbed into the passenger side seat. With an exhale of relief at the sight of the attractive driver, he leaned closer and gave her a kiss before asking, "How have you been?"

With a smile on her face, she replied, "Good thanks. How was the trip?"

"It was good, and everything went according to plan. We had smooth water out in the gulf, which helped to make the transfers easier, and we didn't see any Coast Guard patrols on the way back in."

"Neither did any of the other boats."

"So you have heard from the other driving teams, and everything is alright?"

"Yes, they each contacted me on the burn phone and everything is fine. They are all headed north."

"That's good to know, and we should be on our way as well."

Unlike each of the other five vans, Kyle and his wife Ashley headed west on highway-82 toward Port Arthur Texas. From there it would take them several hours to reach the Tillman ranch via a series of smaller highways that traversed southeastern Texas, but they were looking forward to the peaceful time together before they each headed off again on subsequent assignments. Once they arrived at the ranch, the plan was to unload their portion of the cargo that had been transported from Eastern Europe into a secure location of the mansion. Then in conjunction with Samuel, the crates full of black market weapons and ammunition from South Africa and the Czech Republic would be inspected before arrangements could be made for their eventual transfer to the training facility.

Although traveling separately, the other vans had a different agenda. Employing a method of using smaller highways in southwestern Louisiana as they moved north of interstate-10, each would eventually join up with interstate-49 in either Alexandria or Natchitoches. That major traffic artery would then carry them for nearly the entire subsequent duration of their northerly trek. Once beyond the larger city of Shreveport in northern Louisiana and into the southwest corner of Arkansas, the vans would be nearing the completion of their assigned task. Just a few miles before reaching the city of Texarkana that straddles the state line of neighboring Texas, they would turn west to circumvent the area and enter their home state. Then the vans would head for a warehouse facility owned by Tillman Freight to unload their precious cargo.

CHAPTER SIXTEEN
WEDNESDAY, JUNE 17ᵀᴴ

Having flown to Fort Stockton from the Houston County Airport in Crockett on the family jet, and subsequently transferring into a twin engine propeller aircraft for the remainder of the journey, Samuel and Mason returned to the training facility. Banking to the left while lining up for final approach, their pilot said, "If you would like to see it gentlemen, the landing zone is now clearly visible to our left."

Glancing to his left for verification, Samuel could make out three distinct rectangular shapes of white painted objects within a cleared and smoothed out portion of the barren terrain. Then he replied, "Thanks for pointing that out. They look good from here, and it's exactly what our air personnel will need to properly train."

After landing, he and Mason met with the three men who had been responsible for bringing the training facility, under the cover of the West Texas Skydiving School, into fruition. They were then provided with a brief tour of the facility, and in the process, were introduced to any of the forty-two men and training pilots they had not previously met. Seizing the opportunity, Samuel asked one of the recruits, "What are your thoughts on the landing zone?"

"It's easy to hit sir, even with some of the windy conditions that exist here. It should be no problem for any of us to fine tune the landings even with the extra weight."

Not wanting to come across as being ignorant to the meaning behind the statement, Samuel replied simply, "That's good to hear young man. I like your enthusiasm."

With a nod of comprehension, the man said, "Thank you sir. We won't let you or the cause down."

Moving toward another recruit, Samuel asked him, "How many jumps have you done before coming here young man?"

"Hundreds sir, and many of them with gear similar to what will be required of us for this mission."

"That's excellent, and I'm confident that you will all be ready when called upon."

Then while moving back toward the plane with the three recruiters, Mason unknowingly took the pressure off his father by asking, "What did the first guy mean when he mentioned the extra weight?"

The lead recruiter replied, "At this stage of training the men are getting used to the landing zone and specific quadrants within it by coming in with just their flight suits and boots. In short order we will introduce weight belts for each of them, and then increase the load to simulate all the gear they will be required to carry for the mission. In actuality though, that final weight will be easy for them and less than what they have jumped with before."

"These men have jumped with more weight that what we will give them?

"Most certainly. They have all been on missions that required them to carry fifteen days of food and water rations along with the other gear."

Suddenly realizing that such a need would be necessary in each man's past training and job specifications, Mason replied, "Of course, that makes sense."

The recruiter nodded and continued with, "We will also begin tandem jumping very soon, and then work our way up to the full grouping of seven. That way they can be well practiced at the choreography that will also be required during the upcoming mission."

Having listened to the explanation of his lead recruiter, and being thankful that his son had asked the questions, Samuel said, "That sounds like an excellent plan. The three of you have once again proven why I maintain total confidence in your abilities and commitment to the cause. I will contact number twenty three and inform her that it's nearly time to send in the ground support teams for the eastern targets. What do you think about having them brought in just after July fourth?"

"That sounds good number two. That way they will have four months to get in good physical shape before the mission."

"That's true, but from what I have heard, they are already in good shape from their current and previous training."

"Well if that's true, then it should make their transition to this facility a little easier. Do you want us to inform the men of their pending arrival?"

"Not yet. Although the air personnel and training pilots will be happy to learn that they will have twenty women among them for several months, we should keep that information to ourselves for the time being. We don't want the men to lose focus on the business at hand, and it will be a pleasant surprise for all of them when the ground personnel do arrive."

"I understand number two."

"Good. Now there is an additional element to consider, and you should warn the men of it when the women arrive. Each of them has been trained extensively in the use of hand to hand combat."

Another of the recruiters then said, "Well that should make all of the introductions, and any of the subsequent attempted jousting, quite interesting."

"Indeed, but we can't afford to have any serious injuries during that process. With only one exception each of the women, as well as the men that the three of you and number seven recruited, are all in their twenties or thirties and single with no children. Although those factors were one aspect of the criteria needed for their potential recruitment, it would only be natural for people of that age to have physical needs. Being that they will all be here together for several months, we need to recognize that something is bound to transpire in that regard. Besides, it would be foolish for any of us to believe that we could somehow monitor and prevent such an activity from happening even if we had the time to do so. With that said, please make it very clear to each and every one of the air and ground personnel that fraternization with each other will not be forbidden, but they need to understand that such action cannot interfere with the long term objective."

Smiling in response to the calculated way that his superior had phrased the statement, he replied, "I agree with your assessment number two, and we will make sure that your point on the matter is clearly understood."

"Thank you."

Having forgotten that for Samuel the day could be measured with extreme levels of both pride and anguish, the lead recruiter then uttered what he thought to be a wish of good faith. Without realizing what he had done until after saying the words, he stated, "Oh and by the way, I hope that you and the family can all enjoy a nice father's day together this coming Sunday."

CHAPTER SEVENTEEN

JULY 4ᵀᴴ MORNING

lthough pleasant throughout the process, the security tandem stationed at the front gate was meticulous in their duties. They cross checked the driver's license of each man in the car with the manifest of invited guests that had been provided, and took note of the make, model, and license plate number before clearing the vehicle for entry. Once approved and waived on through, number thirty one slowly advanced the car through the set of stone pillars that supported the ornate entrance gate.

His lone back seat passenger asked, "Is that it up there?"

Looking ahead and to his right, the driver could see the massive mansion perched on the top of a small rise. Then he replied, "Yes, that's the Tillman's home. It's going to take us a few minutes to get up there, so just enjoy the property and the view."

The man questioned further, "Is there another checkpoint that we have to pass through on the way?"

"Normally it's just the front gate, but there could be another check point today. Why do you ask?"

"Because you just said it would take us a few minutes to get there."

"That's because it's slightly over a mile from the entrance arch to Samuel and Victoria's home."

The comment gave cause for the front seat passenger to enter the conversation by asking, "That house is a mile away?"

"Yes it is."

"It must be massive if it looks that big from here!"

"It is, and the mansion is beautiful with great views of most of their property and a small portion of Houston County Lake beyond."

What the three men in the car hadn't realized was that the security personnel, who had helped to protect Samuel and Savanah on New Year's Eve, were already calling the main house to inform their boss of the latest arrivals. The men in the car were part of the early wave of guests that would swell to over one hundred fifty for the late afternoon and evening festivities, but first there was business to discuss. Cresting the gentle hill and leveling off as the roadway opened onto a driveway area that could support perhaps fifty cars, number thirty one followed the advance directive of number two by backing into a space near the eight door garage. Before emerging from the car, his inquisitive rear seat passenger asked, "How many times have you been to this ranch?"

Always mindful of security measures, even among those that were already fully vetted, he replied, "I'm not exactly sure, but I'm always hopeful to be invited again."

Just then their host and his wife stepped through the front door and waited for them on the front porch. As the three men approached, Victoria said, "Happy fourth of July gentlemen. We are so pleased that you could join us today."

While offering his hand in gratitude, the driver replied, "Thank you Victoria. It's a pleasure to see you again. How is everyone in the family?"

"Well they are all just fine thank you, and how are your lovely wife and children?"

"In the peak of health, and they look forward to seeing you again later this afternoon."

"That is excellent news, and I look forward to seeing them again as well. Now, who are these two young gentlemen?"

"Please excuse my manners. May I introduce Mr. Capra and Mr. Fisk who are joining us today from El Paso. Like each of us in the present company, they are loyal Texans and Aggies through and through."

Looking at them with a welcoming smile while extending a hand, Victoria replied, "Well it's always good to shake hands with fellow Aggies, but it's even better to know that you are both loyal to the cause. It's a pleasure to meet you gentlemen, and welcome to our home."

As if in chorus, the two men replied, "Thank you for the hospitality ma'am."

"It's our pleasure. Now then gentlemen, please come inside for some refreshments."

Each man then shook the hand of their host Samuel Tillman before moving through the door into the massive foyer. Once inside, they were then escorted by Victoria to the bar area, and given instructions on where they could also find food, restrooms, and the pool if they so desired.

Samuel then asked, "Alright gentlemen, this meeting could last a little while. What can I get you to drink before we discuss your flight of this morning and the progress of the overall plan?"

Amazed at the openness of the statement, the inquisitive Mr. Fisk was silent for a moment. Then he became further amazed when his hostess snuck up on him from behind. Placing her hand on his shoulder, she said quite plainly, "Well isn't that just the cutest thing Samuel? Either our new friend Mr. Fisk doesn't have a thirst for something cold at the moment, or he doesn't believe that I know anything at all about the overall plan."

Then after a gulp of astonishment, Mr. Fisk replied, "I beg your pardon ma'am, I didn't mean to imply…"

"Oh you most certainly did young man, but that's just fine with me. Your momentary silence was actually a good sign, because it shows me that you are mindful of security measures in this matter."

"Well yes ma'am, I am."

Then with a slight increase of her grip pressure upon his shoulder, the tall and slender sixty five year old Victoria Tillman with short greying hair added, "Very well then Mr. Fisk, we shall address your concerns. Now let me tell you something sir, and this goes for you as well Mr. Capra. I'm a southern bread woman of deep tradition, and I cherish my husband Samuel along with everyone in our family. I love being the matriarch and the woman of the house so to speak, but in assuming that role, it doesn't mean that I'm not a modern thinker. I know it's only natural for many men, especially former military men such as the two of you, to believe that I or other women should be left out of important matters such as this. Unfortunately for those who maintain such a belief, they have not yet realized that it's a thought process of another era. I'm fully aware, and "read in" as some of you like to say, of everything that there is to know about the plans of my husband and our good friends. That of course includes aspects of the roles that the two of you played this morning in Austin, and will continue to play throughout the coming months. Now having others, both on the inside and outside of the organization, believe that I'm ignorant to the subject matter can be useful in creating a wonderful cover for the family should that need ever arise. With that said gentlemen, please don't ever underestimate my knowledge or resolve in the future!"

Having been eloquently put in his proper place by a woman of obvious breading, education, and conviction, Mr. Fisk then spoke humbly. He said, "Ma'am, and you too Mr. Tillman, I realize that there has been a misunderstanding on my part. I intended no disrespect toward either of you or your family home, and ask that you please accept these words as an apology on my behalf. I'm truly sorry, and shall never underestimate Mrs. Tillman's knowledge of the overall plan ever again."

With that Victoria smiled while lessoning her grip and put the man at ease. She replied, "Well now. That is how a proper Texas gentleman shows respect for his hosts through an apology, and I gladly accept it as such. Your parents must have raised you correctly sir, and if they were alive today, they would be proud of you for what you have just conveyed."

For an instant Mr. Fisk wondered how Victoria Tillman could possibly know that his parents were dead, and that he had served in the military, but he didn't inquire. The young man realized that he had no desire to underestimate her knowledge of events ever again.

Then his host Mr. Tillman spoke up by asking, "Now then, can we all have a cool drink and get down to the business at hand before many of our other guests and their young children arrive?"

Victoria replied, "That is an excellent idea Samuel, but I must bid you all a temporary farewell. I need to go over a few things with Ms. Holloway, as the catering group we have hired should be here soon. Perhaps you and the gentlemen can retire to your office to discuss business. I'm sure that you all have many things to cover about various aspects of the plan, and that may take some time."

Samuel nodded with agreement, and motioned for his three guests to follow him into his office. Then after closing the door, he began what would become a lengthy conversation by saying to his old friend, "You have done well number thirty one, and I once again thank you for your continued efforts."

Ever conscious of security measures, he responded without the use of a numbered identity. Instead, number thirty one merely stated, "Anything for the cause Samuel."

With another nod, Samuel turned toward the men who had accompanied his old friend and stated, "So number thirty one informs me that both of you received your initial instruction while attending Texas A&M, and that you have since developed an excellent skill set when it comes to flying helicopters. This morning's flight over Austin was just the beginning, as your collective skills can and will be of meaningful use to our cause. I'm pleased to say that the vetting process for each of you is complete, and both of you have passed with no issue. Therefore Mr. Capra and Mr. Fisk if you will accept, on behalf of those in the organization I welcome you to the party."

CHAPTER EIGHTEEN
JULY 4ᵀᴴ EVENING

Savanah and a few of her friends who came with their parents to the big celebration barbeque were having a wonderful time splashing about in the pool. The doctors had conveyed to her parents Kyle and Ashley, as well as the rest of the family, that time in the pool with the stretching and exercise was good for Savanah. With that in mind, the family had given Savanah every opportunity to get in the water during the warmer months of the year. However with the sun sinking low and becoming one with the western horizon on this hot and humid late evening, the time had come for her to change into dry clothes and watch some of the many fireworks shows.

Beyond what could be viewed on the giant holographic screen in the family room of fireworks extravaganzas in the eastern megacities of Boston, New York, Philadelphia, and of course Washington D.C., Savanah was excited for what was to come. Her grandparents had promised her a good show right here on the family ranch, and they had never failed to keep a promise to her. During the dazzling shows on the screen, Savanah listened to the opinions of the adults in the room. They spoke of how each of the first three cities had played an important role in the birth of America, and therefore had earned the right to celebrate her two hundred fiftieth birthday on this July day of 2026. She also heard them speak of how Washington D.C., as the capitol city of America, had not earned that same right. Their collective thought was that many of those working within the elected government structure and multilayered entangled bureaucracy of Washington D.C. had done more to destroy the concept of America in recent times than to help improve upon the many problems that existed. Although Savanah certainly didn't understand the finer details of all that was being discussed, or the definition of many words that had been tossed about, one thing was abundantly clear to the bright young lady. Each and every adult at the party had nothing good to say about what went on in the nation's capital.

CHAPTER NINETEEN
MONDAY, AUGUST 17TH

A Soviet made MIL MI-8 HIP-C helicopter that Samuel had arranged to purchase during his visit to Nuevo Laredo had begun a revival to its former glory just a few days after his initial meeting with Mr. & Mrs. Flores. As the fuselage measured only inches short of sixty feet in length, the bird had been brought across the border into Laredo and northward on interstate-35 toward Austin by use of a huge flatbed truck and accompanying "wide load" pace vehicles. After retrieving the helicopter from a surplus field near Monterrey, the spectacle viewed by hundreds at the border crossing had been interesting, yet tedious. The height of the fuselage at more than eighteen feet had posed a problem, so the landing gear tripod needed to be removed before she could be loaded onto the truck. With the five overhead rotor blades and three tail rotor blades also removed for transport in a separate truck with that landing gear, the MIL MI-8 HIP-C took on a completely different appearance. She suddenly looked more like a huge pale guppy than some form of military aircraft. Even so, the officials from the United States customs and border control had taken an inordinate amount of time searching through the fuselage with drug sniffing dogs. Much to their collective dismay, they found nothing within. It was in their nature to assume that something of that size must be used for hiding drugs or other illegal contraband while crossing the border, and in most cases they probably would have been correct, but Samuel had no such intentions. The helicopter had been purchased legally under a falsified name, and Samuel had the bill of sale and proper identification to prove it. Beyond the fake identity, the cover story created for customs officials, and anyone else who might be inquisitive, was actually true. The helicopter, if refurbished to operational readiness in time, would become part of a grand aerial showcase over Austin for the July fourth celebration. If not, then she would become one of many military aircraft on the ground that people could view and photograph. The intent of this particular helicopter was to acknowledge the Mexican American influence and citizenship that existed within Texas and the aircraft would be painted in military colors for the event.

Work crews had taken five weeks at a feverish around the clock pace to complete the refurbishing, but she was ready in time. Every inch of the mainframe, both of the engine compartments, and the flight deck instrument panel had been disassembled and inspected by a team of men and women. Then each part was cleaned, repaired, or replaced by newly manufactured parts as they were put back together again. The landing tripod had been inspected for structural integrity and necessary repairs were performed, while the old rotor blades, both overhead and on the tail section, had all been replaced with new ones.

Made ready for test flights only days before the July fourth celebration, the bird had performed well. Then while in formation with other vintage aircraft, she had been flown by Mr. Capra over the University of Texas and the Capitol Complex in Austin during the festivities. In the course of doing so, he and his co-pilot Mr. Fisk had an excellent overhead view of the empty Darrell K. Royal–Texas Memorial Stadium and the playing field. Such an opportunity provided them with valuable perspective.

Now in mid-August, the MIL MI-8 HIP-C had since been stripped down of any unwanted weight within to hopefully create a slight increase in speed and fuel efficiency. Repainted in a special pattern of red, white, and blue to resemble the Texas state flag, the helicopter had been flown out to the training facility with logos for the fictitious "West Texas Skydiving School" emblazoned upon each side panel door.

Throughout a large portion of that restoration process and subsequent transformation into its present state, Kyle had been working on another special assignment. From nearly the moment after the delivery and inspection of the weapons that had been brought into the gulf by the Madura, he had begun what was thought to be a difficult task. Although challenging and time consuming in the research phase, Kyle was to locate and procure additional aircraft that would be needed to compliment the role of the refurbished helicopter. The task eventually proved to be far less than impossible, as while scouring potential sources throughout the nation he had come across something useful in the Orange County area of southern California. There were several small jets, similar in size to that of the Tillman Gulfstream G280, which had been repossessed by banks from those who had failed to maintain the payments. Kyle had learned from his studies of the human endeavor that some people were known to be extremely vain, so such occurrences weren't a surprise to him. Those people who fit that mold were always attempting to outdo their friends and neighbors in order to maintain a level of self-worth, and as a result, some had become overextended financially. Such habits had created an opportunity that Kyle could exploit, as he learned of an early August auction in that portion of the country at the Chino Airport in neighboring Riverside County. The auction would have a selection of high end vehicles, boats, and most importantly, planes.

After notifying Samuel of the discovery, they took a trip west for the auction. Arriving separately to the event, they had each assumed the cover of business men from different locations. While one supposedly hailed from Atlanta and the other from Chicago, the common thread between the supposed strangers was that both they and their families loved skiing in western Colorado. Therefore it was completely understandable for those representing the auction process that each of them would be interested in purchasing a plane for direct access use to the airport near Aspen. Two identical Cessna Citation Latitude jet planes that were slightly smaller than the Gulfstream G280 were purchased with cash, so another aspect of the plan had come together. Each of the used planes were capable of comfortably carrying a flight crew of two and eight passengers, while the fuel range and flight maneuverability of the small jets would be more than adequate for the task ahead.

Ten days before the MIL MI-8 HIP-C had been painted and on its way to the training facility, Samuel rented a car for the short drive to the Chino Airport from the John Wayne Orange County Airport. Then with the two vetted pilots that he had pulled from a group of recruits, he and Kyle rode shotgun in the co-pilot seats of each Citation Latitude as they were flown from the southern California area to Aspen Colorado. While in the course of that action, the Tillman family plane that had deposited the group of four in Orange County, headed east for another rendezvous. When the newly purchased planes reached Aspen, where they would remain until needed, another car was rented for the purpose of a scouting road trip. If anyone had bothered to pay close enough attention, the four within could have potentially been identified as a father and his three adult children. While acting as tourists, they followed the twisting mountain highway-82 to the east over Independence Pass at slightly more than twelve thousand feet. After descending into a valley region, they rolled south through the small towns of Granite and Buena Vista before reaching Poncha Springs. From there they turned east onto highway-50 for the journey through Canon City, and stopped soon after to have a detailed look around. Feeling satisfied in what they had taken note of; they continued east to exit the last of the rolling foothills and onto the plains as they closed on Pueblo.

After turning in the rental car at the Pueblo Memorial Airport, they boarded the Tillman Gulfstream G280 that had arrived several hours earlier and headed for Texas. As Samuel, Kyle, and the two female pilots had been dropped off and retrieved by the family plane at different airports than those of the flight plan for either of the newly purchased Cessna's, there would be no cause for the FAA or any other governing body to believe that the travel of the three planes were somehow related.

CHAPTER TWENTY
LABOR DAY WEEKEND

As another weekend of grand celebrations were taking place all across the nation, the men and women at the training facility continued to hone their respective crafts. The women had been running miles each day both on the flatlands surrounding the facility, and on nearby Bird Mountain via a lift from the helicopter. As a consequence, they were in better physical shape than when they had arrived. Additionally, each of them had continued to practice their hand to hand combat and martial arts techniques, while also learning some basic medical skills in the event they were needed. The group of twenty that had been assigned to be evenly split between the two eastern sites had arrived at the training facility on July seventh, and had been joined by five others in the late days of August. Those five most recent arrivals had been recruited for missions that although less lengthy, contained more complexities than what would be required of their sisters in the east. Unlike the drivers back east who would mainly be used for the retrieval of the attacking forces and their subsequent safe return to Texas, the drivers for the singular western assault had mission assignments both before and after the day of attack.

Three black suburban's would need to be driven from Amarillo to various locations throughout Colorado, Kansas, and New Mexico during the days surrounding the impending attack, with two of those women drivers being called upon to impersonate government officials on a least one occasion. Recruited solely for their skills as jet pilots, the final two women had a more dangerous task ahead of them. As such they focused on little else than increased physical fitness to assist with that task, and how their flying skills could be best utilized. That personal quest was aided by intense study of various maps which detailed the exacting terrain for their upcoming flights.

Although offered to receive time off from her labors for the holiday weekend as she was the only one with a husband and children, the eldest of the now twenty-five women had declined. Having been designated as their leader, she felt that it would have been an unfair advantage over the others to escape the late summer heat of west Texas for a few days. More significantly, accepting such favoritism would have also delivered a poor message to the collective that could upset the balance of team unity.

A minimal addition to the forty-two men of the assault teams were Mr. Capra and Mr. Fisk, but like the pilots who had joined the group of women, their mindset was also of a singular focus. Beyond that belief was an exception to their training that would set them apart from the other newcomers. The two helicopter pilots had been informed that they would also embark on a refresher course with regard to the art of parachuting to safety. Although both had performed numerous jumps during the training and military service of yesteryear, neither had utilized such a skill for several years. It was hoped that said action wouldn't be required within the body of the plan, but if for some reason one or both of them needed to bailout, refreshing them on how to do so seemed prudent.

When Mr. Fisk then asked, "Why aren't the women who will fly the jets be going through the course with us?"

The lead recruiter at the facility replied, "Because they won't have any parachutes to jump with."

In a reply of obvious puzzlement, he asked, "They won't, why not?"

"Well think about it Mr. Fisk. The flight status of the ladies is quite different from that of you and Mr. Capra. Most of your flying will be pre-mission during the training stage, and then the repositioning and delivery of the western attack force. With yourself included in the equation, you will be carrying a valuable set of assets on every flight. Should the helicopter develop mechanical problems or failure while doing so; the safety of those assets must be protected. As the attacking air personnel will always have parachutes for those training jumps and flights, it only makes sense that you do as well. In short, we can perhaps replace the helicopter with a back-up, but those of the attacking force or the pilots that will deliver them are more of a challenge."

After a moment of contemplation Mr. Fisk replied, "Alright, I understand your point, but what about during the mission? Won't the two women pilots have parachutes then?"

"No they won't. But if it's any comfort to you Mr. Fisk, you won't have one during the mission either."

Knowing that none of them could be taken alive, Mr. Fisk suddenly realized why he wouldn't have a parachute during the mission. If the helicopter were to be shot down by an opposing force, then he and all hands on board would perish in the act.

With knowledge that the training aspects of the air and ground personnel were firmly under control, and with his son Mason spending much of his time in west Texas under the tutelage of number thirty one, Samuel took the opportunity to offer Courtney a special mission of her own. He had seen something within his daughter-in-law that led him to believe she was capable, but he didn't taint Courtney's decision process by providing her with that insight. Samuel informed her only that if she accepted the challenge, and he wanted her to take a few days to sufficiently ponder over that decision, then there would be no turning back. Her training for the mission, although just as physically and mentally demanding, would be separate from all of the other recruits. The content of her assignment in various locations would be dealt with in complete secrecy. No one other than Courtney, Samuel, and number twenty three as a contact would know anything about her mission parameters from the moment of her initial briefing on through and beyond the execution of those tasks.

CHAPTER TWENTY-ONE
WEDNESDAY, OCTOBER 7TH

Now fully immersed in his senior year as a first classman at West Point, Jason Tillman was enjoying the privileges of being one of the more highly ranked cadets within the corps. Via assistance throughout the previous spring from Kevin Flores before he had graduated as a Battalion Commander, and with the recommendations that were put forth by him in Jason's name, Jason had advanced in rank to the level of being awarded the occasional special favor. Based on not having abused that opportunity since receiving said latitude, and as his one and only request for such a privilege was different than most with a similar opportunity, it was granted without much question. Firing the pre-game salute from the cannon next to Lusk Reservoir at the final home football game of his senior year was Jason's desire, and so it would be.

Aside from that event slated for the near future, life at the academy with its academic rigors and associated cadet responsibilities continued with similar intensity to those of his previous three years. The significant difference between the earlier time and the present term was that Jason had become more efficient with the management of his time, and his friend Kevin had played a major role in that education. As such, Jason no longer needed thirty hours, if he had wanted to get any sleep, to accomplish what would be required in twenty-four.

Like nearly all of the cadets, Jason was in excellent physical condition. Aside from the daily regimented dose of calisthenics and exercise, he had been jogging through the wooded areas of the academy grounds since the dawn of the calendar year whenever regulations would allow for it. In the course of doing so, Jason continued to gather what could be additional valuable intelligence. Per the instruction of his grandfather and number twenty three, he had used the burn phone to report on the first day of every month. In possession of a new burn phone that Samuel had issued to him during summer break in Texas, the same strategy continued into the fall.

Jason's October first report had revealed his keen attention to detail with regard to the organizations questions that were put forth to him, and that he had witnessed no significant changes in the protocol or security during the events of September twelfth or the twenty sixth. Therefore in his estimation, no reason existed to believe that future events would be handled any differently than with the well-established patterns currently in place.

Based on that intelligence report, and at the request of his lead recruiter, Samuel made another visit to the training facility in west Texas. However during the current trip, he brought a supply of goods with him from the mansion. As he was greeted by the three recruiters, Samuel said, "I'm glad that the men have become so proficient with their training, and also that you're prepared for the next step."

The lead recruiter as usual was first to respond. He said, "Thanks number two. We were hoping to get to this point of refinement by November first so that the men could have a week of practice with the weapons, but now there's no need to wait until then."

"It's always good news to be ahead of schedule, but what exactly will they be doing?"

"Well mostly they will be firing into the desert with the blank ammunition that you procured. That way they can all become accustomed to the recoil of the various weapons that some of them have never fired before."

"Alright, that sounds good. I remember that such recoil, especially from the South African model, is something we had discussed from the very beginning."

"Indeed, but now I have an additional thought on how the men can proceed with the extra practice time."

"Knowing you, that will undoubtedly involve another training exercise. So what do you have in mind?"

Motioning toward the other two recruiters, he spoke for them, "We want to determine how that recoil might affect them while they are still in the air."

CHAPTER TWENTY-TWO
HALLOWEEN

As Savanah was looking forward to the big costume party that she, her brother Blake, and their cousin Jennifer, would be attending with her parents and grandparents in a few hours, a double trailered eighteen wheeler rig prepared to depart from Tillman Freight in west Texarkana. Hidden from view within the trailers were three black suburban's, several crates containing an arsenal of weapons and live ammunition that had been safely secured since Memorial Day, clothing, and provisions of food, water, and cash needed for the mission. Topping off the list of cargo were sixteen parachutes, but two of those would be discarded on the afternoon of November thirteenth. The driver's mission was to deliver the rig to a warehouse location in Amarillo within the northwest panhandle region of Texas on the afternoon of November first, and then without unloading the cargo, wait for his female contact to arrive.

An hour after his departure from Texarkana, Courtney got her first real taste of what she would forfeit when Samuel insisted that there would be no turning back. She had accepted the mission he designed specifically for her, and in so doing, would depart for the early stages of her task from the Tillman mansion while many in the family were at the costume party. As with other social gatherings held within the nearby town of Crockett throughout the year, the annual Halloween costume party was an event that Courtney had attended with the family numerous times. She had enjoyed conversing with the adults, and had watched the various children of those friends grow and develop from their toddler stage into a more independent form of young adulthood during the process. This year however, that transformation was hitting close to home again, and the experience was enlightening.

While helping her fourteen year old boy crazy daughter Jennifer with certain aspects of her costume, Courtney suddenly wondered how different the young lady would be by the time she returned from the task in front of her, let alone in the months that followed. Although the subtle changes had been occurring for a few years, the process had recently accelerated. Jennifer's body shape had changed dramatically of late, and at the rate she was filling in, she would probably need to have her tailored holiday party dress altered before it could be used for Thanksgiving. If there proved to be a shortage of material for such intent, a new dress could be easily purchased. There was minor comfort for Courtney in knowing that in either scenario, Ms. Holloway would tend to the need when it arose. Of course she also possessed substantial comfort in a much grander understanding. If something drastic such as her own death were to fall upon Courtney while on the mission, Jennifer would not be left alone. Like with most other things, Samuel, Victoria, and Ms. Holloway would make sure that she was well looked after even if Mason was somehow unable to step up.

As she fought back the welling tears of having her youngest child already entering the next phase of early womanhood, Courtney looked Jennifer over with a smile, and said, "You look beautiful young lady, and I hope that you have a good time at the party."

Just then there was a knock on the door as the voice of Savanah asked, "Jennifer, may I please come in?"

"Sure Savanah, come on in."

With that the door swung open and Savanah bounded in to say, "Oh hi Aunt Courtney. I'm sorry to interrupt, but I was hoping that Jennifer could help me with my hair ribbon if she has the time."

It was an instant reminder to Courtney that her problems with Mason and missing out on some of her daughter's transitions paled in comparison, as Savanah had her own mountain of concern to overcome. The well-instilled manners and bright outlook of Savanah had also proved once again how valuable Ms. Holloway had been to the family with her time and tutelage. With Jennifer then tending to the hair ribbon of her young cousin, Courtney realized it was imperative that she successfully complete her mission for the good of the cause and the overall plan.

Later that afternoon, shortly after the family entourage had left for the party, Courtney headed for the Houston County Airport that was located on the far side of Crockett. Driving past the site of the Halloween party in the process, she then boarded the family jet bound for the Amarillo International Airport.

CHAPTER TWENTY-THREE

TUESDAY, NOVEMBER 3RD

For many decades the first Tuesday of November in the even numbered calendar years had been Election Day throughout America and during this mid-term election cycle it was no different. President Harwell had been elected two years prior in 2024, and as such, still had that same timeframe remaining before votes would be cast for or against him in his re-election attempt. Samuel Tillman didn't care too much about that particular timetable for now, but also felt that the man probably didn't stand much of a chance at a second term as the chief executive. Of course Jordon Harwell's future within that office could be largely determined by the outcome of the overall plan, and how it would be subsequently responded to.

Of more immediate concern to Samuel were the various state elections that would have a federal impact on Congress, and also at the state legislature level. Many of those with regard to Texas were perceived to be already secured, as Samuel and others of influence within the organization had seen to that. The campaigns of supposed high moral character that had gone on for several months throughout

Texas for certain incumbents located in both Washington D.C. and in Austin had been run cleanly without slander toward their opponents. That had won some voters over as they longed for such non-child-like behavior within the political arena. In addition, a behind the scenes financial machine backing those same incumbents had made things rather difficult for any of the opposing unwanted candidates to overcome.

Regardless of the outcomes of elections beyond the perimeter of Texas, Samuel knew that some within the body of both the United States Senate and House of Representatives would soon be on their way out. In the process, one of two things would occur that were basic to human nature. The outgoing personnel would either glide to the finish line of the winter holiday break while pouting that they had not gained another term, or they would be boisterous and overzealous in an attempt to leave a lasting mark on their time in the Capitol Complex with an eleventh hour legislative statement. Of course the latter of those had the potential to create a disturbance or inconvenience for those around them, but in either case, the mood would be short lived. Their eager to prove replacements would begin their shift in the spotlight after the New Year, and would be faced with a brand new set of challenges.

While viewing the evening news for tallies and results, Samuel smiled with pleasure. Then an hour later, before sitting down to dinner with the family, the television media revealed what he had known all along. Every incumbent that mattered to Samuel and the overall plan had been named the winner of their particular office, so no new bumps in the road from the political scope would develop.

CHAPTER TWENTY-FOUR
FRIDAY, NOVEMBER 6TH

H aving flown to Amarillo via the family jet on Halloween evening, and then staying in a local hotel for the night, Courtney met with her contact at another of the Tillman Freight warehouse facilities on the afternoon of Sunday November first. As the man entrusted by Samuel for the delivery, he had driven the eighteen wheel tandem trailer over from Texarkana containing much of the supplies that would be needed for the Colorado portion of the attack scenario. Courtney's part in the transaction was to match the manifest she had been given by Samuel with that of the contents within the truck. In short, she was to ensure that the shipment arrived safely and intact.

Soon after completing a visual inspection to their combined satisfaction, Courtney drove the delivery man to the Amarillo airport for his one way flight back to Texarkana. Then as he prepared to leave the vehicle she said, "Thanks for bringing the shipment over safely friend, and I hope other aspects of your mission go just as smoothly."

With an outstretched hand, the man replied, "Thanks for the lift friend. For the good of the cause, may your mission, whatever it is, go just a smoothly."

Courtney shook the man's hand before he closed the door and then she drove back to the warehouse. Staring at the once again securely locked trailers, she pulled the burn phone from her pocket and hit speed dial. The woman who answered said, "This is number twenty three, what do you have to report?"

Having recently been given a numbered designation by Samuel that even his two remaining sons did not possess, Courtney replied, "This is number thirty seven. Please inform number two that the shipment is secure in Amarillo, and that I'm going dark to proceed with my mission. My next contact will be in two weeks if all goes well."

"I understand the message of secure shipment, and no contact for two weeks. Good luck number thirty seven."

With that Courtney climbed back into the generic vehicle she had rented that morning, and began her own road trip north. Following highway-287, she crossed over the thin panhandle section of Oklahoma and into the southeast corner of Colorado before stopping for the night in Lamar. Then she arrived in the greater Denver area on Monday afternoon by working her way further to the northwest, and checked into a small motel in a rough part of town that wasn't known for asking any questions of its guests. Later that night she began shadowing the movements of a certain individual when he emerged from his office for the drive home, and placed a tracking device under the trunk area of his vehicle after he parked for the night at his apartment complex. The next few days of reconnaissance had revealed that her target, as had been originally noted by number forty three, was a creature of habit with definite patterns in his routine. One of those habits could be useful to her endgame, as every night on his way home from work, the man stopped for roughly forty-five minutes at what had to be his favorite watering hole.

On the evening of Friday November sixth Courtney waited patiently in an unseen location for him to emerge from his place of business, and as with the three previous nights, noted when other employees either entered or exited the building. When her target exited at the usual ten o'clock sharp, she followed his car at a safe distance to that same watering hole. The bar was filled with people as she ventured inside for the first time, but no one seemed to care that she had unknowingly intruded upon a joint usually frequented only by locals. After getting a drink, and then locating and observing her targets habits for more than an hour, Courtney realized that his Friday night drinking had less constraints than during the previous three nights. Understanding there was a need to do so before her target became too intoxicated, Courtney made certain that he had spotted her when she walked past with a smile.

CHAPTER TWENTY-FIVE
ROLLING THUNDER

In the pre-dawn hours of Monday November ninth, four large vehicle carrying trailer rigs rolled onto interstate-30 to begin their journey northeastward from Texarkana Texas. Their combined cargo, consisting of various makes and models of fourteen automobiles, six large vans, and six black suburban's occupied most of the available double deck transport area of the convoy. The suburban's with dark tinted windows, as the only vehicles less than two years old, had been outfitted with special fortifications for use by the men who would eventually occupy them. Additionally, each of five vans that contained no rear compartment seating had been equipped with a less cumbersome array of necessary gear. The last of the six vans would serve a different purpose, and as such, had maintained its normal array of bench seating behind the driver's seat. If all went according to the plan, then each of the four large trucks would deliver their payload on Wednesday the eleventh.

Last minute preparation before the journey began included the collection of all cell phones from any of the drivers except for the lone burn phone that the lead driver possessed. He had already driven a rig to Amarillo just over a week prior, and had used that burn phone to signal number twenty three that he had returned safely as planned via a one way flight. Each of the men had also been reminded that only limited communication between the four trucks would transpire throughout the entirety of the mission. Such rare communication would be necessary only if one truck from the small convoy had been out of visual formation for a prolonged period of time, and then only via the use of coded messages transmitted on CB radios. That type of plan was nothing new for truckers, as before the advent of cell phones, CB radios had been employed for decades as the primary mode of communication for information on traffic accidents, construction zones, or the presence of law enforcement. What made them attractive in this instance was that the CB radios provided a way to communicate under cover without a satellite traceable cell phone footprint. Each driving pair had also been pre-instructed on the sequence of which CB channels would be used for any contact within the various states they would pass through along the way, and that transition from channel to channel would coincide with the crossing of the appropriate state lines.

Once attaining a comfortable cruising speed, the lead driver glanced in his left side mirror to confirm that the other three had fallen into formation. He knew, and was well experienced at having driven many of them before, that a vast network of interstate highways at their disposal could provide alternative routes if necessary. Fortunately the weather forecast of the next seven days in the eastern half of the country implied that there would be only minor storm activity, so each crew of two drivers believed that the primary route could be adhered to.

If that favorable forecast proved to be correct, then the small convoy intended to pick up interstate-40 on the outskirts of Little Rock Arkansas and follow it eastward until the genesis of interstate-81 well beyond Knoxville Tennessee. From there they would take a more northeasterly course through the Shenandoah Valley within the western portions of Virginia. Finally they would pass through a narrow fragment of both West Virginia and Maryland before closing in on their intended drop off location. By employing tandem driving teams in each truck, it was also ensured that the long distance haul could be made without stopping for any purpose other than fuel, food, or restrooms. Additionally, the empty rigs could immediately begin the return journey along the same route only moments after unloading their cargo.

CHAPTER TWENTY-SIX

TUESDAY, NOVEMBER 10TH

With a newly painted body of camouflage designed specifically for the upcoming mission, the MIL MI-8 HIP-C helicopter from the West Texas Skydiving School had completed the first leg of its northerly journey. Like the small convoy moving northeast from Texarkana, those involved with the western attack site in Colorado had initiated their journey the previous day. The relocation process began when the five women still at the training facility were transported to Amarillo via a twin engine propeller plane. Since the arrival of the helicopter in August to handle all of the training jumps, the twin engine aircraft and her sister ship, along with the two pilots, had served little purpose other than to taxi Mason and others to and from either Fort Stockton or El Paso. Now in Amarillo, the plane would remain in a state of readiness until that same function would be needed again.

As for the helicopter, the HIP-C had performed well under all conditions during the twelve weeks since her arrival. With the weight of the helicopter having been reduced slightly, the normal limit of one hundred sixty-two miles per hour could be exceeded by an additional five. Additionally, the previous maximum range of two hundred eighty miles had been stretched another ten. Although the numbers weren't hugely different, they could become helpful if need be. Unfortunately both extended limits couldn't work in concert. If the speed was maximized, then the range would decrease, and if the increased range was needed, a slower speed would be required.

Although there had been many instances when the full complement of two pilots and fourteen jumpers were onboard for practice runs over the training facility, or in flights that hugged the terrain changes of Bird Mountain, the most current flight had been the longest in duration. As such the distance from the training facility to Amarillo exceeded the maximum flight range by roughly one hundred miles, so a fueling stop had been required at the Lubbock Preston Smith International Airport.

Early Tuesday morning in Amarillo, the pressing function of Mr. Capra and Mr. Fisk was that of tending to the needs of the bird. They ensured that all remained in top notch working order by topping off the fuel level and visually inspecting the frame and her instrumentation. As they did so, a black suburban from the trailers inside the Tillman Freight facility arrived. The large vehicle, like the two others that were only minutes behind, would serve multiple purposes. First, each would bring several canvas duffel bags filled with weapons, live ammunition, and a portion of sixteen total parachutes to the helicopter. That cargo, along with additional fuel containers, would be strapped down within the bird. In so doing there would be two negative effects, as both the fuel range due to the increased weight, and the available floor seating area during flight, would be diminished if all fourteen jumpers were to stay aboard. Fortunately that challenge could be rectified until the actual attack flight, as the three black suburban's would take on a total of ten jumpers for the road trip toward

Castle Rock just south of Denver. Combined with the drivers and jet pilots, there would be five people in each vehicle, while the remaining four jumpers and helicopter crew of two had plenty of room for the next phase of their flight north.

CHAPTER TWENTY-SEVEN
WEDNESDAY, NOVEMBER 11ᵀᴴ

Number forty seven and his contingent of guests had been waiting for nearly three hours since the theoretical time of arrival, but there was no need for any concern as of yet. The overall time needed for the lengthy travel had been an educated approximation, but with the presence of uncontrollable factors such as interstate traffic levels or potential issues with the weather being mixed into the equation, that timeframe was less than exact. In short, they all knew it could still be several hours before their friends would turn up.

When the burn phone in his jacket pocket began to ring, it gave promise that the rendezvous was close at hand. Using a level and non-emotional tone of voice, the short and stout man originally from Abilene Texas answered with, "This is number forty seven, what's your status?"

"Ten minutes out. Are you ready to receive us?"

"Yes we are. Call me again when you turn the final corner, but let it ring just once and then hang up. I'll open the big door and you should pull all the way forward once inside."

"Understood, and thanks."

Turning to the assembled group of twenty-eight men and twenty women who were eager to commence with their eastern attack operations, number forty seven said, "We have about ten minutes. Everybody get ready."

The large collective had flown in on four flights from different cities in Texas the previous day under the façade of attending either a fraternity reunion or a corporate workshop, and had since been well rested at a series of hotels for their upcoming task. They all stood and gathered from various chairs and couches along the wall before moving to deposit any forensic evidence such as paper beverage cups and sandwich wrappers into a central garbage can. Then after checking to see that all was in order, the most senior of the women reported, "We're ready to go sir."

Number forty seven was unaware that the woman also had been given numbered status by Samuel, or he would have addressed her by the designation of number forty one. Instead, she received nothing more than a nod of comprehension from him before they, along with the remainder of the collective, waited in silence. When the burn phone rang just once a few minutes later as had been instructed, number forty seven moved to the large rollup door and pulled down on the heavy chain. Then he looked out the open door to get a visual, and the first of the trucks was no more than two hundred yards away. After stepping outside to wave them in, he moved back into the huge warehouse and waited. Just seconds after the last of the four trucks came through the opening, the chain was pulled in the opposite direction to seal it shut from any potentially curious eyes. Jogging at a brisk pace to the other side of the warehouse in order to greet the lead driver as the man stepped down from the cab, number forty seven reached out his hand and said, "Hello friend, welcome to Harrisburg Pennsylvania."

Extending his own hand, the driver replied, "Thank you friend, we appreciate your hospitality. Now, shall we get these vehicles unloaded?"

"Absolutely, what can we do to help?"

Looking at the assembled mass gathered along the wall, the lead driver replied, "Station one or two of them at the rollup door who can repeatedly raise and lower it quickly. As each car or van is unloaded, the designated driver of that vehicle can put on one of the many license plates that have been stored under the passenger seat. Then they can be on their way without waiting for the others. We can do the same with each suburban and their associated groups of passengers, as those vehicles tend to attract enough attention on their own. It will look far less suspicious that way as opposed to a long line of vehicles emerging all at once. When we get to the last two vehicles, you or one of my drivers can take over the duties at the door."

"I understand. Consider it done."

"Once everything has been unloaded and all of the drivers have departed, we can help you to finalize your preparations before we drive the rigs out of here and head for home."

"That sounds good, but most of what I need to do has already been taken care of."

"Excellent, now how are you getting to the airport for your flight home?"

"I have an escape route on foot mapped out, and then I can catch a cab twelve blocks from here after I'm sure that things have gone according to plan. Given the distance from here, no cab driver searching for a random fare will be suspicious. Add to that the time of day, and only a few homeless individuals in the area could possibly see me during the trek. No one should be any the wiser."

"Excellent, now let's get to work."

Within ninety minutes all twenty six vehicles had been unloaded, various state license plates had subsequently been affixed to them, and they were on their way. Thirty minutes after that the four now empty rigs had also vacated the area, so another phase of the overall plan had moved forward. As number forty seven made his way stealthily away from the warehouse, he began to think about the logistics of all that would transpire in the next few days. Then he began to visualize what his next assignment might be, but had no idea when he would be called upon to carry that assignment out. As those thoughts raced through his head, he suddenly remembered the words of someone he had admired for years who once told him to be certain that one task was completed before becoming concerned with another. With that he stopped briefly to glance over his shoulder, and he could already see thick smoke and a blaze of fire beginning to rise from the warehouse.

CHAPTER TWENTY-EIGHT

THURSDAY, NOVEMBER 12TH

Without knowing that she had done so nearly two weeks prior, the three black suburban's that had been unloaded from the twin trailers in Amarillo had followed the nearly identical route of Courtney toward their destination south of Denver. The only minor difference occurred within the final dozen miles of their trek, as Courtney had turned north from highway-86 onto highway-83 at Franktown while the trio of suburban's stayed west to Castle Rock. Arriving on Wednesday evening, rooms had been reserved for a three night stay with a Saturday morning checkout at the Best Western, Hampton Inn, and the La Quinta Inn. False identities had been created for the fifteen travelers, so one suburban could check into each hotel. During the course of their road trip, the helicopter had also advanced further north. While flying low, the six men within had passed over mostly uninhabited regions of land along the Colorado and Kansas state line. Then after crossing above interstate-70, the bird set down in the remote rolling foothills near the South Fork of the Republican River, but had nearly reached the maximum fuel range of the helicopter in the process. In so doing the men and their arsenal became well-hidden from curious eyes roughly fifteen miles southwest of St. Francis Kansas, and would most probably encounter no interruptions while addressing the fuel issue. With a planned overnight stay and a hold on their current position for the majority of the following day; there would be plenty of time to resolve the problem by unstrapping the fuel containers to quench the thirst of the helicopter. Then when the time was right, they could liftoff and easily reach the southern reaches of the Denver area on the night of Friday November thirteenth.

On Thursday morning in Castle Rock, one of the black suburban's departed with a driving pair and the two female pilots after they had all enjoyed a restful night. The four ladies were headed west toward Aspen, a journey of slightly more than two hundred miles, as twin Cessna Citation Latitude jets that two of them had flown in from southern California in August were waiting to become airborne once again. The road trip through the mountain passes of interstate-70 was beautiful with earlier snow falls having created accumulations at the higher elevations, but they had been lucky with clear road conditions and a favorable weather forecast for the upcoming days. Once at the Aspen-Pitkin County Airport, the two pilots checked in with flight operations and filed a flight plan for the following morning. Then the suburban was driven onto the tarmac so that stores of food, water, and clothing could be loaded onto the planes. As the foursome then prepared to split into pairs, one of the drivers said, "Here's to our collective success and that of the overall plan. Happy flying and we will see you back in Texas."

A pilot replied, "Thank you for the lift ladies, and good luck with the next few days."

Then after the two in the suburban had departed for the trek back to Castle Rock, the other pilot asked her partner, "Well, should we eat dinner in your plane or mine?"

CHAPTER TWENTY-NINE
FRIDAY, NOVEMBER 13ᵀᴴ

y six o'clock eastern time on Friday evening, the fourteen cars and six vans with a lone driver in each had been repositioned to various safe locations within a few miles of where they needed to be the following day. While in the course of that transport from Harrisburg Pennsylvania toward each of the two eastern attack sites, each driver of a car had stopped for purchases of food and water that would be needed by their passengers during the upcoming days. In doing so, they collectively maintained the cover of non-threatening housewives or mothers while also making sure to use cash only for all of their transactions. Before topping off their respective fuel tanks and calling it a night, each of the women driving the escape vehicles had one last task to perform. Within the course of their training in west Texas, each had committed to memory a series of turns, and the distances between them, that would be used for the getaway. Now that burned in knowledge attained by studying maps of cities and towns could be put to practical application via a trial run, and each woman practiced the route that had been provided to them via the advance scouting.

The four or five men within each suburban had used slightly different tactics with regard to repositioning as no supplies were needed, but they had also adhered to cash only purchases during refueling stops or when dining in groups. With a more physically demanding day requiring total focus in front of them, each had been instructed to forgo a late night and the possible opportunity of companionship in order to get a full nights rest.

CHAPTER THIRTY

A RUSE ALL DRESSED IN BLACK

At nine thirty mountain time, roughly thirty minutes before shift change, a black suburban with government plates pulled into the parking lot not far from Courtney's position. Two women dressed in black pant suits then emerged to enter the control tower building at Denver's Centennial Airport. Well rested after their drive to and from Aspen on the previous afternoon and evening, the two ladies were ready to take on the next aspect of their collective mission. Although they were not part of the normal foot traffic for the facility that had been noted during the previous several nights, there was no need for concern. Based on the intelligence provided to her by Samuel several weeks before, Courtney knew exactly who they were.

With the proper look and mannerisms needed to be convincing, brilliant although completely false identification, and just a hint of flirtation from behind a supposedly stern and impenetrable veneer, the ladies presented their request. They informed the shift supervisor that the local FBI section chief had tasked them with finding a suitable place for a military helicopter to be stored for a short time, and they would be in big trouble if they didn't locate one. The ladies expressed that their boss wasn't pleased with their work of late, and felt that he had given them an impossible assignment so that he could subsequently transfer or fire them. They further explained that the helicopter was already inbound from western Kansas and potentially low on fuel, so they needed his help. When the man expressed possible reservations about the legality of such a request, one of the ladies offered up a verbally convincing heartfelt appreciation for any assistance that he could render. Then she and her partner assured him that the helicopter would be gone early in the morning, which became the tipping point in the conversation. With anticipation of a positive reply the first woman drove their manipulation attempt home with a seductive smile, and the request was granted.

A few minutes later Courtney witnessed them emerging from the building, and soon after, a large helicopter landed near the far end of the runway. The women had not known of Courtney's existence within the parameters of the mission, let alone her observational presence of less than two hundred feet from their suburban. That of course had been the intent, and now based on their apparent success, she could move forward with her own mission. After watching them depart, Courtney looked at her watch and realized that they had cut the timing of their ruse close as the relief personnel for the control tower would be arriving within minutes.

As if on cue, three cars pulled into the parking lot a moment later, and the occupants appeared to be having a jovial conversation as they gathered to walk inside. When her target hurriedly emerged a short time later at three minutes after ten o'clock, Courtney followed him at a distance until he arrived at the same watering hole where he had overindulged the previous Friday.

CHAPTER THIRTY-ONE

BIRTH OF AN ASSASSIN

Courtney Tillman had been asked to provide a special service that went beyond her previous self-known skill set, but now that it was done, she felt pride in having played a small part in the overall plan. The past few months, not to mention the last several hours, had brought back a zest for dangerous adventure that made her feel invigorated again. She hadn't felt that way in many years, and although times were difficult with her husband Mason, she appreciated Samuel's faith in her and his attempts to bring her out of an obvious funk. Now, Courtney believed within herself that Samuels trust in her was well warranted, as the evening shift control tower supervisor from Centennial Airport that he had sanctioned her to kill was now dead in his south Denver apartment.

Per the advance intelligence reports of number forty three regarding the man's typical late night habits, which had subsequently been confirmed by Courtney, he entered a bar at ten thirty-five filled with those in search of little more than carnal pleasures. After a close pass of his position near the taps fifteen minutes later, Courtney sat down a few stools away and offered up a coy smile in his direction as she ordered a beer. The man took the bait with eagerness, and slithered in her direction while asking, "Excuse me, but didn't I see you here last Friday wearing a green sweater?"

While surprised that he had remembered the detail of what she was wearing at the time, Courtney replied, "I was here last Friday, and yes, I remember you too."

The ensuing conversation of more than an hour revealed that the man was quite arrogant given his less than attractive features, and he proudly boasted that he had given permission for two federal agents to park a helicopter on his tarmac for the night. Pretending to be enthralled by his self-proclaimed power of labeling the overnight staging spot as his tarmac, Courtney flirted with him over a second drink and waited for the man to advance. As the hour struck midnight and it was now the fourteenth of November, he asked if she wanted to have another drink back at his place. Courtney agreed, but as she supposedly had an appointment during the late morning, would do so only if she could follow him in her car.

Moving through the door to his apartment that he had held open for her, Courtney made sure to not touch a thing with her exposed hands. Then he said as he closed and locked the door, "Make yourself at home. Kick off your shoes and relax if you'd like."

Having heard the deadbolt turn as she took note of her surroundings, Courtney spun toward him with a smile and replied, "Thanks, I think I will after you get me that beer you promised."

He returned the smile before moving toward the kitchen, as the thought of eminent conquest flashed through his mind. Then while leaning into the open refrigerator he asked, "So do you prefer Coors? Or would you like something a little stron..."

Courtney hadn't given him a chance to finish his inquiry, let alone attempt to act upon his thoughts of what could transpire during the next few hours. She had followed him into the small kitchen with complete stealth and fired two shots from her silenced weapon into his back as he spoke. Then with the body crashing forward and slumping into the now broken shelves that caused the contents of food and drink to spill upon the floor, she stepped closer and put one more bullet into the base of his skull for good measure.

In reviewing the events of her actions, Courtney came to a self-realization. The act of killing a man had been easier to carry out than she would have ever believed, and the release of some of the hate felt good. She wasn't really sure how she had gotten to that point of needing such a release, but Samuel had obviously recognized the need for it. Courtney wondered if the hateful feelings were perhaps due to pent up frustrations over Mason, and whoever the woman was that she believed he was seeing on the side. Or perhaps it was because of the death of Chance many years before. He had been a wonderful brother-in-law during the early years of her marriage to Mason, and she, along with the rest of the family, missed him dearly. Maybe it was due to the fact of what Savanah had to face. She was such a sweet young girl with a love for life, but there was a chance that her life would end before she would be old enough to love a man with all her soul and bare children of her own.

CHAPTER THIRTY-TWO
SATURDAY, NOVEMBER 14ᵀᴴ

Having been notified by the graveyard shift of the arrival the previous evening, no one during the transfer to day shift gave it much thought. As the men and women within the control tower at the Centennial Airport were either preparing to depart, or pouring a cup of coffee to begin their six o'clock Saturday morning shift, a helicopter parked at the extreme southern end of the facility requested clearance for departure. According to the log books, the helicopter had been parked overnight at the request of the local FBI section chief, as it was to be part of the planned celebration at the Air Force Academy in the coming hours. Also noted within the log was that two women wearing black suits had shown proper identification as federal agents, and had requested that a fuel truck top off the helicopter that night as opposed to waiting until morning.

As Travis Connor, the morning shift supervisor, read the log entry, he asked no one in particular, "Federal agents. Alright, but what agency were they from?"

The graveyard supervisor who was just about to exit heard the generalized question and said, "Well his entry said by the request of the local FBI section chief, so I assume the agents were FBI."

"Well that would make sense, but he made no mention of that or the agents names. For that matter, there's no information about an arrival time of the helicopter or a flight plan. I just wish he would leave more detailed log entries, so I wouldn't have to ask him those questions the next time that I see him."

"I agree that he should provide more detailed reports, but I'm afraid that's just wishful thinking by the both of us. The helicopter probably came in not long before I started my shift, but when I tried to get some information, he seemed upset that I wanted to keep him a few minutes for questions after his shift had already ended. If he intended to stick with his regular pattern, then I was standing in the way of him going out to begin his weekend with some late night debauchery. Besides, he outranks both of us with his seniority and rarely lets us forget it. If he cleared the helicopter to be here over-night then who are we to argue, especially since we already cleared it for departure?"

What Travis Connor and his counterpart had overlooked, in spite of actually mentioning it during their conversation, was that the timing of both the arrival and the departure had been intentional. It was a well-known fact that the best time to pull something over on someone with regard to security measures was either at the very beginning, or at the completion of, their work shift. That was when most employees and supervisors, including those such as their high and mighty evening counterpart, were likely to suffer from their worst loss of focus.

After being granted clearance for departure moments before the discussion in the control tower had concluded, the MIL MI-8 HIP-C helicopter lifted off and was well on its way to being clear of the greater Denver area. According to the planned intent, it followed a southerly course set to the west of interstate-25 and hugged the foothills while flying low for added camouflage. From the crews perspective the easiest aspect of their mission had just been accomplished, and they were aware that things would get increasingly difficult before the day was through. When reaching the first of the intended rendezvous locations, the two pilots would need to top off the fuel tanks of their bird once again and take on some extra containers for when they were needed as accelerators. Then there was the human cargo element, and the need for all of them to gear up properly for the pending attack. Of course the vital and most challenging aspect of that first landing would be to remain undetected in that location for several hours.

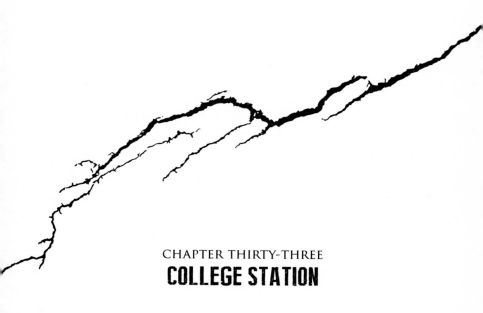

CHAPTER THIRTY-THREE
COLLEGE STATION

Seated comfortably within the luxurious family suite at Kyle Field on the campus of Texas A&M University, Samuel and Savanah watched their beloved Aggies warm up forty-five minutes prior to the gridiron battle against the L.S.U. Tigers while Victoria conversed with some friends. As per the norm for all home games, Samuel and Victoria had arrived from their ranch the previous evening to enjoy dinner and comfortable hotel accommodations close to campus. Then several hours before kickoff they made the short drive over to their reserved parking spot, ascended to the confines of their stadium suite, and enjoyed the spoils of what multiple years of large donations to the university had helped to provide. A short time later other members of the Tillman family would arrive, with Savanah then usually occupying her current seat next to her grandfather during the game.

On this particular day, as it was the final home game of the season, Samuel once again flashed back to the fond memories of his youth when as a boy he attended all the home games with his parents. Then his thoughts shifted to a few years later when he proudly became a third generation student at the university. Throughout those four seasons he never missed a home game as the Aggies were one institution within the now defunct Southwestern Conference. Samuel passionately cheered them on while standing for the entirety of every game in true twelfth man tradition as a faithful member of the corps of cadets. It was during one such occasion that he had kissed his future wife Victoria for the first time, as another valued school tradition dictated that those cadets lucky enough to have female companionship during the game would kiss that young lady after an Aggie touchdown. Of course all of those visions in Samuel's memory of time spent in and around College Station also included the witnessing of several pep rally bonfires, and the tragedy involving loss of life which forever changed how those celebratory events would be managed. Samuel, along with many others, also witnessed one entire side of the stadium being imploded for renovation purposes. As a result of that massive renovation project, the suite that his family currently occupied for the home Aggie games came into being before the 2015 season.

Samuel and Victoria were indeed proud to boast, like both sets of their parents before them, that they were native Texans and Aggies through and through. As alumni and major donors of both academic and athletic endeavors for Texas A&M University, they had developed long term relationships with the senior administrative teams and power brokers within the university structure. In recent years they had used their influential power with the athletic director to schedule a home game on this particular weekend, and then more recently, had parlayed that into another favor. From the perspective of Samuel, it was of vital importance to the overall plan that an earlier than usual morning kickoff of eleven o'clock central time for the contest would be scheduled. Eager to please the Tillman's and a large group of substantial donors that had echoed that same desire, and having learned that a network would be willing to televise the contest, the university administration had complied with the request back in early March. They were easily caught up with the prospect of how much additional revenue would come from scheduling an earlier start time, so it never occurred to any of the administrative team to question why it had been requested.

With Savanah now moving about the suite and securing herself a pre-game snack, Victoria brought Samuel back from his thoughtful state into the reality of the present moment. She placed a hand on his shoulder and quietly asked, "Well dear, the day is finally here. Has anyone checked in yet?"

Returning the soft tone, he replied, "I have heard from number twenty three that number forty seven has reported in."

"That's good, is everything on schedule?"

"Yes. The drop off in Pennsylvania went according to plan, and the warehouse and any evidence that it may have contained has burned to the ground. She also informed me that number forty seven has successfully returned home on a flight to Dallas. He awaits further instructions, but understands they are contingent upon what unfolds today."

"That's excellent news, and number forty seven has once again proved his worth."

"Indeed it is, and yes he has. I'm confident that everything for today will go according to plan, or at least close to it, in the two eastern locations."

"How do you feel about the west?"

"Not as confident. There are a lot of moving parts to mesh properly."

"Has twenty three heard from forty three?"

"Yes and no, which is part of what concerns me. Forty three checked in on the first day of the month like he has been since I stationed him there in May, but he had been instructed by number twenty three to make additional contact a few times during these final two weeks."

"And he hasn't done so?"

"He made contact on the fourth and the seventh, but nothing since then. At this time we can't be sure if he has been compromised or not, so we just have to wait and see."

"What about our other contact there?"

"Beau has done well up to this point as was to be expected, and has reported that security measures have gone unchanged. We won't hear anything from him today, but after things calm down and an accounting of the cadets has been taken, they will probably allow each of them to notify parents or a family member of their safety. He will surely contact Mason or Courtney sometime Sunday I should think."

CHAPTER THIRTY-FOUR
ONE O'CLOCK EASTERN TIME

While the earlier than usual game at College Station had been under way for an hour, events that would define the success or failure of the planned attacks continued to unfold. At Camp Smith Military Reservation a few miles to the south and on the opposite side of the Hudson River from West Point, three black suburban's with the combined cargo of fourteen passengers and their fortifications had been cleared to pass through the main entry gate. Each man had been asked to provide identification, and the falsified documents in their possession representing various government agencies easily passed inspection. The jet black vehicles with dark tinted windows had been fitted in the pre-dawn hours of that Saturday morning with counterfeit government license plates to complete the ruse, and the carefully hidden arsenal within each had gone undetected.

Once inside the gate, the suburban's proceeded slowly toward the cluster of buildings near the parade field while those not driving began to remove the weapons hidden within seat cushions, adjoining backrests, and shallow floor compartments of the interior space.

Those weapons included two Hawk MM-1 MGL semi-automatic grenade launchers for a pair of jumpers within the first wave, and Denel PAW-20 Neopup semi-automatic grenade launchers for the remaining twelve of both waves. The former was a cold war relic of American design that used 40x46mm ammunition in a twelve round rotating drum magazine, and the weapon had an effective range of nearly two hundred fifty yards. The South African made PAW-20 Neopup, at slightly over thirty-three inches in length was eight inches longer than the American Hawk, with the 20x42mm point detonated ammunition being delivered from a six round rotary drum. Although possessing the benefits of roughly three and a half times the effective range as the Hawk at eight hundred seventy five yards, and being much lighter when fully loaded, the rounds were not designed to create the same level of structural damage that the Hawk could produce. Their intent was to have more pinpoint accuracy with regard to the desired impact location, and spray out from that detonation point with a killing radius of about ten meters.

In addition to the grenade launchers, each of the fourteen assailants would also be carrying another shoulder holstered weapon. An American made semi-automatic AR-15 rifle had been selected over the Czech made AK-47 for the simple facts of having a more reliable and accurate range along with a lighter overall weight. Although the AK-47 had been widely used by various factions throughout the globe for many years, its limited range of precision at perhaps one hundred yards would not be good enough for the current undertaking. Along with the various weapons themselves, Samuel and his black market contacts had been able to procure thirty round magazines that could be emptied in about seven seconds for the AR-15's as opposed to the standard issue twenty round clips. With a loaded magazine and eight more accessible reserve clips on their person, each man was equipped with two hundred seventy rounds of 5.56x40mm killing projectiles that were easily reloadable and could be fired in less than two minutes. As a final weapon, each of the fourteen would have a thigh rig for a handheld 45-caliber pistol containing a ten round magazine with an additional bullet in the pipe.

Once parked, the fourteen men dressed in black suits carrying large duffel bags of gear were hardly noticed as they moved toward the nearest building. Intelligence reports from a friend stationed inside the Pentagon had provided the organization with the location of which building would be used by the jumpers as they prepared for the upcoming drop, so with that knowledge, the black suited force quietly commandeered a large interior room that would be suitable for their purpose. Then they began a systematic attack on those men who were scheduled to jump in a few hours.

One by one each of the fourteen parachutists were singled out and distracted by a man posing as a government agent on a fact finding inspection tour, and subsequently taken from behind by another with a strong arm and a hand held rag full of chloroform. After being rendered unconscious and relieved of their respective jumpsuits, each was tied and gagged in the event that the drug wore off prematurely and moved into one of a series of small closets. No hoods were necessary to eclipse their vision of the attackers should they awaken, as none of those soldiers would ever see the light of day again. Once all fourteen had been accounted for, each man was injected with a lethal dose of nerve toxin. The toxin had been developed by United States government labs to shut down the human circulatory system within minutes, and the hope was that the claim would be accurate. If so, then the men would never be conscious of the injections effect on them. Unfortunately a few of them convulsed with open eyes near the bitter end, so a harsh truth was revealed.

CHAPTER THIRTY-FIVE
HIGH NOON IN COLORADO

All had gone well up to the present moment, as the early morning landing of the helicopter had either gone unnoticed or uncared about by any locals in the small town of Monument. The three black suburban's then arrived at the remote rendezvous spot less than an hour later via dirt mountain roads to unload their cargo of the ten jumpers who hadn't stayed with the helicopter, and some extra fuel containers. Each vehicle had long since departed, and if nothing kept them from their intent, the two driven by the women who had posed as federal agents the night before would already be a few hundred miles from the Monument area. One would have used the tracking device given to her in order to pinpoint the exact location of where the helicopter had been hidden Thursday night and most of Friday in the northwest corner of Kansas. That way she could retrieve all of the spent fuel containers that had been deposited at the landing site and the two discarded parachutes that were no longer needed by Mr. Capra and Mr. Fisk. Then after making her way slightly to the east, she would turn south onto highway-27 for the journey toward and through the panhandle region of Oklahoma and into Texas. The other would be in northern New Mexico heading for an observation point where she hoped to report the movement of aircraft later in the day. Remaining in Colorado, the plan called for the third Suburban to be repositioned to the southwest within visual range of the Fremont County Airport in Canon City.

Now hidden in a saddle between two rises of the foothills just west of town, the helicopter piloted by Mr. Capra and Mr. Fisk was ready to go and awaiting the call. One of the jumpers who had been stationed as a lookout roughly one-hundred yards away signaled once again that all remained clear. After relieving another man from an hours watch, he had been flat on his belly to stealthily peek over the top of the rise for half of that time. The continued absence of hikers, bikers, or off road enthusiasts coming up from Monument was a welcome relief, and was probably attributed to either the season, or the game that would soon transpire.

Glancing at his watch, Mr. Fisk, said, "We should be hearing something very soon. If not, we may have a problem."

Mr. Capra nodded with confirmation without saying anything, and then a moment later, the burn phone that had been given to him a few days prior by number thirty one began to ring.

CHAPTER THIRTY-SIX

GAME TIME IN NEW YORK

Each of the helicopter flight crews had been briefed several days earlier as to the specifications of this particular flight, and those specifications were much the same as those parachute drops they had piloted previously. There were a few differences though, as aside from needing two helicopters instead of one for the amount of jumpers and their gear, the major change for this mission was the destination of the flight after their cargo had bailed out. Now with all the pre-flight checks taken care of, the engines warmed up sufficiently, and having been cleared for departure from the parade field, all that was needed before the helicopters could liftoff were the fourteen jumpers.

Switching his microphone on, the pilot of the lead ship, Major Bates, radioed the other helicopter and asked, "Hey Scrib, do you know what's keeping them?"

Captain Scribner replied, "No Major, we haven't heard anything."

Before Major Bates could contemplate the implications of the delay any further, his own co-pilot pointed toward the cluster of buildings and said, "There they are now sir."

135

Looking in the direction of his co-pilots pointing finger, Major Bates nodded and said, "Good. Our available time for flying to the proper jump position is already tight enough, so we don't need any delays. Just imagine what the general would do to us if we were late."

A moment later the fourteen men who had jogged across the grassy parade field divided into two groups of seven, and boarded the respective helicopters. Hidden behind their dark protective face shields, each man was loaded down with gear and weapons that were designed to simulate the standard issue equipment for dropping into a combat zone. Additionally, each man except the last had a large flag representing one of the original thirteen colonies strapped to their backs under the parachute pack. They would be followed by the modern day fifty star version of the American flag via the final jumper, as each would unfurl behind the men once their respective Air Ram rectangular parachutes were self-deployed.

For decades there had been jumps far too numerous to count over a multitude of stadiums throughout the country for one celebratory fashion or another, but none of those had matched the intended purpose of this day. In a spectacle that had been choreographed to the minute, fourteen parachutes drifting down over the stadiums for each of the three military service academies would create a splendid visual to commemorate Veterans day in America's two hundred fiftieth year of existence. Due to the late arrival and hurried boarding of the jumpers, neither Major Bates nor any member of the flight crews on either helicopter noticed that something wasn't quite right before lifting off.

After a short flight of fifteen minutes to obtain the proper altitude and jump position, the twin helicopters slowed their forward momentum to hover high above Michie Stadium and the surrounding grounds of the United States Military Academy. Based on a combination of factors that included an improved Army football product on the field of play, the geographic proximity of their opponent, New Jersey's Rutgers University, and the planned celebration surrounding the Veterans holiday of three days prior, Michie Stadium was filled beyond the normal level of spectators. That assembled crowd approaching the stadiums capacity of thirty-eight thousand included the presence of several dozen generals and senior officers within the Army ranks, with some of them having taken leave from their overseas postings to fly in for the event. General Osborne, currently serving on the Joint Chiefs of Staff and per the directive from President Harwell, had traveled from Washington D.C. for the festivities and was seated next to the current commandant of the academy.

Drifting down from the cloudless sky above their target of Blaik Field within Michie Stadium, fourteen parachutes and the men dangling beneath them could now easily be seen by the spectators within the crowd. Upon reaching a level just a few hundred feet above the playing surface, while having adjusted to their own predetermined choreography, the first four men focused their attention on the Hoffman press box area atop the second level of the west side stands. Simultaneously, the three men descending close behind aimed toward the northern portion of the east stands where the corps of current cadets stood in mass. Then each of the seven began firing their shoulder holstered grenade launchers into strategic locations on both sides of the stadium. Crashing through the large window panes on both levels of the press box, the ensuing explosions caused by grenades launched from the two Hawk MM-1 MGL magazines effectively destroyed the entire media center located within. The network television feed, radio transmission, and all other communication abilities that had been established to cover the celebratory pregame festivities and the events of the gridiron scuffle, were instantly lost. Shrapnel and the concussive force of the grenades had left dozens of human bodies lifeless within the media center, while also tearing multiple holes through the walls of the superstructure.

Had the attack taken place a decade earlier, eliminating the communication center within the stadium would have been a less meaningful endeavor. During the time of 2016 the cellphone craze that had swept through American society was nearing its peak, so a significant percentage of those in the stadium would have been video tapping or "selfie" photographing each other at the game instead of actually watching the events unfold. That would have created the potential for thousands of video files that authorities could subsequently sift through in search of damaging evidence. Fortunately for the attacking force, most Americans had found that habit to be passé by 2024 as they redeveloped a desire to experience life once again instead of constantly starring at a tiny screen in the palm of their hand. That societal transformation meant that very few of the spectators gathered for a game in 2026 would have had the ability, or the desire, to film portions of the attack or those who had perpetrated it. With that lack of civilian captured evidence, an opportunity within the stadium had been created and the attacking force could not afford to ignore it. Although only a minimal amount of military personnel would be located within the media portion of the Hoffman press box, the area became a primary target in modern tactics much as it would have been fifty years earlier. The destruction of the media presence would aid in slowing the release of information, and the gathering of video evidence, with regard to the attack.

A smattering of debris fell upon the outer entrance concourse below the back wall of the Hoffman press box, but as most patrons were already seated within the stadium, only a few lives were impacted as a result. On the press box side facing the field, a massive amount of debris including glass, fragments of concrete, wood framing, drywall, and sound insulation material had created a much higher injury and death toll as it showered onto the crowded seating area below. When a large television camera that had been dislodged from its mount as a result of the blast concussions then followed suit by tumbling downward, it claimed the lives of three more people in an instant.

Roughly one-hundred fifty yards to the east across the playing surface, smaller grenade explosions from the PAW-20 Neopup launchers were ripping through the corps of cadets and sending bodies flying in all directions. When those who had launched the grenades then opened fire with their automatic weapons before touching down, the carnage was multiplied. Just seconds behind them, the other wave of seven drifted in and repeated the assault with the same three and four man directional focus. The only alteration in their tactics was that they began by firing their automatic weapons in a merciless barrage, and held the grenades back in reserve. Once they had all touched down onto the newly defined battlefield, each of the seven emptied their grenade launchers into the superstructure that supported the upper deck of stadium seating. Their hope was that the salvo would cause a stampede of panic as shards of concrete from various pillars and aisle ways began to fly.

Under the cover of that overhanging deck, the explosions caused massive amounts of casualties, and many of the top Army officers in attendance, including four star General Osborne from the Joint Chiefs of Staff, were killed. Those patrons seated within the areas of both end zones or the southern portion of the east stands consisted mainly of non-targeted civilians, and were therefore far less affected by the assault. It had been understood by the attackers that no gun fire or grenades would be aimed toward those sections of the stadium, but some collateral damage was expected. A few injuries had indeed been caused by stray pieces of flying debris, but the majorities of the injuries in those locations, as had been anticipated, were self-inflicted due to panic after the attack began.

Within the lower level of the Kimsey Athletic Center at the south end of the stadium complex, both football teams of the Army West Point Black Knights and the visiting Rutgers Scarlet Knights were massing in the corridor before taking the field. The pre-game schedule dictated that each team would wait to emerge until after the fourteen jumpers had landed and they, along with their parachutes, had been subsequently collected and moved towards the sidelines. Then the teams would take the field and observe a moment of silence with the assembled crowd in honor of America's veterans within all branches of the military who had served. After that America the Beautiful and the National Anthem would be sung by the Corps of Cadets choir, followed by the ceremonious coin toss at midfield, and finally the game itself would begin. The clearly defined schedule designed to coincide with identical proceedings at the Naval Academy in Annapolis Maryland and the Air Force Academy just outside of Colorado Springs would no longer be adhered to however, as the horrific impact of the surprise attack had altered the course of events.

After having stood in frozen amazement during the moments of the attack, a member of the stadium security staff partially regained his composure and rushed into the corridor leading towards the locker rooms. Then he shouted, "The stadium is under attack, take cover!"

Having clearly heard the horrific sounds of multiple explosions overhead, the head coach of the visiting Rutgers team, who had previously served in the military, shouted back, "That's obvious you idiot, but who is attacking the stadium?"

Before that all important question was brought to light, each of the fourteen assailants had unclipped their parachutes and flags, expelled all of their collective ammunition into the crowd, discarded their now empty automatic weapons onto the playing surface, and began the process of attempting to escape under the cover of panic that surrounded them.

The stadium security representative in the tunnel had taken offense to the personal comment of the Rutgers head coach, so as he ran past him he curtly replied, "How would I know who is attacking us? I only know that it's much safer in here than it is out there!"

Realizing that the man scampering by in gross neglect of his duty was neither a cadet nor a member of the armed forces, the Rutgers head coach had no reservations in yelling a trailing response of, "You are a coward who doesn't deserve to be a representative of our stadium, let alone this one."

CHAPTER THIRTY-SEVEN

COLORADO SPRINGS

A s the two attack waves assigned to West Point had been drifting down from the sky to begin their assault, the two waves of their brethren over Colorado Springs had begun theirs just seconds earlier. Having risen moments before from the hiding place near Monument, the camouflaged MIL MI-8 HIP-C helicopter slid into a lower altitude position of two thousand feet over the intended target mere seconds ahead of the twin helicopters from The United States Air Force Academy airfield. At that moment, they began what would become a tightly choreographed dance requiring precise timing.

Many of the spectators within Falcon Stadium had no clue that something was out of order, but the commandant of the academy, seated next to his superior officer from the Joint Chiefs of Staff, was not one of them. Motioning with his hand for an aide seated behind him to lean forward, Brigadier General Vickers turned his head away from the higher ranking general. Then he quietly asked the aide, "Has there been a change in the scheduled format for the pregame festivities?"

"No sir. I haven't been informed of any changes."

"Then can you tell me why there are three helicopters positioned above us?"

There was no time to contemplate the inquiry, as men began to bail out from the larger one hovering at the lower altitude. Within seconds their Air Ram rectangular parachutes had been self-deployed, the designated flags behind each jumper began to unfurl, and the helicopter quickly moved off to the west. The men and flight crews of the higher pair at two thousand five hundred feet were confused. They were witnessing a jump that they had been ordered to undertake, yet they had not been informed of another group in a different model helicopter joining them. Additionally, they had not been instructed to abort their mission, so the lead pilot ordered the human cargo of both birds to continue as planned.

Within the stadium, the commandant, along with nearly everybody else, was watching the jumpers drift down from the sky. Then when he saw the second group begin to freefall, he motioned for his aide once again. With a quiet yet stern voice he said, "Well something isn't right Major, and we need to find out what happened. Make a note that come Monday morning, I will want to speak with whoever just sent two separate flights and two groups of jumpers to perform the same mission while the highest ranking officer in the Air Force was here to see it!"

Knowing that he had not been responsible for the ill-timed foul-up, but feeling as if he had been, the aide replied, "Yes sir general. I will find out who was responsible for this error, and have that officer in your office first thing Monday morning."

There was no reply, as his commanding officer was once again looking skyward. Then the first wave of seven began to alter their course somewhat with the easily maneuverable parachutes, and it looked as though they might not be able to land on the field of play as was intended. A few seconds later, the commandant uttered, "Wonderful. Not only do we have too many parachutes drifting down toward us, but now they are going to show a nationally televised audience that they can't hit the target."

Already experiencing a level of displeasure toward the overall performance of his subordinate currently in command of the academy, coupled with the insult of then being ordered by President Harwell to sit with the buffoon during the proceedings, had made General Brooks more irritable than usual. Having heard the statement that had just been uttered, and the prior whispering conversation between the commandant and his aide, General Brooks of the Joint Chiefs replied to his subordinate, "I sincerely hope that you are incorrect general. The Air Force already gets enough grief from the Army and Navy about somehow being inferior to them, and both you and your men are not helping our cause to stifle that belief with this midair foul-up that is currently underway!"

What hadn't been realized by the man with four stars on his shoulder boards, or by his subordinate with only one, was that the first fourteen jumpers coming down knew exactly where they were headed. That was proven in earnest a few seconds later, as they used their shoulder slung grenade launchers to begin an attack on the press box area of the stadium and the seating area below. At first many of the spectators didn't know what was coming their way, and the voice of one completely oblivious man claimed, "How cool! What a great promotional idea to have the parachute guys shoot balled up t-shirts towards us."

Before anyone could realize that the objects were far too small, and coming in way too fast, to be such a benign item as the claim had suggested, the first set of grenades pierced the glass frontage of the press box and media center. Seemingly an instant later, they exploded to send a shower of concrete and glass down upon those below. The salvo continued into the seating area until the launchers were empty, and then the automatic weapon fire began. Screams of panic were then heard as wounded patrons cried for help while most others began to climb over the motionless bodies of the dead in quest of cover.

Seated on the opposite side of the stadium, many of those in the crowd looked on in amazed horror. Then seemingly in mass, they began to gaze skyward once again. Another two waves who had jumped from the higher altitude helicopters were floating down, but they were perhaps still a minute from landing. Realizing that their location could be the intended target of the additional waves, a desperate attempt to exit began by patrons of the stadiums east side. Unfortunately for those involved, the stampede did little more than cause injuries that never would have transpired. While the actual attacking fourteen floated out over the northwest rim of Falcon Stadium toward their landing zone, the helicopter that set them loose just moments before had circled back around from the west and swooped down to retrieve them. Having unclipped and abandoned their respective gear, the fourteen men sprinted a short distance across the parking area to the rendezvous point. In an action that resembled a drop off or pick up of ground forces in the combat zones of Viet Nam, the MIL MI-8 HIP-C barely touched the ground as the men climbed aboard through the aft ramp and were quickly whisked away.

Within the stadium that was ripe with fear and panic, members of the Air Force Academy Falcons and the visiting University of Nevada Wolfpack football teams emerged from their respective locker room areas to a horrific scene. Expecting to run onto the field in preparation for the gridiron scuffle a few minutes later, they had heard the explosions and came out early to investigate. With the press box area and portions of the stadium below it engulfed in thick smoke and small fires, they witnessed the air corps of cadets which included Beau Tillman spill from their seats onto the playing surface. While seemingly uninjured or fired upon during the attack, and with a desire only to prevent additional death or injuries within the stadium, the cadets exhibited a true level of grit. Their collective intent was to subdue additional jumpers before those landing could continue the attack, and they would not be merciful while doing so. Unaware that the fourteen actually scheduled to perform the pre-game festivities were unarmed; the leading edge of the cadet wave tackled the first few of the jumpers as they landed and began to pummel them. Given the circumstances of the frenzied moment, the move on their part was both understandable and brave. Unfortunately it was also short-sighted, as their overzealous response to the situation had proved to be too much. Although one man would not succumb to the injuries until later that evening, three of the fourteen innocent jumpers lost their lives as a consequence.

CHAPTER THIRTY-EIGHT
THE COVER OF PANIC

Under normal circumstances the teams would access the playing field at Michie Stadium by utilizing the large opening between seating areas at the southeast corner, and that was where the group of fourteen attackers began their daunting task of escaping the scene without capture. The plan was to use the crowd and the panic of the moment for their much needed cover, as each was now armed with nothing more than a silenced side arm. They would force their way through whatever resistance that might be encountered during the first few hundred yards, while staying as tightly formed for added security as possible. The 45-caliber pistols that had been secured to their thighs during descent were intended to be fired upon only those military personnel or stadium security that could potentially jeopardize the intended escape route. However, there would be no hesitation in waving or pointing them towards civilians to effectively clear a path through the crowd if necessary. Each man also understood that if they encountered a civilian hell bent on becoming a hero, they would be required to strike that person with their weapon repeatedly if need be. Above all other things, it was imperative that none of the fourteen be taken dead or alive.

The group successfully made their way south from Michie Stadium along Mills Road with more ease than was expected, while Jason Tillman did his part to ensure that they wouldn't encounter a surprise flanking from their left side. As the senior cadet stationed at the cannon on the east side of Lusk Reservoir, he had ordered the men under his brief command to follow him away from the potential flanking position by taking the walking path along the north shore of the reservoir toward the stadium. His directive toward the handful of cadets was obeyed without question, as there were surely people within the stadium that needed assistance, be it medical or otherwise.

During the escape along Mills Road, only a few rounds of fire, one into the leg of a pursuing West Point football player and two others into the legs of stadium security guards had been required. That action effectively halted the advance of civilians, as most had then hit the deck out of fear. Now moving away from the stadium complex with more ease, the assailants neared a downhill section of road leading toward a large parking and tailgating area used by the fans. While descending into the mass of several hundred vehicles, the men located three large vans with identifying flags flown overhead and quickly moved toward them. There was one each painted red, white, and blue in separate quadrants within the field of vehicles, as they had been parked several hours earlier by three of the group of female drivers. The intent of the vans was simple. They were to provide a brief sanctuary for the attackers, as they changed into the civilian attire that had been stashed within them. Using the keys placed under the rear bumper of each, the men climbed into their pre-assigned vans via the rear doors. A few moments later, each man reemerged after having removed the jumpsuit, face shielded helmet, and surgical gloves that they had worn for the drop and assault upon the stadium. Then before moving on, the last man out of each van set a Fugas thermite bomb with a delay of five minutes. The explosions created by them would be small with minimal damage to the surrounding area, but the intense white heat from the thermite element would completely melt the van from within in short order. Any potentially damming evidence that each vehicle contained would therefore be made unrecognizable and irretrievable in just minutes.

Now dressed in clothing more befitting a patron of the game, each of the three smaller groups regained their brisk pace to the south within the panicked mass of spectators that had caught up to their position. Just minutes later, and not long after the vans had become engulfed in the intense heat of the Fugas bombs, each of the fourteen men moved through the Thayer gate with hundreds of other civilians to exit the academy grounds. Their move had been accomplished before any level of order was restored to initiate security lockdown measures, so the task of apprehending the assailants suddenly became more difficult.

Roughly two hours earlier seven getaway cars of various 2022 through 2024 makes and models rolled into the town of Highland Falls not long after the three vans had entered the academy grounds. Parked near restaurants and local businesses, each of the vehicles and their female drivers appeared to be just another aspect of everyday life within the community as they waited for their human cargo to arrive. As the fourteen attackers dispersed into pairs and moved toward their respective transport vehicles, one of the waiting drivers finished cleaning and then safely stowing away her silenced weapon within a fitted pocket under the passenger seat. She, like Courtney in Colorado, had been given a numbered designation after being selected by Samuel for a specific mission beyond that of driving an escape vehicle. Having recently returned with great pride in the completion of that special assignment, number forty-one took a moment to fix her hair and ponder the magnitude of what she had just done.

Per the intelligence report that was initiated more than ten months earlier by her son Jason, and based on the instructions from on high, Ashley Tillman had located her target exactly where it was believed he would be. Then by use of flirtation, and her well-toned body that had resulted from four months of intense high altitude preparation in west Texas, she was able to seduce and lull the man into a false sense of security at his place of business. During the moments that followed, Ashley called upon her hand to hand combat training of previous years and immobilized her lethargic opponent by breaking one of his arms and destroying both of his knees in short order. With the man crying out in pain and sweat beginning to pour from his forehead as he writhed on the floor, she removed a silenced weapon from her purse and pointed it toward his groin. The man instantly froze to the best of his ability, and with cat like quickness she was on him.

While pinning his good arm under her knee as she straddled him, Ashley pushed the barrel of the gun into the man's mouth. Then she glared into his eyes with a cold blackness of her own and whispered, "I'm sure this is quite different than the way you envisioned me straddling you, but life can be funny that way. Now that I have your full attention, there is something that I must say to you. We have learned that the first cadet you harassed twenty years ago was my husband's youngest brother Chance, and you need to know that he was killed in the action of an unnecessary war on Father's Day just a year after graduating from West Point. Another of the cadets that you picked on less than a year ago, and threatened with physical violence on that same day, is my oldest son Jason. He remembers his uncle Chance with fondness from the days of pre-school, and chose to follow in his educational footsteps. Jason, like his uncle before him, will graduate from West Point this coming spring. It is for both of them, and the many other victimized cadets who came between, that I do this now."

As the man's eyes grew larger with fear, she removed the barrel of the weapon from his mouth. Before he could cry for help, Ashley Tillman quietly killed the obnoxious overweight man with two bullets into the chest and then one more into his temple for good measure. In so doing, she had made sure that Mr. Nick Spano would never bully another West Point Cadet.

With each of the seven vehicles having received their pre-designated cargo of two attackers, and in some cases one of the van drivers, they were driven southward out of town at a leisurely pace so as not to attract attention. When clear of the immediate area, the vehicles then scattered further by using a variety of routes leading them into northern New Jersey or directly into eastern Pennsylvania. From there, they would individually access interstate-80 when possible and head west through Pennsylvania toward Ohio.

CHAPTER THIRTY-NINE

THE ANNAPOLIS RIPPLE

Having utilized the same infiltration method of three black suburban's with counterfeit government license plates, and federal agency identification for those within, gaining entry onto the appropriate military base had been easy. Subsequently, the removal of the assigned parachute jumpers and the substitution of them by that different group of fourteen attackers had also proved to be no problem. In so doing, the early phase of the Annapolis segment within the three pronged attack had gone according to plan. Even the jump had gone well with significant damage being inflicted upon Navy Marine Corps Memorial Stadium and the military personnel present for the game. Where the plan had run into snags, was during the attempted escape from the target area in the moments following the attack.

Unlike the Air Force Academy in Colorado, or the United States Military Academy in New York, the Naval Academy in Annapolis Maryland plays their home football games at a facility that is not actually on the academy grounds. Although certainly in close proximity, the stadiums location is adjacent to route-70 part of the way north from campus toward the nearby east/west directional traffic artery of highway-50. A portion of the surrounding area is residential, with many of the streets and roadways providing alternate access to the same highway. With understanding that the fourteen attackers needn't be concerned with a potential security lockdown of the academy following the attack, one could theorize that their escape would be made easier. Unfortunately for those fourteen men, there was a known factor that would balance, if not tip the scales, in the opposite direction.

Navy Marine Corps Memorial Stadium, through a series of upgrades after the dawn of the twenty first century, had become nearly completely enclosed around the playing surface. The south end of the stadium would provide no avenues for ease of escape, while the north end offered only two possibilities that could both prove to be difficult at best.

It was therefore decided during the planning stages of the attack back in late March that a few of the point detonated PAW-20 Neopup grenades would be kept in reserve to aid in establishing an escape route. As a consequence of that decision less would be launched toward certain areas of the crowd, but it was a necessary sacrifice. Unfortunately that issue became slightly magnified when the attack plan also called for an assault on three regions of the stadium as opposed to the two main zones at West Point. Unlike the three and four man formation within each of the two waves of jumpers that would strike West Point, the plan for Annapolis was to have each wave in a two, three, two formation.

Floating down with flags trailing into their prearranged choreography, the first two with the larger and more potent grenades from the Hawk MM-1 MGL launcher focused on the east side and the modern media center housed within. The other five split their attention onto two separate areas of the west side, with the three man group striking first at the older multi-level press box with grenades. Then they used their automatic weapons on the lower level seating area where many of the high ranking naval officers were located, while the final two of the seven simultaneously concentrated all of their collective firepower where the current Midshipmen were standing in the sections just north of their superiors. The second wave, scarcely more than an instant behind, had used the same attack pattern, but they were the ones who held back some of the ammunition for the escape.

With those in attendance rendered either dead, injured, or in a state of disbelief and shock, the attacking force shed their parachutes, flags, and all of their empty weapons just as their brethren in both New York and Colorado were simultaneously doing. Then the men turned away from the stadiums closed in southern portion where both teams of the Navy Midshipmen and the visiting Wake Forest University Demon Deacons were located, and made for the large grassy hill beyond the north end zone. Unfortunately, even though the Midshipmen in attendance had been thinned out considerably, some were still available to potentially block the intended escape path.

Scampering up the hill of the northwest corner between the Middies and those civilians with end zone seats above the grass embankment, the tight formation of fourteen began to encounter more resistance than had been anticipated. Waving their silenced side arms as a deterrent, the outer ring protected those few who still had their grenade launchers from many of the advancing hoard. Then when two of the grenades were used to blast a gaping hole in the perimeter fence, the group attempted to spill through unscathed while heading for the adjacent parking area. In so doing, one attacker was tackled by a trio of civilians who were braver than their appearance would imply. Before he could rise, two of them began punching him repeatedly in the kidneys and the backs of his legs while the third kicked him forcefully in the ribs several times. Fortunately there were two of his fellow attackers nearby, and as one held the crowd at bay, the other knocked two of the civilians into unconsciousness with the butt of his grenade launcher before shooting the third with his silenced sidearm. Then joined by yet another of the attacking force, they helped their battered friend stager to his feet and pressed on.

Another of the force, while moving into the mass of parked cars for cover, was shot in the arm by a Maryland State Trooper from a distance of about twenty-five yards. To hit a moving target at that range with a 45-caliber Smith & Wesson would have been difficult for a civilian, but the Trooper was a different matter. The wound created by the jacketed hollow point round was not severe enough to keep the man from continued forward movement, but it did knock him off his feet momentarily which created the additional misfortune of having his silenced sidearm slip from his grasp to slide far beneath a car. As he attempted to rise, he heard another shot from the direction of the trooper, and the safety glass window next to his head exploded into hundreds of pieces. Fortunately for him, it was the last shot that the trooper could squeeze off in his direction, as the law man was then eliminated by two silenced close range shots from behind.

Waiting beyond the parking areas were three escape vehicles, two vans and one car, which sat at pre-designated locations for what had been intended to be a quiet recovery of human cargo. The driver of the blue van which had been positioned in the large parking area east of the stadium a few hours earlier, and then remotely detonated after the attack as a diversionary tactic, now waited in the white van with her counterpart. While perched in the window frame with head and shoulders above the roof line, she looked through a set of binoculars and noticed that the attacking force had run into some difficulties. Sensing the need, she climbed from her perch to stand upon the roof in order to signal members of the attacking force. Having then spotted her position on Farragut Road from a distance, six of the fourteen attackers, which included the two slightly wounded men, made their way toward her. The other eight moved further to the west where another vehicle and the red van were waiting along Cedar Park Road near the corner of Farragut. As that group closed to within fifty yards of their rides, they saw the white van pass by and then turn right onto Glen

Avenue. Within seconds they climbed into their own getaway vehicles, and each of the drivers informed them that their counterpart had held up a closed fist followed by a single index finger when she drove past. She had repeated the gesture as verification of her signal that she had picked up six members of the attacking force. Although it was now confirmed that all fourteen jumpers had been accounted for, their successful escape from the area was far from secure.

CHAPTER FORTY

POST-GAME ENLIGHTENMENT

Samuel and Savanah sat in quiet dejection, and felt helpless as the precious time on the game clock ticked away. There was less than one minute remaining, and the outcome was no longer in doubt. The L.S.U. Tigers from Baton Rouge had gained possession of the ball, and they would not need to surrender it before time ran out. They would win this game by the score of 24-14, and in honesty, had outplayed Texas A&M in the process. The visiting team deserved to win, but that didn't make it any easier for Samuel or Savanah.

They shared a wonderful grandfather to granddaughter relationship that was filled with past fun times and fond memories, but Texas A&M football bonded them together more than anything else. As a bright eight year old during the 2026 season Savanah was really beginning to understand how the game worked, and would ask questions to learn more. Samuel had become a willing and eager mentor in her learning process with good intent, but Savanah had unfortunately picked up on one of his traits that could at times become difficult for those around him. Whenever their beloved

Aggies were defeated as was the case on this particular Saturday, their collective inner pouting child would rise to the surface. Of course the pouting of Savanah could be understood for a girl of her age, but Samuel was painfully aware that his behavior was a less acceptable shortcoming.

Glancing at his watch, Samuel knew that the time had come and gone. There had been no information relayed on the stadiums public address system as of yet, nor had there been any type of interruption seen on the televisions within their stadium suite. That could only mean one of two things. Either all three of the attacks had somehow been foiled, or they had all been successful in causing serious damage to the media centers at each location. Of course word of the attacks would eventually get out via one form of communication or another, and Samuel knew that as each of the carefully planned assaults had begun roughly twenty minutes earlier, that information could come at any time. The intriguing aspect of the moment for him to ponder was how would said information be conveyed and subsequently received.

The reaction to the attacks, if they had been carried out, by the local, state, and federal authorities, as well as individual hosting universities across the nation and the governing body of the NCAA was unclear. Samuel believed that there were three distinct options, and felt that each had the possibility of existing during the coming hours. There could be nothing done at all in order to avoid a large scale panic, and for games that were nearly complete that may be the best option. Other games could be halted in mid-action for fear of additional attacks, but that would probably be the least favorable option. Unfortunately for those institutions choosing that path, the panic that could ensue would probably cause more harm than good. Of course a third option would be along the lines of what had been employed after the terrorist attacks of September eleventh 2001. That Tuesday morning attack created the postponement of all sporting events in the United States for several days, and college football games slated for the upcoming Saturday were rescheduled for available dates in late November or early December. If such a decision were to be made in the current situation, it would most certainly impact the majority of the west coast universities who had not yet begun their respective contests. With each of these potential scenarios in mind, Samuel had effectively taken Kyle Field and Texas A&M out of the equation back in March when he convinced the athletic director and other members of the university administration to have an early kickoff for this particular game.

His first indication of how the event would be handled then came, as with the game clock at zero and the teams shaking hands at midfield, the public address announcer made a statement. He said, "Ladies and gentlemen. On behalf of Texas A&M University and our guests from Louisiana State University, we would like to offer thanks for your patronage of today's game. Please understand that there is no cause for alarm and that you are not in any danger, but we have an announcement of grave concern that we feel you should all be made aware of. A moment ago our media representatives received word that the three military academies located in Annapolis, Colorado Springs, and West Point were each attacked by an unknown military force. Those attacks apparently transpired simultaneously roughly twenty minutes ago, but unfortunately we have no other details to offer you at this time."

As many of the Texas A&M alumni had served in the military, and perhaps along with some of the current corps of cadets had at one time aspired to attend one of the impacted academies, they expressed more sorrow at the announcement than a typical civilian may have. That sorrow came without panic however, but the same could not be said for many civilians within the stadium. Samuel noticed that the stadium cleared out much faster than at the completion of most games, and he theorized that the traffic leading away from Kyle Field would soon become a nightmare as people attempted to reach the perceived safety of their homes. That didn't much matter to Samuel and the rest of the

Tillman family, as they usually stayed in their stadium suite for an hour or so after the game. Regardless of how others reacted in the current moment, Samuel had his answer to the question of if the attacks had transpired. The fact that news of the attack had not become national via the media for perhaps fifteen minutes was the bonus he and the other attack planners had hoped for, as those minutes would surely aid in the escape plans of those involved. What Samuel needed to do next over the course of the upcoming days was to observe and study the subsequent impact on American society. Would the events of November fourteenth bring the nation together with the demand of a reprisal toward some foreign entity as he hoped, and if so, would it remain that way for an extended length of time?

CHAPTER FORTY-ONE

IGNORANCE OVER NEW YORK

As the getaway vehicles began their move from West Point toward eastern Pennsylvania, Major Bates and Captain Scribner continued their northbound mission by piloting the two helicopters toward the New York state capitol city of Albany. Their orders were to land in a remote area of the international airport just north of the city to refuel and pick up additional jumpers for another parachute drop. Based on the direction of their flight path, and having no reason to suspect any foul play in the distance behind them, they were unaware that three black suburban's had melted to almost nothing behind a cluster of buildings at the Camp Smith Military Reservation. Those Fugas bomb explosions had been properly set for their timed detonation, as they had occurred within three minutes after the first of the attacking force launched grenades upon the unsuspecting masses at West Point. Much like the three vans in the mass of vehicles on the academy grounds, there had been little or nothing left to sift through for evidence. To balance the scales of ignorance in the current moment, the attacking force was also unaware that the helicopters hadn't returned to a mass of melting suburban's near the parade ground landing zone.

The Governor of New York, in his most typical fashion, had expressed a desire to upstage his counterparts in the states that housed the other service academies. He had called in several favors, including one to his old friend General Norgard, so that he could carry out that intent. The plan was to have personnel from the New York National Guard duplicate the jump over West Point by landing in the Rockefeller Empire State Plaza that surrounded the State Capitol Complex. The Governor would then seize the opportunity to address the assembled crowd, and in so doing, remind them of how his presence in Albany had positively impacted the state of New York. Then a marching band would play some inspirational tunes, with a huge fireworks show to follow. It was well planned pomp and self-propaganda at its absolute worst to kick start his intended presidential run for 2028, but unfortunately for the governor, none of it would transpire.

As Major Bates and Captain Scribner, having flown a northerly heading that for the most part kept them directly above the Hudson River, were now positioned high over the city of Albany, it was time to begin their approach into the international airport. At that same moment, the Governor had just completed what he initially felt to be an intrusive phone call from the White House Chief of Staff. Once he had heard why the call had been placed, he no longer felt that way. An act of terrorism had occurred within the state of New York, and with good reason, the plans for any continued celebration in the downtown area of Albany had suddenly been dashed. After hearing the news of West Point, and acting upon the directive from Washington D.C., the Governor contacted the awaiting National Guard personnel and the airport police. His order to them was clear and concise. They were to secure the helicopters from future flight, and detain the crews who flew them, until federal agents would arrive to begin an investigation.

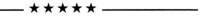

CHAPTER FORTY-TWO
SEATTLE

Seated within the luxury VIP suite on the south side of Husky Stadium, President Jordan Harwell had leaned forward in his seat at high noon when the referee signaled for play to begin. It had been many years since he had attended a game on the campus of his alma mater, and as the first President of the United States to hail from the Seattle area, President Harwell became a welcome an honored guest of the current University of Washington president.

President Harwell had been lucky with the weather for his long awaited return to campus, as the cloudless day was unusual for mid-November in the Puget Sound area of western Washington. On such a day the views from Husky Stadium and the adjoining University of Washington campus were difficult to match, and President Harwell knew that all too well. Just to the east of the stadium stood Lake Washington, which had for decades been used by countless fans for access to the stadium. They would travel in, and then moor their various watercrafts near the shoreline, to enjoy a different style of tailgate festivities before coming on land for the game. Beyond the lake, the distant mountains of the Cascade Range could be seen with the snowcapped peaks revealing evidence of the oncoming winter. To the west beyond the city and Puget Sound suburbs was the region of Olympic National Park, which formed a magnificent towering rift of mountains and forested land between the sound and the vast Pacific Ocean. Finally to the south was Mount Rainer, which stood sentinel as the state's highest peak at well over fourteen thousand feet. It didn't much matter where you were located in the Seattle area, if the skies were clear, then the majesty of the mountain and the views in all directions were difficult to ignore.

Throughout the years of his undergraduate studies at the University of Washington Jordan Harwell had attended many of the home games, but those opportunities faded when he continued on with the more time demanding law school at the same institution. Years later when finances and his work schedule would allow for it, he purchased season tickets to attend the games with members of the family whenever possible. Unfortunately, once he entered the political arena of state office in Olympia and then federal positions in Washington D.C., he could again no longer spare the time.

As President Harwell sat back to relax while play was halted for an injured player, he remembered how those season seats, like the ones he had scrambled for during his years as a student, were far less luxurious than the VIP box to which he currently occupied. Now after many years, he could finally witness a Husky game in its entirety within the warm and hospitable climate of a comfortable suite. At least that's what he thought. Not yet halfway through the first quarter of action, and with the home town team already staking a 3-0 advantage over the visiting California Golden Bears, a secret service man entered the suite to confer with the lead agent of the Presidential protective detail.

After listening to a brief description of what had transpired, the lead agent, Heath Bishop, snapped his head to the right in order to look directly into his subordinate's eyes. Then he quietly asked, "Has this information been confirmed?"

Matching the quiet tone of his supervisor, the agent replied, "Yes sir. It has been confirmed."

"And how long ago did this happen?"

"Information is sketchy, but I would say about twenty-five minutes ago sir."

"Twenty-five minutes ago?"

"Yes sir, perhaps even longer ago than that."

After looking at his watch to learn that it was twelve fifteen, agent Bishop asked, "Why are we just hearing about it now?"

"Sorry sir, but as I said, the information is sketchy."

With a stern grimace on his face, agent Bishop then spoke into the microphone hidden within the left wrist area of his suit. The tone was soft, but his words spoke loudly. He said, "We have a situation that requires immediate attention. Have the car ready to move in less than two minutes, and notify Air Force One to prepare for emergency evacuation. We are on our way down with POTUS."

In his ear piece he heard the reply of, "Understood sir, POTUS will be moving to Air Force One for an emergency evacuation."

Then moving forward, agent Bishop reluctantly placed his hand on the right shoulder of the President and whispered, "Sir. I'm sorry to interrupt because I know how much you have been looking forward to this game, but we must leave immediately."

Understanding that the subject would not have been broached without just cause, President Harwell replied, "What's wrong Heath?"

"Sir I can brief you on the details once we get to the motorcade, but I feel that this location is no longer safe for you. Now please, let's go right now!"

Turning to look directly at agent Bishop who had been on his personal detail since before the election of two years prior, President Harwell could tell that the man originally from Lake Tahoe Nevada was deadly serious. Motioning him closer, the President said softly, "Alright Heath. I understand that you have a well-defined protocol to follow, and I trust you to do whatever is necessary to guarantee my safety. That being said, let's keep this as quiet as possible to avoid a panic."

"I understand sir. Now please, let's go."

Leaning to his left as he stood, President Harwell reached out a hand of thanks toward his host. Then he said softly, "This is probably nothing, but my security detail needs me to accompany them. I will return as soon as possible, or call you later to explain."

Now also standing, the befuddled and rather arrogant University of Washington President, Dr. Edward Plummer, struggled to reply. Then he said, "Well of course Mr. President, but whatever it is I encourage you to stay. I'm sure that the facilities within this VIP suite, or certainly those of my university, can provide you with whatever you may need."

Knowing full well that the statement was grievously incorrect for the present moment, agent Bishop whisked President Harwell out of the VIP suite and was soon joined by two other secret service agents. The four of them made their way through the superstructure of the facility and toward the awaiting motorcade at a brisk pace, while other agents that they passed along the way maintained a vigilant watch on their surroundings. Within minutes they were clear of Husky Stadium and the surrounding grounds without the majority of those in attendance being any the wiser. Unfortunately the safe haven of the President's plane, Air Force One, was still several miles away at Boeing Field just south of downtown Seattle.

The Boeing Field facility had the tremendous benefit of possessing a lengthy runway capable of satisfying the needs of any aircraft, as well as being a complete and separate entity from SEATAC, the region's largest international airport just a few miles further to the south. Simply put, the facility was useful as the preferred site for certain private business or political needs in that substantial ground and air traffic could be avoided with relative ease. That of course meant nothing in the current situation if the motorcade didn't get the President to the plane in one piece. Although he had sent advance word to begin the pre-flight sequencing for a departure that would be several hours prior to the intended plan, and in spite of the obvious benefits and the shorter distance to that field from their current location, agent Bishop wouldn't begin to relax his posture until President Harwell was safely aboard and Air Force One had taken flight.

CHAPTER FORTY-THREE
AIR FORCE ONE

P icking up speed at full throttle as it rolled down the runway toward takeoff, Air Force One was in defense mode. As a consequence of the need for a rapid escape and clear airspace to the south, a temporary hold had been placed on the scheduled departures from SEATAC and the Renton Municipal Airport. The pilot, Colonel Van Horn, with assistance from his co-pilot, Lieutenant Colonel Fleming, pulled back on the yoke to lift the nose of the plane. Within seconds the powerful jets of the modified Boeing-747 had freed Air Force One from an earthly grip at twelve forty-five, and she began a slow cumbersome climb into the sky.

The navigator, Major Hopkins, pressed the headset close to his right ear and reported to his captain, "Sir, an Oregon Air National Guard escort of fighters has been deployed from Portland International Airport. They will be coming in from our right shortly."

"Coming in from Portland Oregon? Isn't there a fighter base closer to us than that?"

"No sir. Unfortunately McChord Air Force Base just south of Tacoma doesn't have a fighter wing at the current time. Their aircraft are mostly cargo and recon."

"Roger that Hop. Can you try to get confirmation on how many fighters from Oregon we should expect, and when they will arrive?"

"Yes sir. I'll get that for you right away."

On the deck below, President Harwell attempted to process the limited information he had been given by agent Bishop while in transit from Husky Stadium. A few key members of his staff who had made the journey west with him were sifting through additional reports, as they would be required to provide insight as to what had transpired. Others had been out of position to meet with the motorcade when it departed the stadium abruptly, and had been left behind. Perhaps transportation back to Washington D.C. could be arranged for them via the FBI section chief in Seattle, but it was surely to be of minor significance in the coming hours and days.

Agent Bishop had made a few calls of inquiry, and while in communication with his boss back in Washington D.C. to confirm the safety of the President, he felt the heavy jet banking to the left in order to obtain a more easterly heading. After listening to his verbal report, the woman praised agent Bishop for taking the initiative to evacuate the President based on the slow intelligence report he had received. Then she relayed word to him that Vice President Sutherland had been taken to a secure location. A moment after that call had ended, another agent approached him and said, "Excuse me agent Bishop, but POTUS has sent for you."

While standing to move past the woman, he replied, "Alright, thanks Carolyn."

In the nose section of Air Force One, President Harwell motioned for agent Bishop to enter his office. Then after hanging up the phone he said, "Heath, thanks for getting me out of Husky stadium without causing a panic."

"You're welcome sir."

"And also for briefing me on what you knew about the West Point attack."

"Certainly sir, I'm glad to be of service."

"You always are Heath, and I won't forget it."

"Thank you sir, I appreciate the thought."

"You're welcome Heath. Now, I'm about to go into the conference room to discuss some rather bad news that goes beyond West Point, and I want you in there with me."

"Yes sir."

"This could turn into a very long day, and I want you by my side until we have figured out what the hell is going on."

"I understand sir, whatever you need me to do."

"Alright then, now come with me."

Within the conference room, staff members stood as President Harwell entered. Then when motioned to speak, one of them said, "Mr. President, at this time we know very little of what has happened at West Point other than that the assailants came in via parachute. I'm afraid that it will be several hours, perhaps even days, before an accurate count of the dead and wounded can be made available to us, but initial reports would seem to imply that the count will be in excess of a thousand."

With a sigh of dejection, President Harwell replied, "Alright, I understand. I'm aware that it will be difficult, but I would like to have those totals sooner than later if you please."

"Yes sir, I will keep you updated."

After motioning for everyone to sit down, and then pointing toward the next person at the table, President Harwell asked, "What do you have with regard to Annapolis?"

"Annapolis? Don't you mean West Point sir?"

"No, I just got off the phone with someone who has confirmed that Annapolis was also attacked."

Caught completely off guard by the news of Annapolis, the man had no information about that attack to give the President. He stood and said, "I'm sorry Mr. President, but if you will excuse me, I will find out what I can about Annapolis for you."

At that moment another staff member entered the conference room and said, "Excuse me for being late sir, but I have just received a report that the Air Force Academy in Colorado Springs has been attacked as well."

All three of the military academies had suffered attacks simultaneously in what must have been a highly organized and well thought out plan, so agent Bishop knew that the President had correctly stated that this could turn into a very long day. Glancing in his direction, he took notice of an expression on the face of the President that was rarely ever seen. With just cause, the man was clearly pissed off. The room fell silent as President Jordan Harwell repeatedly clenched and unclenched his left hand. Then while glaring at the man who had just brought forth the additional bad news, he took a deep breath and broke the silence by asking him, "Has the attack on the Air Force Academy been confirmed?"

The man's voice cracked a little as he responded, "Yes Mr. President, that information has been confirmed."

Then aimed at no particular individual, President Harwell asked, "What about the University of Washington?"

Those seated at the table fell silent once again, and their inadequacy in responding to the question at hand was ill timed. Sensing that his input would be welcomed to break the deafening silence, Agent Bishop broke protocol and spoke up. He said, "Excuse me Mr. President, but I may be able to help with that question."

Turning around, the President said, "Well based on the fact that no one else in this meeting appears to be able to answer my question, then by all means Heath, please do so."

"Yes sir. Once we had you safely aboard Air Force One, I made phone contact with a local agent still on the ground at Husky Stadium. He made no mention of an attack, nor did my direct supervisor in D.C. when I spoke with her a short time ago. I can't confirm at this time that the University of Washington was spared, but the evidence would suggest that it has been sir."

Shifting his gaze toward those at the conference table, President Harwell then added, "Agent Bishop appears to have made a logical conclusion, but we still need confirmation."

One of the men at the table signaled to his aide, and she ran out of the conference room. Then he said, "We will get confirmation on that for you as quickly as possible sir."

Agent Bishop then interrupted again and added, "Mr. President. Since the attack on West Point was accomplished with the use of parachute jumpers, and there is a planned jump into Husky Stadium at halftime, may I suggest that we contact whoever can cancel that jump as a precautionary measure?"

Turning once again to face the conference table, the President said, "Agent Bishop has made an excellent suggestion. Can I assume that one of you will follow up on it immediately?"

Another man at the table picked up a phone with a direct link to the communication center up near the flight deck. Then he said, "This comes directly from the President, so the message is priority number one. Make contact with the flight crew of the helicopter heading toward Husky Stadium, and order them to abort the parachute jump. We are very short on time, so you must act quickly."

After a nod of approval toward the staff member, President Harwell looked at his watch and said, "I hope that we aren't too late."

Then agent Bishop spoke up again by adding, "Mr. President. Although aborting the jump is the prudent move with regard to safety for all those within Husky Stadium, as a result of that action, we still won't know if you were an intended target for some time."

Turning again to face agent Bishop, he replied, "Expand on that thought please."

"Yes sir. If the jumpers for Husky Stadium are part of the same terrorist movement, and aborting that jump has foiled their intended plans, then they could attempt to use the helicopter as a weapon by killing the flight crew and crashing it. That is unless they have already killed the flight crew and one of them knows how to fly it. Then the possibilities of damage are magnified."

"I understand Heath, so what do you suggest?"

"Well sir, they could follow such a course of action and then we would know that you were most probably an intended target. The downside for them by doing so is that it would tip their hand, and that cell, if it is one, could never be used again for anything of significance in the future. On the other hand, if they don't crash the helicopter, and return to base with nothing more than questions of why they had been aborted, that would imply innocence on their part. With their jump scheduled for some time between ninety minutes and two hours after those who hit West Point and the other academies that would seem logical, as they would have no element of surprise to rely on. As for me sir, I would still caution on the safe side by taking the appropriate measures. Having said that sir, I suggest that we detain the jumpers and the flight crew for questioning even if they return directly to their base. That could help us to determine if they are one aspect of the larger terrorist act that included you as a target, or completely innocent of any wrong doing. Additionally, I would have Dr. Plummer from the University of Washington interviewed by the local FBI. Perhaps it is nothing, but he was eager to have you stay in the stadium suite when we were preparing to evacuate you."

After nodding in silence toward agent Bishop, President Harwell reversed his pivot to stare directly upon those gathered around the conference table. Then he said, "Agent Bishop has expressed some keen insight into this matter, and we should act upon it accordingly. We shall wait to see what course of action the helicopter bound for Husky Stadium takes in order to help us determine if I was, and perhaps still am, an intended target. In the meantime, place a call to the FBI field office in Seattle so that Dr. Plummer can be spoken to. While all of that is going on, let's attempt to discover exactly who was a target at the various military academies, and why."

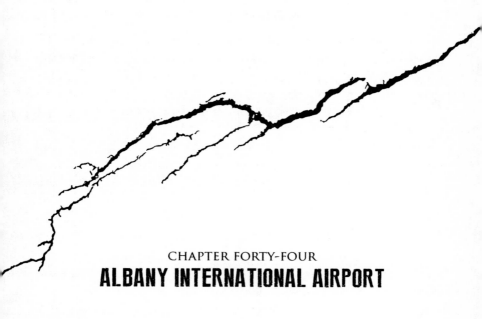

CHAPTER FORTY-FOUR

ALBANY INTERNATIONAL AIRPORT

hortly after President Harwell and his entourage had been safely greeted by an escort of four fighter jets from The Oregon National Guard unit stationed at the Portland International Airport, Major Bates and Captain Scribner were finally given permission from the tower to land their two helicopters at Albany International Airport. Per the orders of the Governor via the White House Chief of Staff, the commanding officer of the local National Guard unit of New York had a squad of troops in position to detain the two flight crews.

During those several minutes of not understanding why they had been kept at bay in a hovering position facing away from the hangar facility, Major Bates heard a strange statement over the headset from a crew member positioned in the rear portion of the craft. The young man had always been a reliable sort, and had played an integral part in assisting jumpers as they prepared to bail out, but what he was conveying in the present moment made no sense at all. He had just added to the mystery of the unusual delay by exclaiming, "Major

Bates sir. There are some soldiers on the ground forming up on our six, and they are all pointing their weapons at us!"

With an inquisitive look on his face, Major Bates replied, "Say again."

After leaning his body further out from the open door for confirmation, the enlisted man replied, "Yes sir. I can see eight men formed into a semi-circle pattern just behind our position, and their weapons are trained on our undercarriage."

Turning to his co-pilot, Major Bates then said, "I think that the corporal needs some time off."

After a smile and an agreeable nod, his co-pilot then purely as a victim of curiosity glanced over his right shoulder toward an area behind the two helicopters. Behind the tinted visor of his helmet, his eyes instantly grew larger as he stared in disbelief. Without returning his gaze toward Major Bates, he clicked on his microphone and said, "Sir, I can't see behind us to confirm the corporals claim, but I can see a group of eight like he described in a position behind Captain Scribner's bird."

Now more baffled than before, and thoroughly concerned, Major Bates increased his tone when he questioned, "So first we were told to hold our position, and now there are ground personnel with weapons trained on us. What the hell is going on down there?"

His question would be answered soon enough, but the answer was less than comforting. After landing, powering down, and then completing the post flight checklist, the crews of the two helicopters heard an unusual request. The lieutenant in command of the ground troops said, "Major Bates and Captain Scribner, please step out of the helicopters and place your hands on top of your heads immediately. When instructed by me both of your co-pilots will do the same, and then we will tend to the crew members stationed in the rear compartments."

Although amazed by the request, with sixteen National Guard troops training their automatic weapons upon them, Major Bates had little recourse but to comply. As soon as the Major stepped down from the helicopter, Captain Scribner followed suit from the other craft. Then with hands on head Major Bates asked, "What's the problem lieutenant?"

"Sir, I have been ordered by the governor of New York to escort all of you into the hanger. You are to be detained until federal agents can interrogate you."

"Detained and interrogated, for what purpose lieutenant?"

Removing his sidearm from its holster, the man in charge of the moment replied, "I'm not at liberty to discuss that with you sir, but all of you must come with me."

Once again understanding that he and the two crews under his command were in no position to resist the young lieutenant and his band of potentially trigger happy soldiers, Major Bates attempted to calm the situation. With a non-threatening tone he asked, "Very well lieutenant, we will come with you to the hangar. But must it be done with all of my men under gunpoint?"

"Those are my orders sir, so that is what I will do."

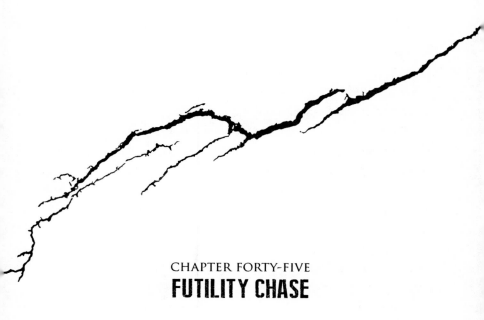

CHAPTER FORTY-FIVE

FUTILITY CHASE

While Major Bates was attempting to fit the pieces of his own puzzling scenario together in New York, a chase of sorts was underway just to the west of Annapolis Maryland. Glen Avenue had been chosen as a direct route away from Navy Marine Corps Memorial Stadium toward route-450, or West Street as it was also known. From 450, access to highway-50 or the smaller route-2, could then be easily attained. Adhering to the pre-determined plan, the white van headed for highway-50 and their westward movement toward Washington D.C., while the red van, with five men in the back, and the other vehicle with the additional three turned south onto route-2 leading toward Londontown.

As the men in the red van had nearly completed changing into their civilian clothes, one of them kept a close watch on the road-way behind through the rear tinted window. Then he loudly asked the driver, "How much longer until we reach the exchange point?"

Matching his volume she replied, "We're almost across the South River now, so five minutes tops at this speed."

Having seen a set of flashing lights in their distant rear which had facilitated the need for his question, he then urged, "Well it looks like we have state troopers on our tail. They are still back there quite a ways, but you better pick up the pace a little."

Trusting his word without debate, she honked the horn twice to warn their partnering escape vehicle and stood on the accelerator with a little more emphasis. The gap between them closed briefly, and then the other car increased its pace as well. Having substantially less weight and mass to hinder the acceleration, the lead vehicle was soon far ahead of the van and would remain so until they reached the exchange point. A moment later, while speeding past the small local airport, the driver of the van said, "Hang on everyone, we have a right turn coming up onto Southdown in a few seconds."

The men in the back, who had already gathered their jumpsuits, face shielded helmets, boots, and surgical gloves into several large easily combustible bags, braced themselves. Then after she had completed the hard banked turn one of them reported, "We are all set when you are."

She replied in kind, "Good. Get ready for a left turn in a few seconds, with a right almost immediately after. Then we will have another left about twenty seconds after that, so we should be at the exchange point in less than a minute."

When she skidded to a stop shortly after completing the series of turns, she spotted the group of vehicles they would transfer into and the one that had fled from Annapolis just ahead of her van. The driver, and the three members of the attacking force that she had picked up, were already out of that car, while the drivers of the others were seated and ready to go. As the doors to the van were flung open, the men brought their bags of gear over to toss them inside with the others. Then a driver from one of the four getaway vehicles waiting to pick up the group of ten asked, "How long do we have?"

The man who had been peering through the back window of the van replied, "Very little, perhaps only a minute or two if the state troopers get lucky with their choice of corners to turn. Just to be safe, let's set the Fugas bombs for two minutes and get the hell out of here."

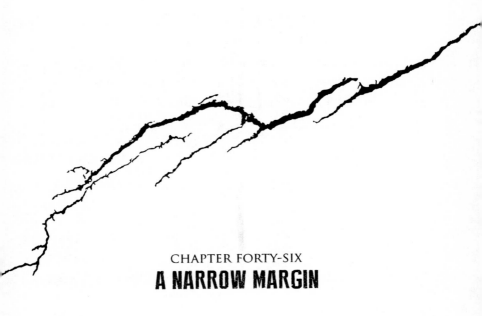

CHAPTER FORTY-SIX

A NARROW MARGIN

T he two Maryland state trooper units that had been in distant pursuit of the red van and car from Annapolis had separated once they arrived in Londontown, and had thusly begun a systematic search in quest of the assailants. Turning onto Southdown Road, and just like he had done back at the corner of West Street and route-2, one of the troopers stopped and rolled down his window. Then he asked a pedestrian, "Excuse me sir, but have you seen a red van driving by within the past few minutes?"

The man responded while pointing at the intersection roughly two-hundred yards in front of the trooper's car, "Yes I did officer. A red van going very fast turned left in front of me as I was stepping off the curb, and then it turned right at the next corner."

With that the officer picked up the microphone for his radio and said, "I have a citizen who has spotted the red van turning off of Southdown Road, I'm moving to investigate."

When the man asked, "What's going on officer? Did the woman driving the van rob a bank or something?"

The trooper replied, "A woman? Are you sure about that sir?"

"Yes officer, I'm sure. What has she done?"

"I'm sure that you will hear about it soon enough, but she is part of something much worse than robbery."

"Well I hope that you catch her officer, for whatever she did."

"I hope so too, and thanks for your help sir."

As the trooper drove away to continue his search with newly discovered information, he also kept an eye out for any women that might be walking along the streets. Turning left and then right onto Stewart Drive as his most recent witness had instructed, he soon came to a T-intersection at Locust Street and glanced to his left. He had found it. Parked about one hundred yards away on the grassy right hand shoulder of the road was the red van, but before he could pick up his microphone to call it in, the van suddenly lurched upwards a foot or two with a brilliant flash from within and came back down harshly on its springs. Thick smoke began to billow from various seams of the doorways, and seconds later the process repeated when a car in front of the van began its own similar death throes.

Then after turning left and rolling forward slowly with his window still down, he could feel an increase in the heat. The trooper stopped his unit, and called in, "We need fire and possible ambulance at the corner of Stewart and Locust. There have been two vehicle explosions, and it is unknown at this time if anyone was inside."

As that call was being placed, the four getaway vehicles, with either two or three new passengers in each, moved south along Pike Ridge Road and spilled out onto route-214 while maintaining a non-alarming pace. At that junction, they all headed west to the intersection of state highway-301 where two of them turned south. The other two remained on route-214 until reaching the capital beltway, and then used the southern portion of that major freeway to cross over the Potomac River and into Virginia. Although the first two also eventually accessed the beltway via route-4, they were not grouped within miles of the other pair.

———————— ★ ★ ★ ★ ★ ————————

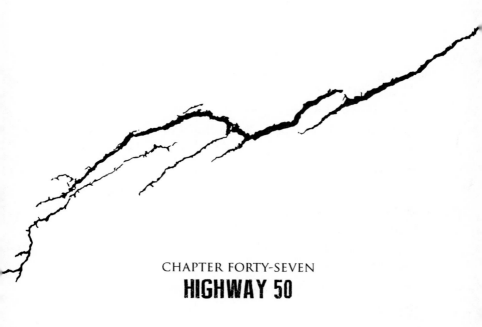

CHAPTER FORTY-SEVEN
HIGHWAY 50

The white van that had sped from Annapolis along West Street to highway-50 was having issues of its own. Local police and state troopers that were stationed near the stadium at Annapolis were receiving reports from a handful of witnesses stating that they had seen a group of people in flight suits and helmets entering a white van on Farragut Road. Although the reaction time had been slower than those who had pursued the group of assailants toward Londontown, there had still been an alert put out to all law enforcement agencies with regards to a white van. Fortunately for the six men, who all but one had completed changing into their civilian attire, and the two women positioned in the front seats, they had the means to discard the white van. That of course, was contingent upon them reaching the exchange point still a few miles to the west just off of highway-50.

With his own gear now stowed in one of the combustible bags, an attacker asked the man who had been shot in the arm, "How does it feel?"

While grimacing with pain as he attempted to remove his jumpsuit, he replied, "Not good, and I can't move it very much."

Then from the front passenger seat, the driver of the sacrificed blue van asked, "How bad is the wound?"

Another of the attackers who was looking at the wound replied, "Well, the bleeding doesn't seem to be too bad at the moment, but I can't see much with his jumpsuit on."

Unclipping her seatbelt, she moved toward the back of the van while stating, "Someone take my seat up front. I need to cut his sleeve and jumpsuit open."

A moment later the collective had the man undressed and his gear was stowed with all the rest in the combustible set of bags. He was ready to change into civilian attire as soon as the bleeding could be stopped. Working efficiently as trained to do so in west Texas, the alternate driver tended to the wound. Then she said while wrapping it with a torn piece of her long t-shirt, "That should take care of the bleeding for the moment, but the bullet must still be in there because I can't find any exit wound. Does anyone know who shot him?"

The man now in the front seat replied, "It was a state trooper, but he has been neutralized."

"A state trooper huh? That means he was probably hit with a hollow point round. Based on that, his pain level, and the inability to move his arm freely, I also think that the bullet struck the bone and broke it."

With a nod of comprehension, the man who had assumed the front seat said, "And what about him?"

Turning her attention to the man who had been beaten by the brave civilians, she asked, "How do you feel?"

While having already changed clothes during extreme discomfort, the man was flat on his back in the cargo area of the van. Looking over he replied, "Not too bad considering, but I do have a lot of pain in my lower back, stomach, and especially in the ribs."

Then the driver announced, "We're coming up on our exit. Three or four minutes to the exchange point."

Pulling into the large parking lot of a shopping center, the van approached the two awaiting sedans and parked directly behind them. As the men began to exit, the driver asked, "How long should I set the timer for?"

"Let's give ourselves plenty of time to get clear of the area. How do you feel about ten minutes?"

"That sounds good to me. Ten minutes it is."

With each sedan having taken on four passengers, including one injured man per vehicle, the drivers who had been waiting for a few hours began the long trek westward. Moving back onto highway-50, they once again joined the semi thick traffic leading them toward the beltway. When they arrived at the busy intersection of freeways, the plan called for both sedans to follow the northerly portion of the loop around Washington D.C. to help disperse the six getaway cars. Like the four using the southern route, they would further disperse once into Virginia and clear of the greater Washington D.C. area. If all went according to the plan, none of the vehicles would ever be closer than a mile or two from any of the others until safely back in Texas.

Shortly before reaching the beltway, the driver of the rear sedan glanced in her side mirror and said, "We have a state trooper coming up behind us."

From the back seat she heard, "It shouldn't be a problem if we don't do anything to attract his attention. Just remain calm, and nobody look back at him."

Then a few seconds later the trooper's lights came on with the accompanying siren, and the driver began to tighten her grip on the wheel. Just as she began to shift lanes to the right, the trooper sped past hers and the other sedan. Everyone watched intently as the trooper increased the distance in front of them, and then breathed a collective sigh of relief when they saw the unit moving toward the closest exit ramp. The wounded man in the back said, "I wonder if someone has identified the van, and he is going back to investigate."

Looking at her watch while sandwiched between two men in the back seat, the woman who had driven the van and set the explosive charges of the Fugas bomb replied, "If that's where he's going, then it's because someone has reported a melting van."

CHAPTER FORTY-EIGHT
ESCAPE FROM COLORADO SPRINGS

Although separated by several hundred miles as it snakes its way through seven different states between Maryland and Colorado, highway-50 would also play a role in the attackers escape from the Air Force Academy. At the junction of state highway-67, roughly five miles east of Canon City Colorado, the Fremont County Airport lay adjacent to that same nation crossing highway-50. What had been envisioned back in May by Samuel and his trusted group of attack planners was bold to be sure, but now it was moments away from either a beautiful realization or complete failure.

Seated with a view of the airport from her northward facing position on a hillside road, the driver of the third black suburban could look through her binoculars to the west and plainly see a handful of single engine propeller driven aircraft and two Cessna Citation Latitude jets near the main building. While her driving sisters of the other two suburban's had by now gained entry into Kansas and New Mexico for their respective mission assignments, she had been tasked with witnessing and reporting the upcoming transfer. Glancing at her burn phone, she realized that the time was near. Rolling down the window for added amplification, she then listened carefully while waiting for the helicopter to arrive.

As anticipated, her wait was a short one. She first heard the reverberating echo of distant rotor blades coming from the canyon to the north, and then after grabbing the binoculars once again, verified that the two jets were beginning to taxi. Estimating that the first would need another minute to reach the end of the taxi-way for a turn onto the runway, she began an intense search of the terrain for the incoming helicopter. The noise level of the pending arrival was beginning to magnify, so even though she couldn't see it yet, the MIL MI-8 HIP-C had to be getting close. Having sped south over a sparsely populated mountain region just to the west of Pikes Peak, the camouflaged helicopter closed on the intended target east of Canon City. Just like the flight from the Centennial Airport earlier that morning, the bird had hugged the terrain as best as possible for added cover and the intent worked to perfection. The flight crew had achieved the upper hand in eluding any pursuers by moving away from the Air Force Academy within minutes after the attack, and their flight tactics had maintained an advantage that was hoped would last.

What Mr. Capra and Mr. Fisk were unaware of as they were finally spotted by the woman in the suburban, was that they had more leeway than either of them thought. The two academy helicopters that also deployed fourteen parachutes over Falcon Stadium were unarmed and ill equipped for a chase, as they had planned on a short duration flight and simply didn't have enough fuel. Unfortunately for those crews, by the time they could refuel and take flight, a chase would prove useless. The aircraft that had been called into a pursuit of the attacking force had lifted off from the nearby Schriever Air Force Base to the east of Colorado Springs, but the order to do so had taken several crucial minutes to be received and executed. That precious amount of time proved to be consequential, as while flying low and hugging the mountainous terrain, the camouflaged helicopter used for the escape could not be spotted from high above.

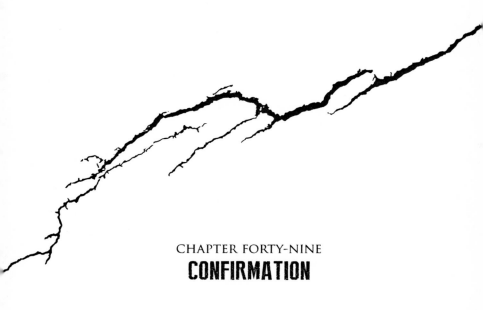

CHAPTER FORTY-NINE
CONFIRMATION

After watching the HIP-C helicopter come in for a landing at the rendezvous point, then counting the fourteen attackers and the two pilots as they transitioned from it into the twin Cessna jets, the woman in the suburban smiled with delight. A moment after the hurried departure of the jets, she could see a bright flash from within the abandoned helicopter and then soon after the fuselage became engulfed with billowing smoke. The subsequent explosion a moment later meant that the extra fuel containers used as an accelerator had also been ignited by the Fugas bomb. As the only individual from the organization to witness those events, she had but one more duty to perform before beginning her drive back to Texas. After setting her binoculars on the seat beside her, she pulled the burn phone from her pocket once again and hit speed dial for the only pre-programed number that it contained.

On the other end of the line a familiar voice said, "This is number twenty three, what do you have to report?"

"Hello number twenty three. I'm confirming that the Canon City package was received, wrapped, and is being delivered according to the plan. Any possible evidence that may have been left behind is melting, and fire crews are just beginning to muster. Please repeat the message back for confirmation."

"You are understood to have confirmed successful landing, transfer, and departure, followed by the destruction of evidence. Is that correct?"

"That is correct. Now please inform number two that all is well."

With that she made her way toward highway-50 and followed it eastbound to Pueblo and the junction of interstate-25. From there it would take several hours to traverse southeast to her destination of Amarillo, at which time her part in the overall plan would be complete.

 ★ ★ ★ ★ ★

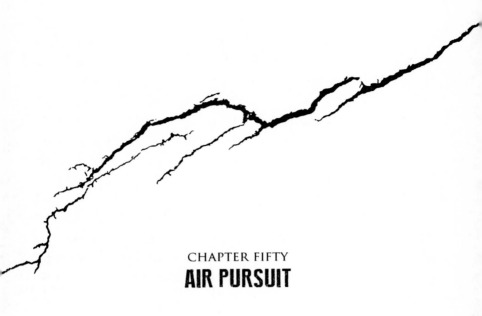

CHAPTER FIFTY
AIR PURSUIT

As Air Force One headed east toward Washington D.C., the flight path had taken it over the northern portion of Idaho and the western portion of Montana. If everyone onboard, including those few members of the press, hadn't been so busy with discovering how and why the attacks could have happened, they would have enjoyed a marvelous view. The mountainous terrain, both vast and rugged, towered beneath the plane with early snows having blanketed the higher reaches of them. Those views had changed drastically however, as the current position of the jumbo jet was over a section of the country that transitioned from mountainous terrain to that of the Great Plains.

While conferring with members of his staff, various reports from each of the three academies began to trickle in. Then an aide entered the conference room and reported, "Mr. President, the communication center on board has received a message from the FAA. They believe that there has been a sighting with regard to those who attacked the Air Force Academy. According to the report of a Major

Fenton, the attack was perpetrated by a group of individuals who were picked up by a camouflaged military helicopter."

Understandably in a foul mood, President Harwell replied, "Well we already know that. Their escape by air is what made the attack different from those of West Point or Annapolis."

"Yes sir."

"So who is this Major Fenton, and why is he reporting information that is already known to us?"

"Major Fenton has identified himself as the principal aide for General Vickers, the commandant of the academy. And sir, he may be in shock and unaware that we already have that information."

After a deep breath, the President replied, "Alright, that's fair enough I suppose. But why didn't General Vickers report directly?"

"The major has informed us that the general and the joint chief were both killed during the attack, so he is from an administrative standpoint in temporary command."

Agent Bishop noticed that the President was clenching and unclenching his left hand again after receiving that terrible news, but was unaware that General Brooks from the joint chiefs of staff had been ordered by President Harwell to attend the game. Then after a sorrowful exhale, the President said, "Alright, we will have to deal with their loss at a later time. Now, you were mentioning something about the FAA contacting our communications center."

"Yes sir. Based on their communication, we now have a lead on the helicopter."

After several long seconds of silence, his reply was sharp. "Well don't keep me waiting, what has been discovered?"

"Yes sir. The FAA claims they have an eyewitness report that such a helicopter landed at the Fremont County Airport in Canon City Colorado."

"Where is that? And more importantly, do we and the FAA consider the eyewitness to be a reliable source?"

"By air it's roughly fifty miles southwest of the academy sir. And yes, she works in the control tower of the regional airport so we believe her to be reliable."

"Alright, so has anything been done to capture those responsible for the attack?"

"Not exactly sir. The eyewitness has informed the FAA that the helicopter landed without identification or clearance on the most distant few feet of the runway from the tower, but then things got weird. Just moments before the unexpected landing, she had given clearance for two small Cessna jets to taxi out toward that end of the runway. One was already in position to take off, while the other was pivoting from the taxiway."

"Is that somehow relevant to the helicopter?"

"Yes sir it is. She reported seeing through her binoculars from the tower that each of the jets opened their doorway, and that several people ran over from the helicopter to climb inside both aircraft. When she attempted to contact the pilots to ask what was going on, they took off immediately without proper clearance. She further reported that while tracking their outbound course on radar, she warned a few other private planes in the area to be on the lookout for the jets as she had no idea of their intended flightpath. While focused on that safety measure, the helicopter suddenly lurched and became engulfed in a huge ball of smoke and fire. Apparently her airport fire crew and that of the community were attempting to contain the blaze when she contacted the FAA, but they were having little success."

"Alright, she sounds like somebody who really knows how to do her job. Does she, or anybody else, still have the jets on radar?"

"Yes sir. The planes are both moving fast in a southerly direction, and based on their radar signature, they must have remained within visual contact of each other. The pair has already entered airspace over New Mexico, and it would appear they are headed for somewhere south of the border."

"Can we get somebody up there to stop them before they enter Mexican airspace?"

"Yes sir, we can scramble some fighters. But unless you order the pilots to shoot them down, they will be out of the country very quickly."

CHAPTER FIFTY-ONE
THE SKY OVER NEW MEXICO

Although the two Citation Latitude jets had set a course from Canon City that appeared to be of no significance other than heading south at their maximum speed of nearly five hundred miles per hour, there was a purpose to it. Once they had entered the airspace over New Mexico, and with knowledge that they had most certainly been tracked on radar for departing without clearance, that intentionally plotted course had lined them up to fly directly over the most populated areas of the state in low altitude. If the connections between the jets, the by now fully melted helicopter in Canon City, and the Air Force Academy attack had been identified, then they could be intercepted by aircraft with orders to shoot them down. With that in mind, the directional heading was imperative.

Within the northern half of the state, Taos, the capitol city of Santa Fe, and Albuquerque were nearly in a direct line, so only minor course corrections were needed by the two pilots in order to remain above them. Frantic communications had come their way from the airport control tower of Albuquerque's International Sunport asking them to avoid commercial traffic by diverting their course, but neither jet had adhered to the plea. A short time earlier, a black suburban parked at a good vantage point near Santa Fe had reported in. The driver within was pleased to disclose to number twenty three that the twin jets had just moved south of her location flying fast and low. They would not have done so if they hadn't received at least some of the attackers that she had dropped off earlier that day some three hundred fifty miles to the north in Monument Colorado.

As the Cessna jets continued over the southern half of the state directly above the traffic artery of interstate-25 that more or less followed the course of the Rio Grande, they flew over a series of smaller towns including Socorro and a place with a befitting name for their mission of Truth or Consequences. Then when approaching the city of Las Cruces near the southern reaches of the state and country, another plea for a course correction from a control tower below could be heard. As with before, it went unheeded by both jets. Closing on the area of the Texas state line and the city of El Paso to the near southeast, the planes veered slightly to the west. There would be a few miles of open terrain with almost zero human population below them, but that also meant that they would be in Mexican air space within minutes if not seconds. After making the latest course correction, the pilot of one jet turned to her current co-pilot who had been on the helicopter flight crew and said, "Well Mr. Fisk, if somebody from Fort Bliss doesn't intercept us within the next few minutes, we should be home free."

"That's true, but we should keep a sharp lookout. We could run into some commercial traffic that's either inbound toward, or outward bound from, El Paso."

While keeping a vigilant watch for such aircraft, they were suddenly surprised when an Air Force fighter jet swooped down from above and assumed a formation position to their left. Mr. Fisk looked out the right window next to the co-pilots seat and could see another forming up on their sister jet. Then they both saw the military pilot to their own left give an unmistakable hand gesture. He was pointing straight down which could only mean that he wanted them to land immediately. With no reply, the fighter pilot repeated the gesture before holding two fingers upwards. It was their second warning to follow his instruction, and it was possible that there wouldn't be another.

Turning to Mr. Fisk, the pilot asked, "We are virtually over the border right now, should we call his bluff and make a run for it?"

"We have no choice. None of us can be caught and you know it. Do what you must to elude him, but keep going south!"

With that the pilot gave the fighter jet a friendly wave, and then pushed forward hard on the yoke. The plane took an immediate steep dive, and she yelled to the seven men in the back, "Hold on everyone, this could be a wild ride for the next few minutes."

The fighter jet dropped into a pursuit of her within an instant, and after a few twists and turns, had the Citation Latitude painted on radar. It had been foolish for the Cessna to try and outfly the fighter even for a moment, and the pilot while smiling with pleasure let his command at Fort Bliss know that he could fire at any second to blow his helpless target to bits. The other pair of jets had gone through a similar dance in the sky with that target now also painted, so all that was needed for both was the order to fire. Much to the dismay of the two fighter pilots who were primed for the rush of a kill, that order never came. President Harwell, per the observation commented upon by Samuel Tillman on President's weekend back in mid-February, had once again been lethargic with his decision making process. He had waited too long while in flight on Air Force One to order the deployment of pursuit aircraft into the sky with permission to shoot. By the time the fighters had engaged the twin Cessna jets, their enemy was already in Mexican airspace.

★ ★ ★ ★ ★

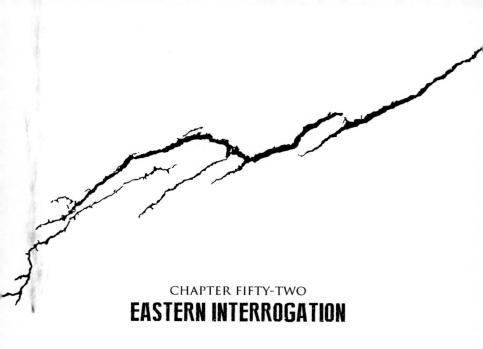

CHAPTER FIFTY-TWO
EASTERN INTERROGATION

Major Bates and his men had been waiting under guard in a hangar facility at the Albany International Airport for more than two hours before authentic federal agents arrived at seven o'clock eastern time to interrogate them. Although held in the relative comfort of an employee breakroom, none of the men had been allowed to speak with one another while being sequestered. Visits to the restroom were taken by one detainee at a time, and always under the gunpoint supervision of at least two New York National Guard troops. The young and eager Lieutenant who led the squad maintained a vigilant watch on Major Bates, and had been fighting the urge to begin his own brand of interrogation. It was a battle that he would have eventually lost if the agents hadn't arrived, as he was concerned over the well-being of his cousin who was currently a first year plebe cadet at West Point.

When the federal agents did arrive, they were accompanied by General Norgard, who was Major Bates commanding officer. After rising and coming to attention with a salute, the Major asked, "Sir, can you please tell me what is going on?"

The two men had never really seen eye to eye on most things, so it wasn't a surprise to Major Bates when his question had been greeted with a stern scowl. He held the salute until it had been reluctantly returned by the general, but the verbal response that followed was stunning. General Norgard drew in a deep breath and then loudly asked, "What the hell is the matter with you Major? Why have you committed treason against the United States by having your jumpers attack West Point?"

Shocked by the questions of accusation, if not by how they had been asked, Major Bates replied, "Treason? What do you mean general?"

"You heard me Major, but I'll spell it out for you very clearly if I must. The men who parachuted out of your two helicopters earlier today attacked Michie Stadium at West Point, and they probably killed hundreds if not thousands of people in the process!"

Still at a loss for understanding, the Major replied, "I don't understand General. If what you say about West Point is true, then how did they do it and how severe is the damage?"

The lead agent of the FBI pair that had come from their Manhattan field office intervened by saying, "Thank you General Norgard, but we will take it from here."

Although not pleased to do so, the general yielded his position to the agent. Then before leaving the room in disgust he said, "Very well. I no longer have any desire to look at or speak to such a treasonous man. The two of you do what you must, and keep the lot of them here all night if you have to."

Realizing that the general had no authority to grant him such permission, and that his departure would expedite the progress of an interrogation, the agent was pleased that the gruff old officer wanted to leave. Then after the door slammed shut behind the general, he turned back toward the pilots and crews and said, "Well gentlemen, we have a lot to talk about."

Major Bates replied, "With all respect, I think that the general is out of his mind. I know nothing of an attack on West Point."

While taking a seat at one of the breakroom tables and motioning for the major to join him, the lead agent stated, "Major Bates, you can believe that what the general has told you about an attack is true, and preliminary reports suggest that the damage is extensive. As to how those who attacked the stadium were able to accomplish their devious act, that's what we intend to discover. Since they all jumped from the two helicopters under your command, our investigation will begin with you!"

CHAPTER FIFTY-THREE
WESTERN PENNSYLVANIA

B y the time Air Force One completed its transcontinental flight to Andrews Air Force Base in Maryland under the ever present fighter plane escort, and President Harwell had subsequently been shuttled over to the White House, Ashley Tillman and her three passengers had already traveled deep into western Pennsylvania. As one of the seven vehicles to successfully escape the area of West Point after the attack, they had only made one previous stop. After traveling for nearly fifty miles of non-toll assessed highways of New York and New Jersey before hooking up with interstate-80, and then heading westward on that super highway for an additional two hundred sixty miles, they used a roadside rest area just west of Snow Shoe for restrooms and the initial change of license plates.

Those rather intense first five hours to cover the three hundred ten miles had included only one location where the vehicle could have been photographed with ease, as there was a toll plaza for the crossing over the Delaware River from New Jersey into Pennsylvania. With the undetected changing of plates from New York to Ohio under the cover of darkness at the nearly vacant rest area, such a photograph, if one existed, had been made inconsequential.

With an additional fifty miles traveled beyond the rest area, Ashley had pulled into a gas station in the town of Falls Creek at mile marker ninety seven, and said, "Alright, let's fill the tank and switch drivers."

As one of the jumpers stepped inside with cash for the transaction, and the other prepared to fill the tank, the woman who had driven one of the vans used for the post attack changing facilities moved over into the driver's seat. Then she said, "When should I wake you Ashley?"

Looking at her watch, Ashley replied, "Well it's about eight thirty, so why don't we say somewhere close to midnight when you come across a rest area. Remember to exit this interstate onto 76 just west of Youngstown before 80 becomes the Ohio Turnpike. That's a toll road and we don't want any more photo opportunities than is absolutely necessary. Interstate-76 will take you through Akron and you should merge onto south 71 sometime before midnight."

"You got it Ashley, no problem. Now try to get some sleep."

As they pulled back onto westbound interstate-80, what the group of four and those in the other six vehicles of the West Point contingent were unaware of, was how perfectly executed their aspect of the three pronged attack had been. After having caused the most damage and loss of life at any of the three academies, their escape had been so clean that there was not a soul in pursuit of them.

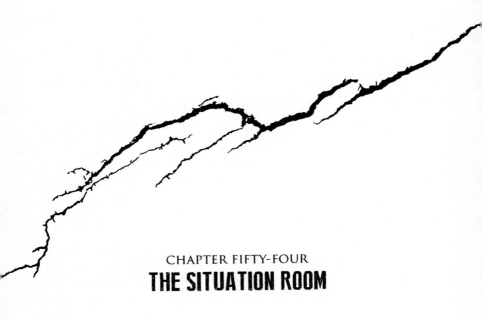

CHAPTER FIFTY-FOUR

THE SITUATION ROOM

he flight from Boeing Field in Seattle to Andrews Air Force Base just outside of Washington D.C. had taken more than four hours. It was less than the generally required five hours for commercial traffic to travel between the two cities, but Air Force One had the advantage of being a faster aircraft when need be, and with priority landing privileges, she was never shuffled into a pecking order with other incoming aircraft. Another thirty minutes had passed before President Harwell, agent Bishop, and others from the entourage were transported via the Marine One helicopter to the south lawn of the White House where his Chief of Staff Christopher Westin was waiting. A moment later they, along with agent Bishop, left the entourage behind and descended into the underground bunker facility. With a three hour loss due to time zone changes from the west to east coast, President Harwell finally strode into the situation room just prior to eight forty-five eastern time.

Before all those present could rise, he motioned for them to remain seated and asked, "What do we know definitively?"

Vice President Sutherland replied, "Mr. President, we know that West Point took the worst hit in terms of loss of life. General Osborne from the Joint Chiefs was killed during the attack, and his principle aide is listed as critical. Many others in the officer ranks were also killed or injured, with the corps of cadets being hit hard as well. We don't have specific numbers yet, but they should be coming in soon."

Knowing that he had ordered General Osborne to attend the game, as well as the man's counterparts from other branches of the military, President Harwell looked at his running mate and asked, "That is tragic news, as he served this country proudly for many years. What do you know about the other members of the Joint Chiefs?"

"Admiral Mendenhall, his aide, and the commandant of the Naval Academy have all sustained injuries, but none are life threatening. Unfortunately General Brooks and the Commandant at the Air Force Academy, General Vickers, have both been killed."

"Yes, we already knew about Brooks and Vickers. A principle aide of the commandant contacted us via the FAA during our flight and reported their deaths."

"Yes sir."

"What about civilian casualties?"

"Reports confirm that civilian losses aside from those in the press box areas are comparatively light at all three locations. It would appear that the attacks were aimed primarily at military personnel."

"Well I suppose that's a small measure of good news. When can you get me an accurate count at each of the locations?"

"We have people working on that right now sir and the civilian count from each academy should be coming in before the military numbers are finalized."

"Where are all the bodies of the dead being moved to?"

"For the present time sir, each of the three football fields is being used as a collecting point for identification purposes. Initially the more seriously injured were being treated on the field as well, but many of those have since been moved to local hospitals. Contact information has also been gathered on those with minor injuries, and after being cleared by local medical personnel, they were asked to return to their homes."

After silently nodding with understanding, President Harwell then motioned toward the head of Homeland Security and asked, "What can you tell me about all of this?"

"Well sir, it's obvious that the attack at each of the locations was well thought out. As the Vice President alluded to, civilian casualties were far too limited for this to have been a random act. Those assailants coming in via parachute knew exactly which area of each stadium to concentrate their fire upon."

"So you are concurring with Vice President Sutherland that the attacks were aimed at our military forces."

"Yes Mr. President I am. But they were also aimed at symbols of our military forces."

"What do you mean?"

"Well sir, the stadiums were also attacked. Although one of them isn't actually on academy grounds, they all serve as a facility of their respective academy. As such, it could be interpreted that the attacks were made upon three of our domestic military bases."

"I see your point, and understand your position on such treachery. But for now, I want to maintain a focus on the human element of the attacks."

"Yes sir."

"So how did the attacking forces learn of where the military representatives in each location would be seated? Do you suspect an inside source of some kind?"

"There is no evidence to suggest that at this time sir. Besides, seating charts or photographs for most stadiums can be easily accessed via the internet. It would have been no problem for the attacking forces to formulate a plan of where to concentrate their firepower based on such readily available information."

"I understand. So do we have any leads on who attacked us?"

"Nothing concrete sir, at this point everything would just be theoretical. There simply isn't any evidence for us to build a case on yet."

"No evidence? What about weapons, finger prints, or something like that?"

"I'm sorry Mr. President. As I said, the attack was well planned out. There were abandoned weapons on the playing field along with all of the parachutes at both West Point and Annapolis, and in Colorado Springs the same stockpile of gear and weaponry was discarded in an adjacent parking area. We do know that an identical arsenal was used at each of the locations, and some of it was foreign made."

"And with all of that you have no evidence to suggest who attacked us?"

"No sir. The weapons they used can be purchased from some foreign governments with ease, and other elements of their arsenal are readily available on the black market. Forensic teams have been going over those weapons, empty shell casings, and anything else that has been recovered, but there are no finger prints as of now. Multiple witnesses stated that they caught a glimpse of the attackers, and their hands were white or cream colored. Based on that and the absence of fingerprints, they were all probably wearing surgical gloves."

"What about their faces or body type?"

"The attacking forces all wore a helmet with dark face shields, which made identification impossible. As to body type sir, they were all described as average height with medium build. Unfortunately that doesn't give us much to go on."

Feeling dejected at the absence of true leads, the President turned to the Secretary of State and asked, "What about your teams? Is there any whiff of who might have done this?"

"Well Mr. President, no element or faction has taken credit for the attacks as of this time. We at state have good reason to believe that the attack was carried out by some group within the Middle East, and based on recent actions; the most likely candidate would be the Syrians. We have teams both here and in the region working that angle in search of tangible proof."

"That's good Mr. Secretary. Please keep me posted of whatever your teams may uncover."

"Yes Mr. President."

CHAPTER FIFTY-FIVE
POSSIBLE COMPLICATION

B y eleven o'clock eastern time, and not long after the discussion in the situation room had ended for the night, one of the six escape vehicles from Annapolis had covered more than four hundred miles as it reached the town of Bristol Virginia on the Tennessee state line. The trip southwest along interstate-81 had gone smoothly except for one additional stop beyond that of restrooms or the recent need for fuel. That stop west of Washington D.C. along interstate-66 had been necessary to purchase some towels and bandages for the injured man in the backseat, as the gunshot wound he had received continued to cause bleeding and severe pain in his left arm. In the hours that followed he lost the feeling in his fingers, and the recent pale blueish appearance of his hand and forearm provided proof that blood flow to that region had been severely diminished.

Located in the middle seat to his immediate left, the woman who had been tending to his wound since they were riding in the white van thought that the man showed incredible bravery. The pain must have been excruciating for him, but he had never cried out in spite of having no more than a pencil from within the glove box to bite down on and a steady regiment of Tylenol. Knowing that additional medical attention beyond what she could provide would be needed long before their return to Texas; she feared that he could possibly lose the arm.

Meanwhile the second injured man was in another car roughly seventy miles behind on that same interstate near Wytheville Virginia. They, like the car in Bristol, had taken the northern loop around the Washington D.C. area before proceeding west on interstate-64 and then southwest along 91. What had slowed them down to create such a distance between was the need for a few extra stops, as the man who had been severely beaten and kicked several times in the midsection was not well. He was developing a fever, had vomited several times, and the latest such episode at a roadside rest area forty minutes earlier included some blood.

In both cases the men were in bad shape, but nothing could be done about that. Checking either of them into an emergency room or clinic anywhere along their intended route back home would have brought forth unwanted questions and an investigation as to how the injuries had been received. Such an investigation would undoubtedly lead to uncovering bits of personal information such as names, addresses, and medical history that could not be revealed. Although each of those could be falsified by use of the documents they each possessed, those documents claimed that the men were federal agents. If those were to be presented to medical personnel in place of authentic identification, the federal employee database would be accessed for verification. When it was discovered that no such persons actually existed, the standard blood sample taken in an emergency room environment would be scrutinized to reveal their true identity via DNA testing. That entire scenario was simply unacceptable to the successful completion of their mission, so the injured men would just have to endure their discomfort and pain.

Further to the east, the four cars that had left Londontown undetected from the rendezvous point and moved around the southern edge of Washington D.C. had driven nearly all the way through North Carolina. Once over the Potomac and then into Virginia they had turned south onto interstate-95 before using a roadside rest area south of Fredericksburg to change the Maryland license plates to North Carolina. Then while maintaining their spacing of a few miles between each vehicle, the uninjured collective of eight attackers and six drivers were able to maintain a quicker pace than the pair of cars further to the west. Upon reaching Petersburg south of Richmond Virginia they followed the more western option of interstate-85 toward the Tar Heel state, and had since rolled past the outskirts of Durham and Greensboro. As the dashboard clock turned to eleven o'clock when the lead of the western pair was in Bristol, the driver within the first of the four slowed to exit at a roadside rest area about twenty miles north of Charlotte.

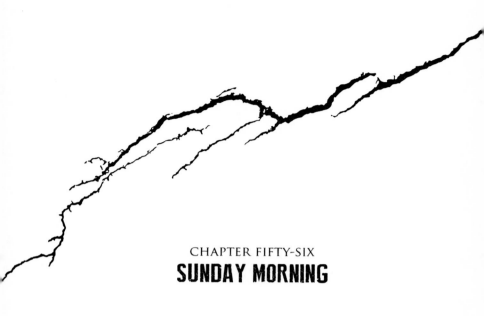

CHAPTER FIFTY-SIX
SUNDAY MORNING

President Harwell finished his hurried breakfast in the White House residence area at seven before briskly walking toward his office. On most mornings he enjoyed the short stroll along the adjoining outside patio area for a moment of fresh air, and on Sunday's he usually slept in a little bit later than all other days. However as he and the nation were now painfully aware, this was not a typical day. The meeting in the situation room the previous night had been long and grueling, and the emotions created by it were a far cry from the joy that he felt during the morning hours while back home in Seattle. Now on this particular Sunday, and most assuredly during the days and weeks ahead, that joy would be further suppressed. The task of identifying who had committed the terrorist attack, and then determining the best course of action toward that element, would be the most pressing issue on his agenda. Jordan Harwell knew that the subject matter would be more time consuming and draining than any other that he had experienced during his nearly two years in office, but such a necessity was part of the job for which he had been elected.

From the personal perspective of President Harwell, it had been comforting for him to learn during the briefing that he had not been a target of the terrorist attacks. That was proven via the thesis of agent Bishop when a lone helicopter scheduled to fly over Husky Stadium for a halftime parachute drop had aborted per the instructions to do so, and returned to base without incident. The crew and jumpers aboard were found to have no weapons of any kind on their persons, nor was the helicopter equipped with any explosive devices. The subsequent interviews conducted by the local FBI in Seattle of those aboard had been completed shortly after Air Force One had landed in Virginia, and revealed no malicious intent. An additional interview with the current University of Washington President had unearthed nothing tangible other than the man's overall innocence, but he had been arrogant in his resounding displeasure of being questioned at all. Such a small bit of comfort at not being a target was perhaps the highpoint of the two hour briefing in the situation room, and although some progress and enlightenment on other fronts had come forth, there were still many questions left unanswered.

In most cases, several key members of the staff would either be enjoying a Sunday away from the office, or if not, would be engaged in a lighter workload than normal. That was not true on November fifteenth however, and Mrs. Dawson would be the first to prove it. While seated at his desk, President Harwell had a moment to reflect upon the memory of men from his joint chiefs of staff that he had personally, although inadvertently, sent to their death. Then while jotting a note of who he must call to send his condolences, his personal secretary of many years came into the oval office. With her customary professionalism she said, "Good morning Mr. President, what can I do to help?"

Knowing that she was rarely if ever present on a Sunday, let alone by five minutes after seven, he smiled and asked, "Mrs. Dawson, why are you here on a Sunday?"

"With all due respect Mr. President, this is not the time for me to have a day off. Now, what do you need me to do?"

The elderly woman meant well with her intent, and her loyalty was unwavering. As one of the few people who truly understood his humor, the President felt that he could be somewhat less guarded with his answer toward her. So he replied, "Well thank you for being here Mrs. Dawson. Although I'm not sure that we could classify this morning as a good one either personally or for the United States, with your help we shall press on."

"Yes sir."

Then he added, "I don't suppose you could turn the clock back twenty-four hours for me? What I really need is for yesterday to have never happened."

"I wish that I could do that for you sir, but that power lies beyond all of us."

"Indeed. So, do you have my schedule for today?"

"Partially Mr. President, but I'm afraid that you will have a steady stream of people without scheduled appointments coming in all morning and afternoon. I hope some of them can provide you with the answers that you seek."

"Thank you Mrs. Dawson, so do I. Now, who's first?"

Throughout the course of the morning the President met with various individuals and small groups who provided him with information not easily absorbed. One such report revealed that the jet planes thought to be part of the terrorist escape from Colorado Springs had been lost, and that the Mexican authorities, as of the time of the report, had no idea as to their whereabouts.

The man providing President Harwell with the negative information said, "The jets were flying so low that radar lost their signal. Their course away from New Mexico suggested that they were heading for the Pacific coast, and many aircraft of that type and size would have the fuel range to do it. The jets would first have to climb in order to fly over the Sierra Madre Mountains, but using their last known course as a guide, then a good guess would be that they were headed for an airport in San Jose del Cabo, Mazatlán, or Puerto Vallarta."

"Well that actually sounds like three guesses to me, but it's a start. Have you and the Mexican government begun a search for the planes in any of those locations?"

"Yes sir. The state department is working on that and other avenues as we speak."

"Very well, please keep me posted of the progress."

"Yes Mr. President."

Another morning briefing revealed that Major Bates, Captain Scribner, and the crews of the two helicopters flown over West Point were innocent of any wrong doing other than not being as attentive as they should have been. Their most notable attribute, if one could call it that, was their casual approach to the entire flight. In their belief, all events leading up to the drop must have been as they were intended to be, and as such, the men were of little help to the investigation. They simply missed any potential clues of slightly incorrect attire or weaponry that may have given them cause to abort the mission. Only one man, the corporal who had notified Major Bates of the New York National Guard soldiers training their weapons on the helicopter, was the exception by remembering something unusual.

When asked by the Federal agents who interrogated them all if he had noticed the surgical gloves while in flight, he replied, "Yes sir, I do remember seeing the gloves shortly after the men came aboard and we lifted off. I didn't say anything about it or ask them why they were wearing the gloves because we were tightly crammed in and short on time. As it was we barely got everything ready for the seven of them to jump before reaching the designated drop zone."

In the crews defense, they had been given a short time window by General Norgard to position the jumpers over West Point, with a continuing time pressed mission beyond that. Additionally, there were no fingerprints on the helicopter other than those that could be matched to the flight crews, ground support personnel, or other members of the military that had legitimate cause to leave them behind. The fourteen soldiers scheduled to jump from their helicopters had been found dead, and initial toxicology reports had revealed that their deaths must have been excruciating. Nothing tangible had been recovered from the three smoldering vehicles used to gain entry onto the facility from which the helicopters departed, and it was doubtful that anything ever would be. In reality General Norgard was the one guilty of improprieties, and would need to answer for his misuse of military hardware by sending the helicopters to Albany for an unsanctioned evening event. That separate investigation would probably cost him his single star via a demotion in rank, but it could wait for the time being.

Later in the afternoon, President Harwell finally received some tangible information with regard to body count, and it wasn't good news. He had known from early reports that the military casualties at each of the three academies would be substantial, but he had also been led to believe that civilian loss of life had been minimal. Those figures, like most every statistic formulated by a government agency, could have a wide range of results depending on interpretation. In this case, the question became what constituted a civilian. Did it include members of the media and employees of the attacked facility, or did they fall into a different classification from those who had an actual ticket to sit in the stands at each game. For that matter, did family members accompanying military personnel in the stadiums create a separate category, or were all of the above to be lumped into one grouping?

As the President listened to the banter of the men and women who had been collecting the data, his aggravation level quickly rose. When he had heard enough, he finally asked quite bluntly, "Can any of you provide me with some numbers, or are you just wasting my time? This has been a tragic event in the history of our country, and I have been waiting for this important information. When I speak to a joint session of Congress tomorrow I would like to have some specifics, and the four of you are trivializing it by creating sub- groups of human souls that were lost. Now for the moment I really don't care how you break it down, as you can always do that later in a more detailed report, but aside from those currently in uniform, how many people were killed?"

With a gulp of fear for having offended the President in the oval office of all places, the lead woman of the fact finding group spoke first. With voice cracking she said, "Yes Mr. President, sorry about that sir."

After a deep breath and a sigh while staring at her worrisome eyes, Jordan Harwell replied, "Yes, fine. I apologize as well, and also understand that your team has been given a difficult task. Now could you please just think about those who have lost a loved one? They, along with the nation, will need answers. I can't help them with that unless you give me something to work with. So now once again, start with the total civilian casualties before breaking them into sub-groups."

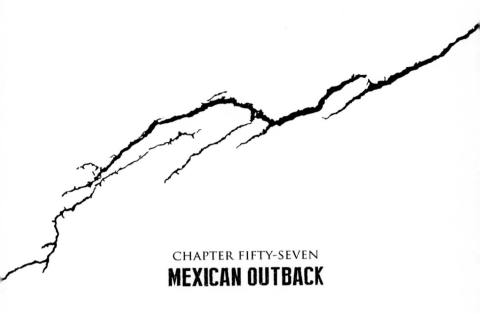

CHAPTER FIFTY-SEVEN

MEXICAN OUTBACK

During the course of the morning briefings at the White House, the sun began to rise over a seldom used airstrip well south of Chihuahua near the small Mexican town of Valle de Rosario. Continuing south from the airspace just inside Mexico when pursuit by the two American fighter jets had been called off, the pilots of the two Cessna Citation Latitude jets brought their total of sixteen passengers in for a safe late afternoon landing. Even while flying in low terrain hugging altitude to help avoid detection at nearly their maximum speed, the fuel range of the aircraft at close to three thousand two hundred miles had not nearly been met. Following a meal of non-perishable rations that had been stowed within the jets a few days earlier in Aspen, and a good night's sleep for the weary souls, the collective could now anticipate their next rendezvous. If all continued to go according to plan, then the second MIL MI-8 HIP-C helicopter that had been mentioned as available for purchase to Samuel by Mr. Flores in May would soon pick them up.

In conjunction with the one that had been brought into Texas at the border crossing of Laredo, and subsequently used for the training and carrying out of the Colorado aspects of the overall attack plan, Samuel had purchased what he considered to be her sister ship. At that time in May, Samuel made a simple business arrangement with the man who helped make that transaction a possibility. The organization would pay for the simultaneous refurbishing of the second HIP-C helicopter, but the work would be done in Monterrey. Then with the bird remaining in Mexico, the Flores family and their business associates could have free use of it when needed in exchange for a few favors. Those favors would be required in mid-November, and although not privy to the events leading up to said act, Mr. Flores would obtain outright ownership of the helicopter after those favors were successfully carried out. The terms were very clear, and the two business men agreed on how their goals should be accomplished. All Mr. Flores needed to do was assure the safety of Samuel Tillman's comrades by retrieving them from a desolate airstrip far to the west, and then transport them all back to Monterrey where they would be given shelter from any and all Mexican authoritative agencies. Then after perhaps a week, the eighteen individuals would be safely smuggled over the border into Texas by associates of Mr. Flores without detection.

Now that the morning hour of seven o'clock central time had come, they all prepared themselves for the pending extraction from the desolate airstrip. Mr. Capra and Mr. Fisk listened carefully for distant rotors, and with their well-trained ears, each picked up the distinct sound before others in the group could hear it. While moving forward a few paces and positioning an outstretched hand in front of his face to shield the rising sun, Mr. Fisk then saw the helicopter. Speaking loudly he stated, "There it is now. I can see the black silhouette of the fuselage just to the left of that small rise."

Seemingly turning in unison, the remainder of the group mimicked his hand position while scanning the eastern horizon. A moment later as the figure grew larger in the distance, one of them replied, "Alright, I see it now."

Flying low to the ground, the helicopter arrived within the next few minutes, and soon after that, the sixteen men waited to climb aboard the HIP-C while watching the two women who had piloted them to their current location perform one final act of brave treachery. With the cabin doors left open for an expedient and desperate escape, each of the Cessna's were pushed to full throttle while the pilots stood on the breaks with all their might. Then with the yoke locked into a fixed straight forward position, the first pilot in line released the breaks and scrambled for the exit. With a light load of no passengers or cargo, the jet had already reached a speed of more than twenty miles per hour before she could jump down without hesitation from the open doorway. When hitting the ground she tumbled and rolled several times before coming to a stop, but suffered only a few scrapes and bruises in the process. Then the second pilot followed suit in her plane, and the two women came to their knees while watching the jets roar down the compacted dirt runway.

Given enough forward velocity even a barn door can fly, but controlled flight is another issue. The two Cessna Citations were no exception, and they both rose slightly above the brush while screaming out over the Mexican outback. Then each had an intensely bright flash within, and quickly nosed gently downward to belly land. The Fugas bomb within each had ignited, and smoke began to billow wildly from the melting wreckage. A moment later, after the two women had climbed aboard the HIP-C into tight quarters with the sixteen men, the helicopter lifted off and did a quick flyby to ensure that the destruction of any potentially damaging evidence was under way. Then while flying at no higher than two hundred feet toward the rising eastern sun, and with a need for only one refueling stop along the way, the collective reached the cradle of protection provided by the Flores family and the city of Monterrey within hours.

—————— ★ ★ ★ ★ ★ ——————

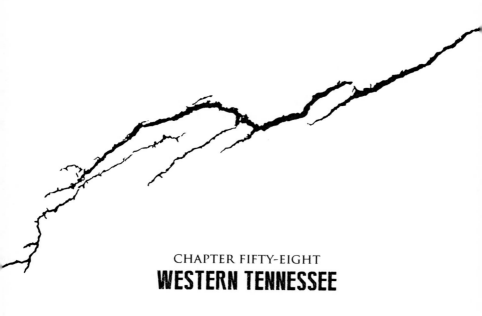

CHAPTER FIFTY-EIGHT
WESTERN TENNESSEE

D riving from Bristol in the northeastern corner of Tennessee via the remainder of interstate-81 and then onto interstate-40 toward Memphis which bordered Arkansas in the southwest would have normally been possible in about eight hours. Unfortunately for the second of the two escape vehicles from Annapolis along that route, things had not gone as smoothly as planned. Already seventy miles behind the first car that had arrived in Bristol at eleven, the car with the battered man continued to be slowed by his condition. Throughout the night his fever increased a few degrees, and the now bloodier vomiting intensified. The first vehicle had switched from Virginia to Tennessee license plates at the roadside rest area roughly forty miles southwest of Bristol, and with the lack of late night and early morning traffic, had been making reasonably good time. The badly wounded left arm of the man in the back seat had been the only cause for slowing beyond the norm of restrooms and fuel, but as had been the case throughout their journey, he continued to exhibit bravery. That stern emotional resolve came in spite of the self-realization that his arm was in terrible condition, and the loss of feeling that now included everything below the wrist.

Already traversing the entire width of the state in only thirty minutes longer than had been hoped, and by gaining an hour on the clock when crossing into the central time zone between Knoxville and Nashville, the car rolled around the northern edge of Memphis at six thirty in the morning. Crossing the Mississippi River into Arkansas a few minutes later meant that the five souls within could begin to feel more at ease. They were now in a state that bordered their own of Texas, and only moments after their brethren had been retrieved from the desolate Mexican desert, the car pulled into another roadside rest area thirty-five miles west of Memphis.

As the clock on the dashboard panel read seven fifteen, the second car had dropped further behind. Parked at a rest area just west of the Tennessee River, that group of five souls was roughly one hundred sixty-five miles to the east of their counterparts. As they prepared to once again press on after refilling water bottles that had been used mostly in a futile attempt to control the fever, the woman acting as caregiver slid herself back into a seated position while gently lowering the wounded man's head into her lap. At that point he had already been stretched horizontally for a few hours with his feet resting on another man's legs in an attempt to ease the discomfort, but the shaking, sweating, and vomiting had not lessoned.

The other woman in the car who was about to resume driving turned to look in their direction, and the return glance of the caregiver seemed to verify her suspicion. Then she asked, "Should we risk going faster on the interstate to make up some time?"

The man seated next to her asked, "Why would we do that?"

"Because we have probably two and a half hours in front of us before exiting Tennessee, and that's if we only stop for fuel."

No one said a word for several seconds, but then the injured man broke the silence. With a weak and raspy voice he said, "Don't risk being pulled over by the law due to excessive speed on my account. I know that we all have a long way to go and are behind schedule because of me, but all of us must get through undetected."

Turning back to start the car, the driver replied, "Is that how everyone else feels?"

Once again there was silence before the woman tending to him said, "Let's just do the best we can while maintaining a nearly legal speed. It's what he wants, and it sticks to the plan. Besides, I believe that he knows the possible implications of additional time being needed to get home. Meanwhile, I will do what I can to keep him as comfortable as possible."

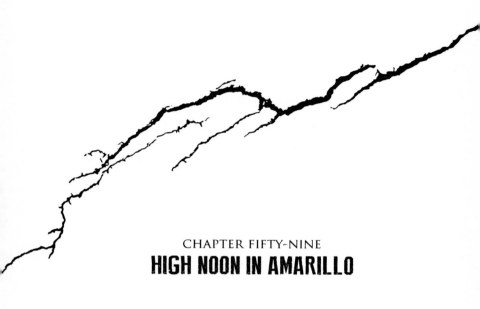

CHAPTER FIFTY-NINE
HIGH NOON IN AMARILLO

By midday Sunday, the drivers of the three black suburban's used for support in the western attack had each been in Amarillo for more than twelve hours. Coming in from various directions of northern New Mexico, western Kansas via the Oklahoma panhandle, and Colorado by traversing a course down through the southeast corner of the state, the three women had all arrived well before midnight. Now after resting comfortably in a local motel and catching up on the morning regional and national news reports of the attacks, it was nearly time for the drivers and their vehicles to continue onward.

Courtney Tillman had arrived many hours before them during the midafternoon, and as the final aspect of her secretive mission, waited for the safe return of the three women. After checking out of her south Denver motel during the early morning hours of Saturday, Courtney had driven directly south on interstate-25 past the Air Force Academy long before the attack had transpired. Then two hours later, shortly after entering New Mexico, she turned more eastward onto highway-87 for the remainder of the distance toward the northern outskirts of Amarillo. By the time forty-two men began jumping out of helicopters to do their dastardly deed, Courtney had already crossed over into the central time zone at the state line of New Mexico and Texas.

Later that night after getting five hours of well-earned sleep, Courtney positioned herself where she could easily record the pending arrival of the three drivers. After the last of them arrived, she broke her non communication mode of two weeks by contacting number twenty three. Courtney informed the woman that her own mission in Denver had been carried out successfully and without complication, while also disclosing what she had observed with regard to the drivers arrival at their designated motel. Shortly after ending that communication, Courtney then began to gather intelligence for something of a more personal matter. The two women that she had witnessed going into the Centennial Airport control tower posing as federal agents looked quite different as they emerged from their rooms in the relaxed attire of jeans and t-shirts. Courtney couldn't blame them for venturing into a country bar next to the motel with the third driver for a late night drink and a bit of relaxation, and in a way, wished that she could join them. Because none of the women actually knew her, she might be able to position herself near them in the bar and listen for confessions or gossip. She didn't possess the slightest bit of evidence to support it at the current time, and perhaps it was just her own imagination running wild, but Courtney's gut instinct told her that one of those women might be sleeping with her husband Mason.

For the Sunday afternoon drive toward Dallas, the three women in the suburban's could travel through the safety of Texas in formation if they so desired. They could take their time moving southeast along highway-287 toward the rendezvous point, and if all had gone well for their counterparts in the east, there would be a reunion of sorts during the coming night. As the vehicles were passing just to the south of the Amarillo International Airport and exiting interstate-40 onto 287, Courtney prepared to depart the area as well. While in the process of returning the rental car that she had used for the previous two weeks, she stewed over what might be going on with her husband. The women had only been in the country bar for thirty minutes before returning to their rooms, so it was fortunate that Courtney had not followed through with another possible course of action. She had wanted to go into each woman's room and search for any evidence that might link them to an affair with Mason, but had she done so, their short visit to the bar would have left her vulnerable to being caught in the act.

As Courtney attempted to dismiss the negative thoughts that swirled about in her head, she turned her attention to the Tillman Gulfstream G280. Per the prearranged plan Samuel had sent the jet to Amarillo for her retrieval, and she was looking forward to the comfort it would provide for the final leg of the trip home. When she arrived at the Tillman mansion and with Mason still in El Paso, Courtney planned to spend a quiet evening with her daughter Jennifer and niece Savanah. Knowing that she would be the lone passenger aboard, she also reasoned that the flight attendant Domonique would have some spare time to join her in a game of cards and friendly conversation. She was a pleasant woman that Courtney had always felt comfortable around, and perhaps one that she could also confide in. If the mood was right, perhaps she would ask Domonique her feelings on if Mason was fooling around.

CHAPTER SIXTY

SUNDAY EVENING

A s President Harwell picked over his dinner in the residence at six o'clock before returning to the oval office, agent Heath Bishop was searching for something to do in his own apartment. After the long day of Saturday and the taxing session in the situation room that night, there was still the requirement for agent Bishop to file a report and be debriefed as to the emergency evacuation order he had issued in Seattle. Although every one of his superiors believed that his actions had been justified, and had once again verbally praised him for them, those events and how they unfolded needed to be recorded. That entire process, which could not commence until after President Harwell had dismissed him, had taken an additional two hours once he returned to the local field office.

At the completion of those duties, agent Bishop was then notified that he would have the following two days off, and it was not optional. He was in no way being suspended or reprimanded for his actions; it was just felt by his immediate superior that Heath earned what would normally have been granted to him after the President's trip to the

Pacific Northwest. Additionally agent Bishop was informed, at the specific request of President Harwell, that he had been cleared of all other duties until further notice. Therefore come Tuesday morning at eight when he would report to the oval office, his lone responsibility was to be at the beckoned call of the Commander and Chief.

Unfortunately for Heath, Tuesday morning seemed years away. He was never much good at sitting on the sidelines, and felt that he could be of assistance to the President now as opposed to waiting another thirty-eight hours before returning to duty. Due to the bene-fit derived from several restful hours of sleep and some solid nutrition, agent Bishop was ready to ignore that order and get back to work.

Meanwhile at Fair Park in Dallas Texas, some of the vehicles returning from the two eastern attack sites had reported in. Hav-ing been slated with the most direct route back to Dallas, the car from Annapolis carrying the gunshot victim had been the first to arrive. After switching the license plates from Tennessee to those of Texas and departing the roadside rest area west of Memphis by seven thirty in the morning, the car then merged onto interstate-30 in Little Rock Arkansas for the final leg home. By eleven they were crossing the state line north of Texarkana where they could increase speed a little, and three hours later they were in the vast parking area that surrounded the old Cotton Bowl Stadium near the heart of Dallas. Unfortunately by the time of their arrival, the wounded man's fingers had turned black, and the loss of all feeling had moved to slightly above his elbow. His traveling companions had offered to take him to an emergency room once they had re-entered Texas, but he had refused sighting the need for every member of the jump-ers and drivers to report in before individual needs were addressed. Now that said requirement had been personally met, the man was taken to a nearby medical facility which was known to be sympa-thetic to the cause. Only time would tell if those doctors or others could save his arm.

In the three hours that had elapsed since the triumphant return of that singular vehicle, the question on the mind of those who had escaped with the gunshot victim was if anyone from the New York attack had been injured as well. However when the first few vehicles from that team began to arrive, including the one driven by Ashley Tillman, the likelihood of said fate became less and less possible. What the occupants reported was that no one had been injured during the attack or while in the process of fleeing from West Point, but it was unknown what may have transpired along the journey home. Based on a more northerly and western trajectory across Pennsylvania, Ohio, Indiana, and Illinois before turning south toward Dallas, those remaining vehicles could have encountered weather issues. The group already safely in Dallas felt completely at ease with their absence however, even though the others were perhaps still a few hours out. It was also well-known that all cars, vans, and suburban's used for ground support during each prong of the attack had maintained a strict code of cash only purchases for whatever services were needed. Therefore each vehicle and the occupants within had accomplished a vital and most challenging task for anyone to achieve in the modern world. They had all effectively stayed off the grid while leaving no tangible tracking evidence in their wake.

The three black suburban's coming in from Amarillo and the four vehicles from Annapolis that had escaped south into North Carolina had also arrived. In the case of the latter, once they had made their way from Charlotte across the northern portion of South Carolina and into Atlanta Georgia via interstate-85, they merged onto interstate-20 for the remainder of the journey. That route brought them through Birmingham Alabama, Jackson Mississippi, and Shreveport Louisiana before crossing into Texas.

When rolling through the city of Shreveport, one of the drivers stated, "Well we just crossed over interstate forty-nine. Do you remember when we were on that highway?"

Then the woman in the back seat replied, "Of course I remember. It was on Memorial Day weekend in late May, and we were on our way through this city toward Texarkana driving vans loaded with crates of weapons and ammunition."

With fond memories of that short but vital mission of nearly six months prior, the car they currently rode in soon crossed into Texas. Less than three hours later they joined many of the others at Fair Park, and within minutes after that, the last of the cars from West Point checked in as well.

Unfortunately several more hours passed before the last of the vehicles from Annapolis reached Dallas. The medical condition of the wounded man in the back seat had continued to worsen, and in spite of numerous stops in western Tennessee and Arkansas in an attempt to keep his fever under control, he had finally lost the battle. The woman tending to his injuries believed that something within him had been punctured via a broken rib suffered during his beating. The resulting internal bleeding coupled with massive dehydration from the feverish sweats and vomiting had probably caused organ failure, and she felt helpless as her limited medical training could provide him with no discernable help. The man was provided with a last comforting thought however, as she woke him and softly said, "Hey, we just crossed the state line into Texas. Hang on just a little bit longer and we can get you to a doctor."

To which her patient drowsily replied, "Thanks for letting me know that. I wanted to hold on until we got back to the greatest land on earth, but I don't think a doctor can help me now."

"Oh don't be silly. A doctor can have you fixed up before you know it."

"You're a sweet and caring woman, and I know you're only trying to soften the blow, but my time has come. At least I will die in Texas."

Then looking up she asked the driver and the other two men in the car if they could stop at a hospital in west Texarkana, but it would serve no purpose. Before she could look back down at the face of her patient, she heard a deep exhaling sigh. The man had just released his final breath, and per his most personal desire, had died in Texas.

 ★ ★ ★ ★ ★

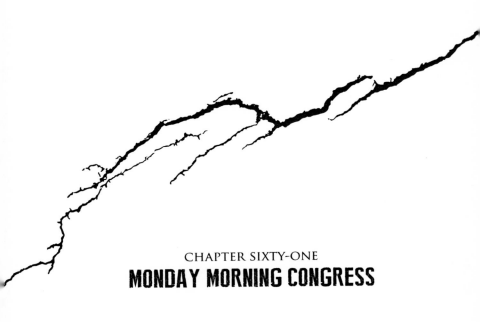

CHAPTER SIXTY-ONE
MONDAY MORNING CONGRESS

After being announced, President Harwell moved toward the platform housing the central lectern, and was greeted with mixed levels of respect. Some, in typical childish behavior that can be exhibited in the political arena, did not applaud the man who was the supposed leader of the free world. Those within the assembled mass who chose that path of disrespect hadn't done so for reasons of substance such as being personally and negatively impacted by actions of the man who was about to speak. Nor was it due to any lack of character that he may have exhibited by his treatment of others. Their dislike of President Harwell was instead based on nothing more than the ridiculous notion that it was acceptable for men and women representing the general populace of the nation to disregard the worth of someone simply because they were a member of the opposite political party. However to be fair, others who applauded him did so simply because the President was a member of their particular political party. In either case, the substance of Jordan Harwell as a leader, humanitarian, or simply a man who could have been their neighbor, was never a determining factor.

When the chamber settled back into a state of anticipatory silence, President Harwell began his speech to the joint session of Congress. The focus of his address, although already known by the collective at least in part, would be to deliver grave news of the three pronged attack. The President would also provide them with accompanying statistics, and as he had learned Sunday afternoon in the oval office, civilian casualties were far worse than originally believed. When combined with the military casualties, the total death count from all three of the targeted military academies stood at eight thousand seven hundred forty-one with a potential increase of perhaps a handful more.

When the President began to break down specific numbers, some within the chamber took notes. West Point had suffered the largest loss of life at three thousand six hundred fifty-two, with four hundred twenty-nine of those being media representatives and other civilian classifications. Another three hundred eighty-one were from the current corps of cadets, which left twenty eight hundred forty-two other active military personnel that had also been killed. That list of seventeen hundred twelve officers and eleven hundred thirty from the enlisted ranks included General Osborne from the Joint Chiefs of Staff, and by succumbing to multiple injuries Sunday morning, his principle aide. That information was received with a collective gasp and murmurs of disbelief, so the President decided to let that sink in a little bit before proceeding.

Moving on to Annapolis, President Harwell reported a loss of three hundred sixty-four civilians, and a higher cadet number than that of West Point as four hundred three midshipmen were lost. As they had been nearer to the route used by the escaping terrorists than those at the other eastern site, the collective of young men and women had become even more vulnerable to harm. Turning to the fifteen hundred thirty-two officers and seven hundred seventeen within the enlisted ranks, the death total reached three thousand sixteen. Of that total, only two civilian deaths had come from apparently precisely aimed gunshot wounds, as one victim was found in a parking area just outside the stadium complex. Not far from his position, a Maryland State Trooper had also been killed via gunfire. Although the two deaths were most probably somehow associated with the terrorist act, what had happened to each of them was a momentary mystery. The initial belief was that the first man had been one of the attacking forces, and that somehow the two victims had killed each other during an old fashioned western shootout. That theory was soon put to rest however, as witnesses had come forth stating the horrific truth of what actually transpired. Additionally, their recollection of events was confirmed when ballistics revealed that separate weapons of a different model sidearm than the troopers 45-caliber Smith & Wesson had been used to slay them.

Turning to the Air Force Academy in Colorado Springs, nearly a thousand less people had perished than at Annapolis. The breakdown of those killed however, was drastically different than in either of the two eastern locations. While one could take solace in that not a single member from the current corps of cadets had been killed, they could also be saddened by the increased loss of civilian life at seven hundred fifty-three. Medical examinations on the scene revealed that very few civilian deaths other than those of the media had been caused by fragments from exploding grenades or any flying debris as a result of them. Instead, nearly all could be attributed to various internal injuries as a result of being trampled by panicked masses. Unfortunately many of those were either children or the elderly out for nothing more than the joy of a football game and the pageantry surrounding it on an otherwise pleasant day. Their demise now meant that parents or family members believed to be somehow responsible for their welfare would inevitably battle inner demons as a result of self-blame and loathing.

The officer casualties stood at one thousand forty-one, and included General Brooks from the Joint Chiefs of Staff and General Vickers who had been serving as the Commandant of the academy. Those from the enlisted ranks were minor compared to their counterparts from the Army and Navy, but two hundred seventy-nine had still been claimed. Included in that total were the three who had been mistakenly attacked by the corps of cadets as they parachuted onto the playing field.

President Harwell reiterated to the collective that within the numbers from all three locations, two members from the Joint Chiefs had been killed while a third, Admiral Mendenhall, had suffered some minor injuries that would keep him in dry dock for the next week or two. What enraged President Harwell beyond the fate of those men and the loss of other military personnel in all three branches was the loss of civilian life. Because of that, he closed by asking Congress to consider voting for a declaration of war against whoever perpetrated the attacks. Although the identity of those scoundrels was not yet known, the President wanted to be prepared for action when their identity was learned.

While taking precise notes throughout, a member of the United States House of Representatives waited patiently for the President to conclude his remarks and exit the chamber. Then soon after, while an hour long recess was being observed, the man walked to his office so that he could compare those notes to some taken by a staff member. When alone in his private office a few moments later, Democratic Representative Braden Donahue of Texas pulled a burn phone from his locked desk drawer and hit speed dial.

A woman's voice on the other end answered, "This is number twenty three. What do you have to report?"

"This is number nineteen. I have the final tally as reported by President Harwell during his recent address."

"Very well, proceed."

"Total dead at all three locations is eight thousand seven hundred forty-one. Of that, fifteen hundred forty-six were civilians."

"Understood and thank you. I shall pass these totals onto number two."

 ★★★★★

CHAPTER SIXTY-TWO
CENTENNIAL INQUIRY

Several hours before President Harwell delivered his address of sorrowful news to Congress and those citizens of the nation watching the live broadcast, Travis Connor from Centennial Airport suddenly bolted upright in bed. It was a few minutes after two in the morning, but he wouldn't need to report for work until six. Unfortunately Travis would be kept awake for the entire time gap due to the revelation that had just occurred to him. The truth hit him hard like a brick, and he would discuss the possible ramifications of that truth with his counterpart when reporting for work to relieve the man in less than four hours.

When hearing of the multiple attacks after the conclusion of his Saturday shift, Travis hadn't given them much thought other than that of sadness for those citizens who had been personally impacted. Throughout the remainder of the day and on into Sunday, he watched or listened to multiple news reports and pondered over how the terrorist action might impact the nation's airports. The events that had transpired a quarter century before on September eleventh had been well documented and used as a case study for all air traffic controllers, as aside from issues of safety for the innocent, all planes needed to be cleared from the sky over the United States as quickly as possible. No such directive had been issued in the current situation, but something with regard to procedure would surely be updated by the FAA in the near future. It was thoughts of such an action while in a dream state that caused Travis to bolt upright from a sound sleep. What he realized was that the helicopter that exploded and melted on the end of the runway at Canon City may have been the same one that he and his graveyard shift counterpart cleared for departure during their shift change early Saturday morning.

With an inability to fall back asleep, or to wait any longer before engaging in a discussion with regard to his belief, Travis finally gave in and left early for work. Once there, he ran up the stairs and bounded into the control tower at Centennial Airport thirty minutes before his scheduled start time. After looking in his direction and then at the digital clock on the wall, the graveyard shift supervisor said, "Well good morning. Are you here early to give me a jump start on my two days off, or for something else?"

While experiencing a slight shortness of breath from his hurried entry, Travis replied, "I wish that it could be for the former, but I'm afraid it's not. If you have a few minutes to spare, I do have something important to discuss with you."

"Sure, what's on your mind?"

"Do you remember that helicopter we cleared for departure during shift change on Saturday morning?"

"Sure I do. You made a comment then about how the logbooks from the evening shift for its arrival were incomplete."

"That's right, and I didn't like that our counterpart was lazy in that regard."

"I remember, so what about it?"

"Well I believe that same helicopter may be the one that exploded in Canon City later in the day."

The man's mouth fell agape in disbelief, and then he replied, "You mean the one that authorities believe was involved in the attack at Colorado Springs?"

"That's the one."

After several seconds of reflective thought, his counterpart said, "Alright, I suppose that would be possible. But if we are to believe that's true, then the authorities will want to hear your opinion. We need to contact the FAA and the local FBI so that they can talk to you, and we should attempt to call our evening counterpart to see what he has to say about the events of Friday night."

"That all sounds good to me. Which of those calls would you like me to make first?"

Those subsequent calls made by each man were somewhat frustrating. In spite of multiple efforts, both were unable to contact the supervisor who was responsible for the helicopter being parked on the tarmac overnight. They then surmised that at the current early morning hour he would probably be sleeping for some time, and had perhaps turned off his phone. The FAA was thankful for the theory of the helicopter that was presented to them, but was more interested in continuing their investigation of the crash site in Canon City. Unfortunately they couldn't, or wouldn't, send an investigator to Centennial Airport for a few days. Although the most responsive, the FBI was still not fast acting. After listening to what Travis Connor had to say, the Denver field office agreed to have a pair of agents on site before the evening supervisor began his shift so that he could be questioned as well.

With no other recourse, all that Travis could do while tending to his normal work responsibilities was wait for them to arrive. Finally at one thirty in the afternoon, two men dressed in black suits with authentic FBI identification and badges entered the control tower to begin their investigation. Travis explained how the helicopter had requested and received clearance for departure at roughly six on Saturday morning, but he was unaware of specific arrival details from the previous night. With their initial questioning of Travis and a look through the logbook completed, they too waited to speak with his counterpart who would arrive for his shift at two o'clock. It wasn't until fifteen minutes after two that the agents became concerned.

With the remainder of the morning shift having been relieved by the evening personnel, Travis turned to those whom he knew but rarely worked with. Then he asked, "Has anyone heard from your supervisor? As you already know, these two FBI agents want to speak with him. If anyone could offer some helpful information as to his whereabouts it would be appreciated, because in spite of his normal weekend habits, it's not like your boss to be late for work."

None of the staff could provide any tangible information, but one of them did offer to call the man's apartment again. To that offer an FBI agent responded, "Thanks, but if he hasn't answered at home throughout the day, then I doubt that he will answer now."

Travis then said to the agent, "I'm willing to stay here on duty a few more hours if necessary, but the two of you need to tell us what we can all do to help you."

"That's good of you Mr. Connor, but can we speak privately for a moment?"

"Certainly, we can step into the hall."

After doing so the agent's first question was direct. He asked, "Is there anyone on duty at this time that is qualified to take over for you?"

Although somewhat surprised, Travis replied, "Yes, one of the staff on duty is the relief for the man you want to speak with. She assumes the role of supervisor two days a week."

"That's good. Please have her relieve you right away."

"Alright, but can I ask why?"

"A man we would like to question has not been heard from in two days."

"Yes, but that's not so unusual for him."

"Perhaps, but your efforts to contact him at his residence throughout the morning have been unsuccessful. Now he is late for his shift, and by your own admission, that is unusual."

"Yes, that's true."

"Well Mr. Connor I believe that the two are somehow related, and the possibility of that merits further investigation on our part. Therefore I would like you to accompany us."

"Alright, but where are we going?"

"The three of us are going to visit his residence."

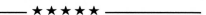

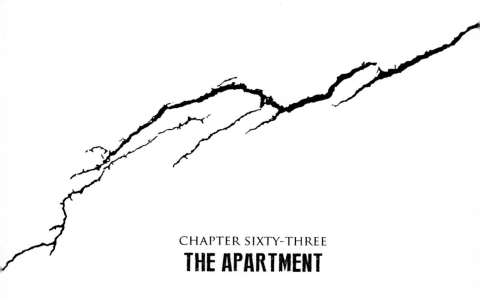

CHAPTER SIXTY-THREE
THE APARTMENT

With assistance from the property manager and his pass key, Travis followed the two FBI agents into the missing supervisor's apartment. The main room was cold and nearly completely dark with only the minimal external daylight permeating through the thick curtains. However a faint illumination of an electrical light source could be seen coming from somewhere around the corner to the left, so before turning on additional lighting, one of the two agents asked the property manager, "What's over that way?"

"That's the kitchen and a small eating area."

After instructing Travis and the property manager to retreat a few paces into the hallway and not touch a thing while doing so, the agent moved cautiously in the direction of the kitchen with his Glock sidearm drawn. Then he called out, "This is the FBI, is anyone there?"

Not a sound was heard in reply, and he soon knew the reason why. Peering around the corner, he could see a motionless body slumped into an open refrigerator with a large pool of blood, other liquids, and various spoiling foods on the surrounding vinyl flooring. There were

242

pieces of glass from bottles of beer and egg shells within the mix too, as several of each had broken when falling from the dislodged shelves. While his partner provided cover from behind, the agent flicked on the light switch for the kitchen and dining areas to ascertain if anyone else may have met with a similar fate. Then with that area secure from threat, he and his partner began a systematic sweep of the entire apartment. Upon completion they asked Travis to once again not touch anything while in the apartment, but they needed him to re-enter and identify the only body, alive or dead, that had been found.

That process only took a few seconds, as the victim's body had fallen forward in such a way as to see one entire side of the man's face. With a quick look Travis said, "Yep, that's him. There's no doubt about it. Now aside from the obvious answer of him being shot and killed, what do you think happened?"

"We don't know at this time sir, but this man's demise may help to support your theory about the helicopter. His obvious murder suggests a possible connection between him and the helicopter that was parked at your airfield on Friday night. It would appear, at least preliminarily, that he was killed by someone that he didn't suspect would do so."

"Why do you say that?"

"His body position mainly. The man was obviously shot in the back twice while attempting to get something out of the refrigerator, but a person wouldn't be doing that if they felt any danger. If I had to guess, I'd say that he was killed by someone that he had invited into the apartment. And whoever that shooter was, they made sure of his death by putting one more bullet into the base of his skull. This has the look and feel of a deliberate hit that was probably done to keep him quiet about something, and that something may have been his knowledge of what transpired on Friday night."

"Alright, I can follow that. But if that's true, then what happens next?"

"I will call the field office in a moment to initiate an investigation into this entire situation. It will begin almost immediately, and will include interviews with others who were on duty in the control tower Friday night. One or more of them may have noticed something that could help."

Less than an hour later, a forensic team from the FBI was dusting the apartment for fingerprints, and checking for hairs or any other evidence that could help to solve the mystery. Although many things were ultimately discovered with regard to his less than sterile existence, there was nothing that would reveal the identity of the dead man's short term guest during the first hour of November fourteenth. Courtney was careful during her brief moments in the apartment, and as she had been expertly trained to do so, was quick and clean with her post murderous departure from the scene. Using her own handkerchief when turning down the thermostat to slow her victims decay and minimize the smell that would arise from it, Courtney assured that she would leave no fingerprints on that wall component or any of the light switches when darkening the apartment. Then by placing the cloth back into her purse next to her silenced weapon after closing the locked front door behind her, she had effectively become a ghost.

CHAPTER SIXTY-FOUR

TUESDAY MORNING BRIEFING

T hree hours after his eight o'clock return to duty at the White House, agent Heath Bishop remained at the ready no more than ten feet from President Harwell. His orders were to be at the beckoned call for whatever might be needed of him by the commander and chief, while also being sworn to secrecy with regard to all that he heard during various briefings and phone calls. Among many other things, agent Bishop had learned throughout the morning that there were still no nations or factions within the Middle East region claiming responsibility for the attacks upon the three American military academies. In addition, no radical Muslim influenced group in any part of the world had stepped forward either. To agent Bishop that seemed rather strange, because history showed that in nearly every case of terrorism, be it large scale or small, there had always been somebody claiming the credit for said action.

Although his primary duty was to help protect POTUS from harm, as a Secret Service agent Heath Bishop was required to remain abreast of international news and current events that could directly or indirectly impact how that protection was provided. Heath had been trained and programmed to root out those who intended to remain in the shadows while hiding from the reach of civilized authoritative justice, and was therefore overly suspicious during the current unprecedented global silence. As such, even with the absence of a true enemy or suspect to pursue, agent Bishop would continue to search for clues that might unravel the mystery behind who had attacked America.

Throughout all of the morning briefings, nothing much of anything was revealed other than frustrating excuses as to why little had been ascertained about the terrorists. But then one briefing finally provided something that a case might be built upon. Concluded roughly fifteen minutes earlier than the one currently underway, the content had held the focus of agent Bishop ever since. He thought about what had been conveyed, and how he, with the approval of the President, had become involved in the conversation when both of them were informed of something interesting occurring in Mexico.

The director of Homeland Security had come into the oval and said, "Mr. President, The Mexican authorities have informed us that eighteen people scheduled for a flight from Mexico City to Sau Paulo Brazil on Monday morning were unaccounted for. When they learned of such a large number missing from the flight, the authorities did a little digging. What they discovered was that eighteen more people under different names had missed an earlier flight of Sunday morning from Chihuahua to Mexico City."

President Harwell had replied, "Alright, so that's a lot of people to not make their flight on one occasion, let alone two. And you're probably thinking that two flights on consecutive days with the same large number of missing passengers must somehow be more than just mere coincidence."

"Yes sir, I am."

"Alright, so assuming this information could be some sort of a lead, what significance do you place on the number eighteen?"

That was when agent Bishop joined the conversation by saying, "Excuse me Mr. President, but I may be able to help with that question."

Turning toward the man, President Harwell responded, "Alright Heath, go ahead."

"Yes sir. We know that fourteen parachutes were used during each of the attacks, and eyewitness reports confirmed that a helicopter retrieved those of the Colorado Springs site. We also know that the perpetrators were subsequently transferred into two small corporate jets for their escape southward into Mexico."

"That's right Heath."

"Well sir, the numbers do add up. If we assume one pilot in each jet, and a crew of two for the helicopter, then combined with the fourteen jumpers we get eighteen."

"The director of Homeland Security broke back in by adding, "Sir, that is a logical conclusion, and it was our assessment as well. I also have additional intelligence from Mexico that could help to clear things up."

"Very well director, please proceed."

"Yes sir. The Mexican authorities have reported locating the remains of two small jet planes that have burned off the end of a remote airstrip well south of Chihuahua. Not much of either smoldering aircraft remained by the time their investigation began, and the small amount of debris indicated that the jets had virtually melted under an intense heat for several hours."

"So they believe that the jets crashed while attempting to land?"

"Yes sir they do. The belief is that the two planes overshot the runway and rolled into the desert causing something to ignite within them."

"And what do you believe?"

"That explanation of the planes crashing seems plausible sir, and I have no reason at this time to believe anything different."

Agent Bishop then spoke up again by asking, "And what about the bodies director? Have the authorities located any sign of human remains?"

Although insulted by the way a mere secret service agent had become involved in such a high level conversation, the director was smart enough to know that agent Bishop was highly regarded by President Harwell. Therefore he showed no emotional response to the younger man for having the temerity to suggest that the bodies hadn't been taken into account. With a measured tone he replied, "That's a good question agent Bishop, but nothing has been found as of yet. The fire was so intense that any bodies within would have been burned beyond all recognition. It will take more time for a forensic team to determine if the eighteen people we have been discussing were all lost in the crash."

"How about transport vehicles, eye witnesses, or something like that?"

"What are you implying Bishop?"

"Excuse me Director, but if the airfield with the crash is well south of their intended departure point of Chihuahua, then how were they going to get from one location to the other? There must be a truck or something out in the desert for their use!"

"Bishop, if there was, it's long gone by now."

Sensing the possible tension that could arise during a continued exchange, President Harwell said, "Alright, thank you director, and please keep me posted on any progress that is made. Now, is there anything else that you would like to add?"

"Yes Mr. President. I have also received a report from the State Department. They have been in contact with the airport authorities in Sau Paulo, and agreed to pay a measure of cash for the information that was received.

"Very well, and what did they uncover?"

"It seems that the eighteen missing people on the flight from Mexico City were also intending to catch another international flight within hours after arriving in Sau Paulo."

"Indeed. And where were they attempting to go?"

"Their flight was bound for Syria sir."

CHAPTER SIXTY-FIVE

THE POWER COUNCIL

Samuel Tillman had gladly driven over to Austin solo on Tuesday afternoon, as the road trip gave him some uninterrupted time to think. The hotel of choice for the next two nights would as always provide the necessary amenities to keep him comfortable, and that included an exceptional service of pressing his suits. As he had set up a meeting with number three for Wednesday morning at nine o'clock in the man's office, Samuel felt that a freshly pressed suit would help give the position to which that man had ascended a deserved level of respect. He also intended to enjoy a meeting and subsequent lunch with number five a few hours later, but the lunch aspect was contingent upon if her schedule would permit the time. If not, they would still have the meeting in her office, and in either scenario his pressed suit would extend the same courtesy of respect toward her position.

When entering the outer office of number three, a staff member rose to her feet and said, "Good morning Mr. Tillman. It's nice to see you again, how are you today?"

"I'm fine thank you, and it's nice to see you too. Is everything well with you and the family?"

"Yes it is thank you, and we just learned that my daughter and her husband in Fort Worth are expecting a baby in late May."

"That's wonderful news. Please give them my best wishes and my hope that the child will be born into a better nation than the one that exists today."

"I certainly will Mr. Tillman, and thank you. Now let me see if the Governor is ready to receive you."

"Thank you."

Less than thirty seconds later, the Governor of Texas emerged from his office with extended hand, and said, "Hello Samuel, punctual as always I see."

"Good morning Governor. I find punctuality to be a trait that serves me well in business of any nature, and besides, I know you attend to many issues that can create a rather tight schedule."

"Well thanks for recognizing that I'm actually doing something while in this office Samuel. There are some that don't believe as you do, and I'm not sure that I could ever convince them otherwise."

"Governor, many of those people just haven't been paying attention. I wouldn't worry about them too much."

"Fair enough Samuel, fair enough."

After moving into the Governor's private office with the door closed behind him, Samuel asked, "So how is everything on your end number three?"

The Governor responded with, "Right on schedule number two. The Lieutenant Governor has been briefed under an oath of secrecy, and he understands his role."

"That's very good number three, and the appropriation of funds?"

"Number seven will get whatever finances he needs should we move forward."

An hour later, Samuel stood and emerged from the Governors private office after their lengthy and productive conversation. They had covered all that needed to be discussed for the moment, but there was much more to be done. Keeping that in mind, he turned his attention to the upcoming meeting with number five.

With some time to kill before his eleven o'clock meeting, Samuel decided to take a little head clearing stroll. He was soon at the edge of the University of Texas campus, and although he would never admit it publicly to any of his fellow Texas A&M Aggies or his youngest grandchild Savanah, the supposed enemy territory was pleasant to view. After a few minutes Samuel began his return to the State Capitol complex, and then entered the outer office of number five. His conversation with the staff member who greeted him was less relaxed and familiar than what he had experienced in the Governors outer office, and this man offered up no personal family information.

With the initial awkward greeting behind them, the staff member said, "Mr. Tillman, Madam Speaker has been able to clear her schedule for you. I have been instructed to inform you that after she meets with you in her office, she will have time for your planned lunch in the House of Representatives dining area."

Samuel replied, "Well thank you, that's good news. Besides, I didn't want to eat in there all by myself."

The relatively new staff member, who had met Samuel Tillman only a few times during recent months, was momentarily baffled by the statement. He was unaware that an ordinary civilian, no matter how wealthy or connected, would be allowed to eat in the formal dining area without being the guest of an elected house member. He soon learned however, that Samuel Tillman was no ordinary civilian.

Emerging from her office, the Texas State Speaker of the House gave her guest a hug and said, "It's always good to see you Samuel. How are Victoria and the family doing?"

"They are well Madam Speaker, thank you for asking."

"And how is Savanah?"

"She is doing well. Kyle and Ashley are optimistic, as test results have shown promise. But we all know that she is far from out of the woods."

"Well Savanah is a fighter. Now, shall we step into my office?"

Once behind closed doors with instructions for her staff to not interrupt unless the building was on fire, the two old friends could address each other by their designations of number two and number five as given by the organizational head. They began their discussion of what was to come, when certain events would transpire, and the continued role of number seven. At the conclusion of the hour long meeting Samuel said, "Very well, that should cover everything for now. We can communicate with each other after today via number twenty three once more of the situation is known. For now, we must focus on becoming fully prepared in the event that we can move forward."

After a nice lunch with her old friend that included a brief visit by several House of Representative members, number five walked with him back toward her office and said, "Well Samuel, this has been great, but I must get back to work."

In re-establishing their respective cover, Samuel replied, "Very well Madam Speaker. I must get back to my responsibilities as well. Thank you for the time, and please give your family my best."

"I will Samuel, and may you, Victoria, and the rest of the family have a happy Thanksgiving."

CHAPTER SIXTY-SIX

SATURDAY, NOVEMBER 21ST

Samuel, like on every other Saturday during college football season when his beloved Aggies played on the road, had arranged his schedule so that nothing would interfere with him watching the game on the giant holographic screen. Seated in his favorite chair with Savanah on the nearby couch, they waited for the game to begin. Although security measures had most surely been heightened in stadiums throughout the country, which probably included the temporary absence of parachute drops into them, Samuel was glad to see that scheduled games for this day were actually taking place.

As the final regular season game of his favorite team unfolded, and it appeared that Texas A&M was on its way to a rather easy victory, Samuel smiled at Savanah and said, "Well, even though we can't win the conference championship, at least the team is playing better than they did last week."

She nodded with a smile and replied, "Yes they are grandpa. They played really bad last week, but I heard you say that at least they lost to a really good L.S.U. team."

"That's right sugar."

"Well I want to watch us beat them next year if we are good enough?"

Recognizing that the most important aspect of her statement was the optimism that Savanah expressed about being able to watch a game in another year, Samuel replied, "I'm sure the team will try real hard, and you and I can watch them win together."

As she turned back to watch the current game, Samuel mulled over what information he received earlier that morning. Number twenty three had communicated to him that she had received a report from numbers thirteen and seventeen less than an hour prior. They had both stated that things appeared to be leaning in the right direction, but deliberation for both sides of the argument had been hotly debated for the entire week. As a result, nothing would be determined until after Thanksgiving. Then she continued by stating that she had received a rare report from number twenty nine the previous evening. His information conveyed that military leaders were posturing for a retaliatory strike, but he had no idea if and when such an event would transpire.

Samuel was intrigued by the information on all counts, but especially from number twenty nine. His cover was deep and established more for the future than at the present time. But still, he had been in his current capacity for more than a year, and the reason that the man rarely reported was because he had to be more cautious about communication than other operatives. His mention of the military leadership posturing for retaliation was good news though, as it implied that at least some of the diversionary bait with regard to Syria was being looked at and nibbled upon.

CHAPTER SIXTY-SEVEN
THANKSGIVING

A t the Tillman family home, the usual Thanksgiving activities were underway with football to watch and anticipation of the oncoming feast. However during this particular year, the collective mindset of the nation toward the day had taken on a different feel. Although sympathetic to how others may perceive the day of thanks, or lack of it, in the current worrisome climate, Victoria Tillman had no desire to take on the collective emotional weight of the country. She was not however completely unfeeling toward the situation, as she had known firsthand what the sudden and unexpected loss of a child or other loved one could do to a person. With this in mind, Victoria's idea was to expand her normal traditions of the day, so she mandated that each person sitting at the table verbally list a few things for which they were thankful before any food would be served.

Ms. Holloway, who for many years in order to fully enjoy the time with her adopted family had been relieved of her duties by a catering staff on Thanksgiving Day, was first to volunteer. She stood with raised glass and said, "I'm thankful for many things each and every day that I'm with the Tillman family, and hope to continue for as long as my body and mind will allow me to do so. You are all so special to me, and I have enjoyed watching each of you blossom into the people that you have become. It's always a pleasure for me to see most of you together for a holiday or any other occasion, and I'm especially thankful that none of you have ever treated me as anything less than a member of your family."

When the elderly lady sat back down next to Samuel, he smiled in her direction while she in turn smiled across the table toward Savanah. Then Samuel looked down the length of the table toward Victoria and asked, "Well that may be difficult for any of us to match, but we must try. Who would you like to go next dear?"

Before Victoria could reply, Savanah spoke up by asking, "Is it alright if I go next grandpa?"

Noticing the smile on the face of his wife that the youngest member of the family had brought forth, Samuel reached for Savanah's hand and replied, "I think that would be wonderful sugar, so please, go ahead."

Rising to a standing position she began with, "I'm thankful that almost everyone in our family is here tonight, because we don't get to spend the whole day and then eat together very often. I'm also thankful for my brother and cousin that aren't here, and I hope that Jason and Beau are safe and with friends."

Seated next to her daughter, Ashley said, "That's very nice honey, you did great. And thank you for thinking of Jason and Beau."

When everyone else in the family had spoken, Samuel stood and completed the mandate of his wife. He said, "You have all expressed wonderful thoughts, and I too am proud to have all of you, including Ms. Holloway, as members of this family. I must also say that we are all incredibly thankful for the one thing that has not been mentioned, as Savanah is beginning to get better. Now with that said, I can only add one more thought."

After a long silence while those around the table pondered her ongoing battle, Savanah reached for Samuels hand and asked, "What else did you want to say grandpa?"

Smiling down at her precious face with those big green eyes he replied, "Well Savanah, I think that we should eat!"

Later that night after Savanah and the two teenagers of the family had gone to bed; Samuel sat enjoying another piece of pie and a strong cup of coffee. Then looking at those within the room, he asked Victoria, "Have the three caterers left?"

"Yes they have. You can speak freely."

"That's good. I wanted to say something before when verbalizing what we were each thankful for, but with the kids at the table and the caterers possibly within earshot, I thought it would be prudent to wait until now. Aside from all that was mentioned before dinner, I'm also thankful for the safe return of many who have given of themselves in behalf of the cause and the overall plan. Our friends in Mexico have provided a portion of our group with protection and safety while in their hands, and I have been informed that all eighteen of them have now completed their undetected passage back into Texas and are without harm. To that end, I would also like to express my thanks to the continued successful progress of the overall plan."

To that several coffee cups were raised into the air as a show of respect for those that Samuel had mentioned. Then Victoria replied, "That's nicely said dear, and I liked that part before dinner about Savanah too."

CHAPTER SIXTY-EIGHT
TUESDAY, DECEMBER 1ˢᵀ

T here had been much deliberation over the matter at hand since President Harwell addressed the joint session of Congress on the Monday following the attacks, and it would surely continue on into the future. Of course the most vocal in favor of the proposed declaration were the Senators and House of Representative members from the three states that had been attacked, but they were certainly not alone. Although none of the elected officials from New York were in office twenty-five years prior when the September eleventh terrorist attacks had occurred, the memory of that day still burned within each of them. Now with the psychological wound reopened by another terrorist attack upon their state, those elected men and women led the charge that screamed for vengeance. With the same level of distain toward the perpetrators of the current attacks, and an understanding of pain over the former attack as neighboring Washington D.C. had also been impacted that day, Maryland stood resolute in her intent for vengeance as well. Not shying away from the flood of emotion, Colorado was ready to go fight on the soil of whoever was determined to be ultimately responsible. Many other members representing states from coast to coast within both wings of the Capitol had similar feelings of a need for retribution, but they were not as vocal as their brethren who were leading the charge. Sympathetic to what had transpired; those men and women also understood that land in their own states had not been attacked. Therefore the impact upon the people they represented could in no way be considered equal. Aside from a few of the current cadets, active military personnel, or random civilians that were in attendance at any of the sites, no citizens of their respective states had been killed or injured.

On the flip side of the argument, there was a belief that no military action or economic sanctions should be carried out until more defining evidence was gathered. It was true that during the now more than two weeks since the attacks, several pieces of evidence had been obtained which could point toward Syria in the Middle East as the underlying culprit. Unfortunately, much of that evidence was tenuous at best and some maintained that it wasn't as concrete as many believed. That voice of doubt was minimal within the chambers, but some still cautioned of advancing upon Syria without truly knowing what the United States would be getting itself into. There was the memory of what had transpired after the attacks of September eleventh to consider, as that administration had been able to prey upon the American citizens and their elected officials after the attacks by pushing through a plan with ulterior motives while everyone was still raw with emotion. In time it was discovered that the war which ensued had been ill advised, as those ultimately responsible were not the same people that the administration wanted to wage war against, nor were they even in the same Arab country. In essence the American people had been misled by the highest office of leadership into financially backing a military incursion for another purpose under the guise of retaliation, and many within the military ranks had been killed or severely injured as a result. With that in mind, a few Federally elected officials questioned the wisdom of voting for a war against Syria in the current climate.

It could be argued that both sides of the debate had a strong case, but as the vote was due to be cast in short order; there was no more time to do so. The answer to the question of America's next move would be answered soon enough, and some felt that opportunity had not come quickly enough. In the minds of the American public, each member of the Senate had been granted more than enough time to reach a decision on the matter. First there was the initial nearly two full days after the attacks before President Harwell's address and the entire five day week of deliberation that had followed. Then there were the nine days of the Thanksgiving Holiday break, and finally the following Monday when back in session to choose a side. Now on this Tuesday morning any final thoughts on the matter had been delivered, so as the last few elected officials entered the chambers to take their seats, the process of the nationally televised vote could finally commence.

Seated comfortably within his family room while staring at the giant holographic screen, Samuel Tillman asked those members of the family in attendance if anyone wanted to wager on how lopsided the vote would be. Mason, who had returned from El Paso on the day before Thanksgiving, smiled and said, "Sure dad, what are you thinking? Something like an eighty to twenty margin?"

Before he could answer, Victoria elbowed her husband gently in the ribs and said sharply, "Don't you answer that question Samuel!"

To which Samuel looked at her playfully and replied, "You are no fun."

Victoria returned the smile with another softer elbow while reminding everyone to ignore her man as this was a potentially serious moment in history. Then as the verbal votes from each man and woman on the Senate floor were tallied and listed in the upper right hand corner of the screen, Samuel smiled. Before long it was obvious, the United States would soon be going to war against Syria.

At that moment President Harwell was also watching the same live coverage while inside the oval office with his Chief of Staff Christopher Westin and Mrs. Dawson. All three were intently focused on the early results and the obvious direction to which the vote was headed. Meanwhile agent Bishop, still on special assignment for the president, stood no more than twenty feet away. While hearing and viewing the results of the incoming tally, his stomach churned with discomfort. Although he would never outwardly express toward the President his displeasure in the now obvious pending declaration of war, he could also not agree that it was the proper course of action to pursue. For Heath Bishop, something about the entire chain of events just didn't quite add up to condemn Syria with such ease, but he couldn't put his finger on why just yet. Although aware that his feelings were irrelevant because he possessed no power to stop what would soon be set in motion, agent Bishop resolved within himself that he would continue to dig for a reason to eventually halt it.

CHAPTER SIXTY-NINE

MONDAY, DECEMBER 7TH

Armed with news of the event he had witnessed via the television broadcast of December first, Samuel immediately contacted number twenty three that morning to set the wheels for the next phase in motion. She had in turn contacted numbers three and five who were also aware of the declaration of war against Syria, so that they could begin the necessary process. The result of that process was now currently underway, and for the moment, had been met with resounding agreement and success. Unaware of how each individual state conducted business within their respective legislatures, Samuel Tillman could easily be considered as normal with regard to most citizens' general lack of knowledge in that area. He, like most, was simply too busy or concerned with other important matters involving impact upon their own lives, so keeping tabs on how any of the other forty-nine states did things was generally irrelevant. However, when it came to his native land of Texas, Samuel understood the political structure quite well and had been manipulating it to his or the organizations advantage for years.

In the structure of Texas, the Lieutenant Governor presided over the Senate wing of the legislative branch. With assistance from the current Governor who Samuel and the organization had helped to retain office on more than one occasion, the former was pleased to help in any way that he could. A special session of the legislature, far later into the calendar year than on most other such instances, had been decreed and was currently in progress. Under strict secrecy number three had previously briefed the Lieutenant Governor of his intent, and as such an unusual event transpired within the agenda of the special session. Samuel Tillman was granted the right to do something that few, or perhaps no others, had ever done by addressing the Texas State Senate as nothing more than an ordinary everyday nonelected citizen. In so doing, he brought forth to them an extremely important message, and Samuel's words resonated with clarity and conviction among the elected body. Now that he had completed that task to a round of applause, Samuel would attempt to do the same in the House of Representative Wing. However before he could do so, house protocol demanded that he be announced to the Madam Speaker and those of the elected body to which she presided over.

Moving toward the lectern, Samuel smiled at his old friend number five and shook her hand while saying, "Thank you Madam Speaker for the opportunity to stand before you and the other representatives today. I'm truly honored as a proud Texan to be in these hallowed halls."

"You are welcome Mr. Tillman, and I thank you as well. We the members of the Texas State House of Representatives are honored to have you speak today. Please proceed when you are ready."

With that Samuel began what he felt would unify the assembly as it had done a short time before to members of the Senate. Public speaking had never been a shortcoming for Samuel in the business world, and he treated this particular audience as if he were conducting just another of those countless meetings. The only difference between each of those past and that of the current address, was the magnitude of the content. In the process of his address to some that he recognized as people the organization had helped over the years, he noticed that many were nodding in approval. They too had been fed up with many of the actions which had occurred during recent days, weeks, months, and years, and were therefore ready to turn a new page.

Perhaps the most galvanizing portion of his riveting address in both wings of the Capitol Building was when Samuel stated, "You must all understand that this is our most opportune moment to strike with conviction. The entirety of our nation's government structure, the military industrial complex, and the vast majority of American citizens, are out of nothing more than misguided habit looking toward the Muslim world in the Middle East as the perpetrators of the most recent terrorist attacks. They have been socialized to believe that if anything of negative impact transpires within the United States, or in the entirety of the globe, then it must be the fault of some extremist Muslim faction or group. That socialization within some American citizens had been brewing for months or years before, but the events of September eleventh a quarter century ago brought it to a head. Osama Bin Laden as the unquestioned leader of the Al-Qaida terrorist movement claimed credit for the attacks upon New York and Washington D.C., and thus the mold was cast. As time went by and his power diminished, those same blameful Americans, whose numbers continued to grow, searched for a new source to bear the brunt of their dismay. Of course the media outlets, ever ready to create an over sensationalized story about anything that they could get their claws into, were glad to oblige. Throughout subsequent years they brewed up a fear of the Taliban, ISIS, and others under a range of labels. Then as each one faded into yesterday's news, another magically came along. The sickening perpetual cycle included the Bishri Zwar, as they became the new horrific threat to peaceful existence in our time just two short years ago. Now I'm not here to claim that any of those fears and blame weren't justified in some respect, as the actions of those radical groups more than demonstrated their malicious intent when given an opportunity. No my friends. I'm here to convey for those of you who aren't already aware of it, that the American society in general, and frankly many others around the globe, look first to the Middle East for blame whenever the mood strikes them. That reflex will never end as long as it is fed by fear, and we can use that fear to our collective advantage. Those growing number of self-proclaimed important figures in Washington, the military leaders, and so forth have absolutely no intention of looking inward for a domestic source with regard to what transpired at each of the three military academies. In addition, those fear mongers don't possess the guts or intestinal fortitude to accept such a reality even if it were somehow discovered to be true. Therefore it is reasonable and prudent at this time for us to proceed with our ultimate plan, and as the door of opportunity is wide open, we must act upon that and move through it within the next two weeks. I have no doubt that our opponent will be caught completely off guard when we swiftly and decisively do exactly that."

At the conclusion of Samuels address, number five stood to applaud. She was joined by many others in rapid succession, and he waved with pleasure in their direction. Then as he turned to depart, the Madam Speaker said to him, "Thank you Mr. Tillman. You have just conveyed so strongly what many loyal Texans have believed for years. As an elected representative body we have much work in front of us, and I shall contact you personally through my office to inform you of any decision that this quorum arrives upon."

CHAPTER SEVENTY

WEDNESDAY, DECEMBER 9TH

Seated in his private office at four in the afternoon, Samuel Tillman concluded his conversation with number twenty three. As had been agreed upon with number five during their meeting and subsequent lunch prior to Thanksgiving, number twenty three was relaying vital information from her that could lead to the next phase of the overall plan. Although certain specific details had been omitted for the time being, such as how or by what level of ease the forwarded news had been achieved, for Samuel and those in the organization the message content was fantastic. After slightly more than forty-eight hours since his address to each wing of the Texas State Legislature, the all-important question had been acted upon and answered with clarity.

After setting the burn phone down and moving from his office into the kitchen area, Samuel found Victoria and Ms. Holloway engaged in a typical conversation over a cup of coffee. Then he asked, "Are any of the grandchildren around?"

Victoria replied, "No Samuel, Jennifer and Blake are both at basketball practice. Although for Jennifer, it's really more about watching the boys practice than anything else."

"Yes, that young lady definitely needs some focus."

"Jennifer is focused Samuel, just not on what you would want."

"Alright Victoria, I hear you. So then where is Savanah?"

"Ashley has her at physical therapy, so none of the grandchildren will be home for more than an hour."

"Very well, then I have some news."

"Alright Samuel, what is it?"

"It is done. I don't have specifics, but I just concluded a conversation with number twenty three who was passing along the confirmation from number five."

"It's done? Well that happened faster than you anticipated."

"Yes it did. I asked them to be decisive one way or the other by the end of the week so we had ample time to prepare, but they surprised me by actually doing so. The information number five passed on included that the deliberation had moved swiftly with little resistance during the time since I departed. A motion for a vote was put forward early this afternoon and then seconded immediately. Apparently they concluded less than an hour ago."

"That's wonderful. So what's next?"

"I will be on the burn phone in my office several more times this evening I'm sure. I have instructed number twenty three to initiate contact with each of the five operatives in Washington D.C., and she should be able to reach all of them rather quickly. Perhaps number twenty nine will be a challenge in that regard, but at least for the time being, he is the least important of the five to receive and respond to my message."

"And what is that message?"

"I asked number twenty three to deliver a simple message from me that the light is now multiple shades of green for their requirements within the Capitol Building and on the opposite side of the

Potomac. The operatives will in turn each contact me for discussion and instruction. After those conversations, numbers eleven, thirteen, seventeen, and nineteen will begin their final preparations for what they hoped would be coming, and exactly how to play their part in the grand orchestration. Each has been well prepared, but they will still have questions of me as to the specific date and precise timetable when their actions should commence. Beyond that, I need to contact number seven directly and inform him of his next assignment as well. Numbers three and five have done their part for now by helping to guide things along in the proper direction, and they each showed an extreme level of expediency for any level of government during the process. But now because of what will happen due to the wheels being set in motion, number seven will need as much time as possible to prepare for the upcoming responsibilities of those he commands. So as I said, it will be a busy night for me."

Ms. Holloway, who had known for decades to never speak of certain business matters that were discussed within the Tillman mansion, then asked, "It sounds as if you could be missing out on the family dinner tonight. Would you like me to make something for you to eat right now Mr. Tillman?"

"Thank you for the thought Ms. Holloway, but I will probably just get something out of the fridge when I'm through with the business at hand."

CHAPTER SEVENTY-ONE
FRIDAY, DECEMBER 18ᵀᴴ

On Friday morning, the last such work day before the annual two week holiday break for Christmas and New Year, United States Republican Senator Nathan Pearson of Texas arrived at his office earlier than usual. Although no special need to do so existed, as every document of significance generated during his tenure had already been either secretly shipped back to Texas or destroyed, the Senator wanted to enjoy a peaceful cup of coffee alone in his office. His intent was possible only because the entirety of his staff and interns had also been dismissed from duty the previous evening. If nothing had interfered with their schedule, they were already bound for Texas on early morning commercial flights.

Sitting patiently at his desk in quiet contemplation, Senator Pearson visually scanned his office for the final time while reflecting upon his years in Washington D.C. and what he had done to deserve such a splendid opportunity. Then when the latest in the line of burn phones rang to break the silence, he quickly answered it with a simple greeting of, "Good morning. This is number eleven."

In response he heard, "Good morning to you as well number eleven. This is number three."

"Yes sir."

"Are you ready?"

"Yes I am. Our final session before the holiday break will begin in less than an hour, and I will make the announcement shortly before we adjourn this afternoon."

"Excellent, have you spoken to number seventeen?"

"Yes I have, and she will address her collective at the same time with number nineteen close at hand."

"And number thirteen?"

"She will stand with me when the time comes."

"That's excellent. I know that you will all do a splendid job, and I look forward to seeing each of you soon."

With that Senator Pearson ended the call, placed the burn phone securely within the inside breast pocket of his suit jacket, and exited his office. Before moving toward the Senate chamber, he felt that it was important to enjoy one final walk through the Capitol Rotunda. As the centerpiece of the United States Capitol Building, the room directly beneath the dome was magnificent. It housed a series of individual statues positioned in a circular perimeter, with each representing one of the fifty states. On the ceiling above, there was also a massive painted mural depicting a brief history of the United States. While gazing upon the varied artwork for several minutes, the man who had just been re-elected the previous month to a fourth term in office pondered all that had, and hadn't, been accomplished by the elected body during his years in Washington. Then after strolling into the Senate chamber, he met with a few colleagues for a moment of lighthearted conversation before taking a seat at his desk.

At three that afternoon, Senator Pearson knew that the time was at hand and stood to be recognized. After receiving a signal that his intent would be honored, he turned to catch the eye of his counterpart, Democratic Senator Denise Walker of Texas, and gave her a nod. They both realized from observing the actions of the day, that no one in their present company had any clue as to what was about to transpire. Then a moment later a voice from the head of the chamber said, "At this time Senator Pearson of Texas is recognized."

Rising from his chair and moving toward the nearest lectern, Senator Pearson then replied, "Thank you sir. I'm pleased to see that most of this elected body is in attendance on this final day of session before we recess for the holidays. The past several weeks have been difficult to be sure, with long hours and much discussion over the central question of going to war yet again based on a conflict with some party residing in the Middle East. As each of us seated here represents a portion of those who have been tasked with that daunting decision, I must say this. I understand that the vote of this Congress has carried to indeed pursue such a course of action that will once again plunge this country of ours into a war. This will not be the first time that our military forces will be required to engage with an oppositional force in that region of the world, and mistakes have been made in the past as to our grasp of the true resolve of similar forces. I fear that we are headed down the path of overconfidence again, and in that spirit I ask once more that this collective forgo such an undertaking. I have voted against the action of war, and shall continue to stand by that decision. I ask in near desperation for many of you to stand with me if this country is to avoid another irresponsible decision of going to war against Syria. Such an action by this nation and its military will undoubtedly have serious economic implications for many years to come!"

As residing President of the Senate, Vice President Sutherland interrupted briefly to ask, "We all understand your conviction in this matter Senator, as you have expressed it now on numerous occasions, but what are you hoping to accomplish at this time? What's done is done Senator. The vote has been cast and passed resoundingly by this elected body to declare war against Syria, and this nation shall do so."

Knowing fully that his well-rehearsed speech would be received negatively, and also aware that it would have made no difference in the overall plan even if the response had miraculously been positive, Senator Pearson smiled inwardly. Then he calmly replied, "I understand that sir, but this nation will do so without the great state of Texas."

"What are you talking about Senator? You are more than aware that just because you privately disagree with how this Congressional body has voted, you don't have the right to refuse acting accordingly with regard to that legislation. In the event that you have somehow forgotten that fact Senator, then let me remind you of something. We stand as a nation in this decision to go to war."

Now smiling outwardly, Senator Pearson replied, "With respect sir, that's not exactly true. Senator Walker and I have been given specific instructions for this day from our Governor and the Texas State Legislature."

After several long seconds of silence, Vice President Sutherland finally replied, "Alright Senator, would you care to elaborate by informing us of those instructions?"

With Senator Walker having joined him at the lectern, Senator Pearson said, "Yes sir. Our instructions are to inform you and this elected body that Texas is now formally declaring its intent to once again become a Republic of its own."

Not believing what had just been heard, the Vice President asked, "I'm sorry, I don't think I understood you. Could you please clarify your statement for me Senator?"

"Most certainly, as we don't want any misunderstanding in this matter. When the New Year commences at midnight on the morning of January first, two thousand twenty- seven in the Central Standard Time zone where our great capitol city of Austin is located, Texas shall sever all ties with the United States. At that moment we shall once again become the Republic of Texas, and will not adhere to the laws or restrictions set forth upon any of the other forty-nine states as mandated by the federal government. Additionally, we shall not become involved by way of financial resources, or the use of our military personnel, in any of the actions taken by the United States with regard to hostilities toward any foreign nation."

Now even further amazed by what he had heard, the Vice President leaned forward from his chair and asked, "Excuse me Senator Pearson, and please understand that this question is being asked due to my many years of knowing you and the concern over your declaration and what feelings those words have brought forth in me. But are you insane?"

"I understand that some may think so, but I can assure you sir, I'm quite sane."

"Then why would you, as a multi term elected official for the state of Texas make such a ridiculous declaration?"

"Sir this is a legitimate declaration that needs to be taken seriously by you and the other Senators here with us today. You should be made aware that as we speak, our counterparts within the House of Representatives chamber at the opposite end of this grand complex are currently submitting an identical declaration. Texas is indeed separating from the United States in two weeks, and as you have already professed to me just moments ago, what's done is done. Texas maintains a sincere desire to separate from her parent country as cleanly and smoothly as possible on the date that has been proclaimed, and we fully expect this government to aid in any logistical matters within that process."

"Have this government aid Texas in the process? You are sadly mistaken Senator Pearson. I don't believe that this country would allow such an action to transpire at all, let alone with our aid. On a more personal note, if you truly believe in what you have just said, then I think it would be best for you to seek professional help. You need to speak with a doctor who is trained and well versed in how to best cope with illusions of grandeur."

"There is no call for that course of action sir or for the slander upon my faculties that you intend by suggesting it, as it is you who are mistaken. I would like to remind those of the Senate who may not be aware, but Texas is the only one of this nations fifty states that has the absolute right by treaty and law to separate from the main body of the United States if, and when, she so desires. Let my words, under the direction of those who I represent, serve as a formal declaration. Texas desires to exercise that right at this time and become an independent Republic once again. Do you understand that decree sir, and will you for the record formally acknowledge that the words of said declaration were directed at you and this elected body at such a time as when I had been formally recognized by you to address them."

Still flabbergasted by the events of the past several minutes, Vice President Sutherland tossed his hands into the air in disbelief. Unfortunately, he had no choice but to carry out one of his many sworn duties. With that in mind, he stood and replied, "Very well Senator, for the record then. Yes Senator Pearson, the United States Senate hereby acknowledges and accepts that the state of Texas has proclaimed a desire to separate from these United States in order to form a Republic unto its own."

With those words now embedded into the official record, Senators Pearson and Walker breathed a collective sigh of relief. Then Senator Pearson closed his speech with, "Thank you sir. Now that I have proclaimed the intent of Texas, my colleague and I understand that we will not be a part of this collective governing body after today. Therefore I must say this. I personally harbor no ill will toward any of you, and have very much enjoyed working and deliberating with each of you over a myriad of subjects. I sincerely hope that some of us can remain friends in the future even though we will be citizens of different nations. I wish each of you and your families a safe and joyous holiday season. Thank you for your attention."

The timing of the declaration had been perfect, as there would be little time for the federal government structure to act upon said intent before it came to fruition. Both Senators from Texas knew that Congress would adjourn for two weeks in less than an hour, and when reconvening after the New Year began, could then debate a course of action to pursue with regard to Texas. Additionally, several new members of Congress in both legislative wings would be sworn into office during those first days of 2027. Combined with the war against Syria, they would face two hugely significant issues possibly before learning where the washrooms were located. By then, Texas would no longer be required to adhere to the whims of what those deliberations brought forth. With a broad smile on each of their faces, Senators Pearson and Walker gathered up their personal belongings before exiting the stunned and silent Senate chamber.

 ★ ★ ★ ★ ★

CHAPTER SEVENTY-TWO
THE UNIMAGINABLE CALL

S eated in total dismay, Vice President Sutherland watched the Texas delegation exit the chamber before glancing at the clock on the wall. Then he put his arms out to the side and correctly stated, "Well, we are due to adjourn in less than an hour for the holiday break, and I obviously have an important call to make before then to President Harwell. He will need to know immediately of what has just transpired, and in spite of any leaks of information from this and the House of Representatives chamber that are most assuredly already taking place, the President will want to hear the details directly from me. Now with that said, I can't imagine that any of you have something on the agenda that will trump what we just heard. Therefore, I suggest that while I excuse myself to call President Harwell, you all use what limited time you have to begin a constructive discussion about Texas that will surely have an impact on the holiday season for all of us. If no one is opposed to that course of action, then I believe that would be more beneficial than introducing a new topic or sitting around staring at each other."

Although openly invited to do so, there wasn't much discussion regarding the Texas declaration. The larger concern was still the upcoming war with Syria, but the Texas issue would add a wrinkle to the plans for that war. The military leaders, including those who were temporarily filling the two vacated Joint Chiefs positions, had already developed a plan based on the declaration of December first. That plan called for the deployment of additional Army and Marine Corps troops to the Middle East with an up scaled presence of both the Air Force and Navy in the nearby eastern Mediterranean. With much of the equipment and troops already in the repositioning phase, an all-out assault had been slated for just after the New Year. Without a doubt when word of the declaration of Texas got to the news media, there would be a feeding frenzy. Both issues would be of significance to the collective mindset of the nation's citizens during the final days before Christmas and well beyond. How much of a negative impact upon the upcoming holidays would occur as a result was an unknown factor, and the depth of such was yet to be determined.

While standing to speak on the phone with President Harwell, Vice President Sutherland decided there was no way to sugarcoat the news. Therefore he said quite plainly, "Sir, I'm afraid I have some bad news. If there's a good way to inform you of this then it currently escapes me, as Texas has decided to part ways with the United States!"

After a long silence, President Harwell replied, "Mr. Vice President. You and I have known each other for several years in the political arena, and have enjoyed many laughs throughout that time, but this is not a good day for jokes."

"I understand that sir, and believe me please, this is no joke."

After another long pause which included his chief of staff Christopher Westin entering the oval in a hurried and somber state, the President said, "You're not kidding are you Mr. Vice President?"

"No sir. I'm afraid not."

"That's preposterous. When did this happen?"

"Their formal declaration was received by me less than ten minutes ago."

"They gave you a formal declaration? Couldn't you refuse it?"

"No sir, not legally anyway. I can explain in more detail if you wish?"

"Well who presented the declaration?"

"Senator Pearson."

"I want you to speak with him privately to find out what the hell he is trying to do. Then I want both of you at the White House as soon as possible to meet with me in the oval, and you can explain to me in more detail then. Do you understand me Mr. Vice President?"

"Yes Mr. President. I'll get him over to the White House as soon as possible."

When Vice President Sutherland finished the less than pleasant phone conversation with his boss, he prepared to visit Senator Pearson. Waiting in the outer office before he could begin the quest, a trusted aide intercepted him. With a touch of panic in his voice, the aide announced, "Sir, I'm sorry to report this. I have some news that could be of interest to you."

Looking at the visibly distressed young man, he replied, "Alright, but I'm in a hurry at the request of the President. What is it?"

"I have already attempted to contact the office of Senator Pearson thinking that you would want to speak with him, but no one answered the phone. So I walked over there to find out why, and found the offices empty."

"You mean that he let his staff go early today. That's not so unusual. If it hadn't been for the bombshell that Senator Pearson dropped on all of us, you and the rest of my staff would be leaving in a few minutes as well."

"No sir, that's not what I mean. Everything is gone except the furniture. There are no paintings, personal effects, nothing but a lone coffee pot and a single cup."

"What? Are you serious?"

"Yes sir."

"What about his files? Did you see any?"

"No sir, all the file cabinets have been totally cleaned out and the computer equipment is gone."

Realizing what may have happened, the Vice president quickly ordered, "Have someone check the offices of Senator Walker right away to see if she has done the same. Then have someone else contact the house wing. I need to know if that delegation from Texas has indeed given an identical declaration of separation, and if so, did any of those representatives also clean out their offices."

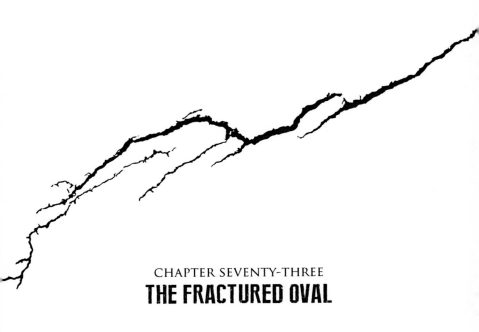

CHAPTER SEVENTY-THREE

THE FRACTURED OVAL

With the White House Chief of Staff and Mrs. Dawson by his side, President Harwell began to wonder what had been keeping his running mate for so long. More than two hours had passed since Vice President Sutherland was ordered to report to the oval office with Senator Pearson in tow as soon as possible, and there had been no contact from either man. Even though Washington D.C. can have difficult traffic at times just like any other major city in America, a motorcade transporting high level elected officials was immune to such inconveniences. The two men should have been standing in front of the President by now, and their absence made an already fatigued and overwrought Jordan Harwell more disagreeable than usual.

Turning to Mrs. Dawson, he said gruffly, "Give his office at the capitol another call please."

As she left the room to place the call, Christopher Westin who had entered the oval office in a state of shock while the President was first hearing of the declaration commented, "This is not normal for the Vice President to be so inconsiderate of you."

"That's true Chris, but these are not what one would call normal times."

"Even so sir, he should have communicated with you at some point during the past two hours."

Fully aware of that obvious fact, and now short on patience, President Harwell replied, "Well that can't be changed now can it? However, with everything else going on during the last five weeks and the bombshell of two hours ago, I will reprioritize my thinking and speak with the Vice President about your perceived inconsideration of me. Will that make you feel better?"

The Chief of Staff had no reply, and silence fell over the room as he felt nothing could be said in the current moment to ease the tension. Then Mrs. Dawson returned to say, "Mr. President, I'm told that the Vice President is in route to you now."

"Thank you Mrs. Dawson."

As if on cue, Vice President Sutherland strode into the oval office a moment later, but he was alone. Throughout much of the two hours he had been involved with some investigating at the Capitol Building, and what he discovered was not good news. With trepidation in his voice the man out of nothing more than force of habit said, "Good evening Mr. President. Sorry to keep you waiting."

Now with sarcasm entering the mix of frustration and anger, President Harwell replied, "Now what could possibly be good about this evening Mr. Vice President? And where is Senator Pearson? I instructed you to bring him to this office with you."

"Yes sir, I know you did, but he can't be located."

"What do you mean?"

"Sir, his offices have been completely emptied out with the exception of the furniture and what was nailed down. The same goes for Senator Walker and every member from the House representing Texas. Everything is gone sir, and they all scattered like the wind."

"That doesn't make any sense, you must be mistaken."

"Pardon me sir, but I'm not mistaken. Senator Pearson is gone from the hill, and neither I nor any of my sources can locate him. He and the others probably vanished to avoid an inquisition."

"An inquisition, is that what you think he was going to face?"

"Well being ordered to bring him here certainly gives that impression sir."

"And you think that is improper?"

"I didn't say that sir."

"Then what are you saying?"

"I'm attempting to understand why you wanted me to bring him here sir."

"I wanted to talk some sense into the man of course, why else?"

"So you thought that you could somehow change his mind about the Texas declaration? That makes no sense to even try sir, as this is a serious move on their part that could not have been taken lightly. No sir. You can't view the intent of Texas as something that was just conjured up within the last few hours of today. I doubt that you, me, or anyone else, would have the power to change their mind."

Infuriated that his underling would speak so candidly while in the presence of others, President Harwell began to clinch and unclench his left hand. Then he replied, "Well that may be Mr. Vice President, but I do have the power to attempt it. Now remember this. Don't be condescending or impertinent towards me in this office ever again. Is that clear?"

"So am I to understand that having a viewpoint somehow different from yours is deemed to be impertinent Mr. President?"

"In this case yes, and don't ever do so again or I will find myself another running mate for the next election. There is no way that this nation is going to lose one of its states under my watch. Is that understood?"

Not wanting to further aggravate the man, he replied, "Yes sir, perfectly."

"Good! Now I don't care what resources you need to tap into, legal or otherwise, but I want Senator Pearson in this office as soon as possible!"

Vice President Sutherland stood in momentary disbelief to what had been said. Was his boss truly concerned over the welfare of the nation, or how a fracturing of it during his administration would paint him in the history books? Suddenly the Vice President realized that there was a huge question beyond those of the war with Syria and the Texas declaration for him to personally consider. Did he want to be Jordan Harwell's running mate again in the re-election campaign of 2028, or did he want to make his own bid for President against the man? Pushing the thought aside for the moment he then responded, "Yes sir Mr. President. I understand and will bring Senator Pearson here to converse with you. Now will there be anything else sir?"

"No, just find him!"

Agent Bishop stood silent less than twenty feet away throughout the entire exchange, and continued to do so after the Vice President had left the oval. He had not been asked for any insight during the evening, nor did he feel this was the proper time to step forward and offer it. What he did find intriguing was one specific comment that the Vice President had made while the President was too enraged to absorb it. Texas just didn't conjure up their intent during the previous few hours.

CHAPTER SEVENTY-FOUR
NEW YEAR'S EVE

T he grand catered event had been spectacularly festive for several hours, and was easily outshining that of the July fourth barbeque. Much like that event, security at the front gate had been diligent in their efforts by crosschecking names of each guest invitation with photos that Samuel and Victoria had provided for them. The two security men that Samuel had with him in Manhattan the previous New Year's eve were in charge of the entire detail of men and women that were also patrolling the grounds. There were some major figure heads with regard to the future of Texas present, and Samuel didn't want to take any chances with their safety or identity.

Savanah and the other two of Samuel and Victoria's grandchildren who were still of minor age had taken a nap for a few hours during the earlier portion of the evening. All three had reluctantly done so at the instruction of their parents and Ms. Holloway, so that they could be awake and alert for the massive celebration that was yet to come. Although she had been defeated in her attempted protest, the most vocal reluctant voice was that of Mason and Courtney's daughter Jennifer. She, at the advanced and ever wise age of fourteen, believed that she could endure and stay awake into the early hours of the morning. Ms. Holloway knew that in truth, the now fully blossomed young lady just didn't want to be labeled as a non-adult any longer.

When the clock then struck midnight in the central time zone of the United States of America to usher in the year 2027, the point had been well proven. As a joyous roar rose up from all those assembled within and around the Tillman mansion, Savanah, her brother Blake, and her cousin Jennifer where all awake and alert to witness it. Based on the decree to Congress nearly two weeks prior, it was now official. Texas had just moved into a new era, and was once again a Republic of its own. There would be numerous challenges in the future without a doubt, but those involved in the structuring of a new nation were confident that those challenges would be met with character. Glancing around the room, Samuel internally identified many of the major players within the organization who had been instrumental in carrying out the elaborate scheme. Numbers three, five, seven, and twenty three had done a masterful job with each of their respective responsibilities both before and after the attacks from their offices in Austin. The first three of that list would all have new roles to assume as of this day forward, while number twenty three would remain as the focal point of secretive communications.

Additionally, those from their former positions in Washington D.C., numbers eleven, thirteen, seventeen, nineteen, and twenty nine had performed exceptionally well. For number twenty nine, his undercover role would continue on indefinitely, as his position of authority within the Pentagon could provide valuable intelligence for Samuel and Texas. As for the other four that had done their duty in Washington D.C., their knowledge of those within the leadership structure of the United States would prove to be quite valuable as time moved forward. Perhaps there was a place for some of them within the hierarchy of the new Texas government structure, but that would be determined at a later time. Not to be forgotten was the work of number thirty one in El Paso. Through the advance scouting, planning, and organization of assets, that pivotal region of Texas appeared to be in good hands as his duties would escalate in the coming days and weeks.

Of course those without numbered designations such as the six attack planners, the three men responsible for the operation of the training facility, and Samuel's two remaining sons Kyle and Mason could not be ignored. Each in their own way had done what they could to look at every conceivable angle, and then identify how to best achieve success that would assist in the completion of the ultimate goal. Without their efforts, the work of all the numbered operatives wouldn't have amounted to much more than wishful thinking. Pleased as a father for how each of his sons had performed throughout the entirety of the year and before that, Samuel also laughed inwardly with the knowledge that neither had a clue as to their wives being granted numbered status while they had not.

Finally there was the support staff for all those he had mentally listed. Although perhaps uncertain of exactly where their respective contacts and superiors had fit into the grand structure, they also deserved some credit for their collective effort. No matter who it was, or what part they had played, it was nice for Samuel to see many of them present to celebrate the birth of a new nation. Each of those individuals had been part of a larger team that helped to create it, and therefore they should enjoy the spoils that went with it.

Realizing that the time had come to do so, Samuel seized the opportunity to acknowledge those who had given so much to the success of the overall plan by offering his sincere and heartfelt thanks. While clasping Victoria's hand for temporary balance, he climbed up onto a sturdy table and said loudly, "Can I please have everyone's attention for a moment? I have an announcement to make."

It took several minutes, and a few repeated calls for their cooperation, before all those gathered on the large outdoor patio area settled down, but they eventually did. Then a flow of those who were in the family room or other portions of the mansion made their way outside while Samuel remained patient. He didn't begin speaking until after he heard Kyle report, "I think that's everyone from inside the house dad."

Then with his booming voice he replied, "Thank you Kyle. Now ladies and gentlemen, I'm sorry to interrupt the festivities for a moment, but I wanted to thank everyone for the part that each of you played in the overall plan. Some of you have not met before this evening, but I can assure you, that was never intended to be a personal slight upon any of you. Please know within your heart that you played a role in re-establishing the independent Republic of Texas, and that tight security measures were vital in attaining that goal. Personally speaking, I shall never forget those efforts that each of you put forth. I have also spoken with number one earlier today, and was asked by the leader of our organization to convey thanks and congratulations to each of you. Additionally, I was asked to provide a special acknowledgement on behalf of number one to those brave men and women who were members of the air and ground assault teams at each of the three target locations. I believe it's proper at this moment to ask that each of those brave souls raise their hand so that we as the collective can recognize them and give them the well-deserved round of applause that is due."

After having done so, and hearing a various round of shouts such as "Here's to those on the front line" and "Long live Texas, may she never forget you", everyone took a drink from their glass to salute each member of the assault teams.

Then Samuel asked for quiet again and continued, "Ladies and gentlemen, I would also be remiss if I didn't add one other thing. All told there were twenty-eight men who parachuted into the eastern stadiums, along with twenty women who provided them with ground support by retrieving them and driving them safely back to Texas from New York and Maryland. Another group of five women and two men were responsible for both ground and air operations with regard to the fourteen additional men who jumped into the Colorado stadium for the western attack. Although three drove back home from their mission, the other four of that support group were responsible for flying them away from the stadium toward Mexico. Then that collective of eighteen persons needed to wait within the borders of our foreign neighbor for more than a week until the opportune moment to re-enter Texas from the south was presented. Within that entire assault and support force of sixty-nine persons, there was only one injury that required medical attention, and one death. The man who died was part of the Annapolis team, and internal injuries caused shortly after the attack were the cause. His teammates with him in the escape vehicle provided the best medical attention they could offer under the circumstances, and asked repeatedly if he wished to go to an emergency clinic. Knowing that such an action could potentially expose the entire operation, he bravely declined. With no family members to assume the care of his body, it became an extreme honor for both me and Victoria to have his remains put to rest upon the property of this ranch next to our youngest son Chance. Now I must ask one final thing from everyone. As it was proper for all of us a moment ago to provide applause and a toast to those brave souls who came home to us, it is also fitting and necessary that we share a moment of silence in the memory of the one who has fallen."

After a long moment in which no one seemed prepared to be the first to raise their head or utter a word, Victoria took the lead. She broke the deafening respectful silence by saying, "Thank you for your attention everyone, and for paying proper respect where it was due. Now please, let's all get festive again by celebrating what that man felt was a cause worth giving his life for."

Throughout the course of the next few hours, and the several kisses to celebrate the New Year and the newly reformed nation, Samuel and Victoria were interrupted from time to time by well-wishers from various factions of the organization. One such interruption was made by the approach of a man with a bandaged left arm. Then when reaching with his right hand, he said, "I would like to offer my thanks for the evening Mr. and Mrs. Tillman, but especially for what you said about the man who fell after Annapolis."

Reaching to shake the man's outstretched hand, Samuel replied, "You are welcome sir, and how is your arm?"

"The doctors at Baylor were able to save it from just below the elbow as you can see, and they say that was due largely to the care that I received during the drive back from Annapolis. Unfortunately the bullet had shattered the bone in my upper arm, so chances are that even with my soon to be fitted prosthetic, I will never again have the full range of motion that I previously took for granted."

Victoria intervened by stating, "I understand that the past seven weeks have been difficult for you young man, but please don't despair. The medical staff at Baylor is top notch, so you keep working hard on the rehab and your new Republic will cover the expenses."

Turning to his hostess, the man replied, "Thanks for the encouragement ma'am, and I will work hard to regain mobility so that I may be of further service to Texas."

Then Samuel added, "Regardless of your range of mobility, there will always be a place for you in the organization sir. Texas will need to defend herself from a foreign enemy at some point in the future, of that I have no doubt. When that day comes your services will be welcomed, if not on the front line, then perhaps in the role of an instructor."

"Thank you sir, that's kind of you. Please know that I shall be ready for the call."

The man departed to try his luck with a woman near the pool who had caught his eye, and having watched her initial reaction to the bold advance, Samuel stated to Victoria, "I think he may stand a fair chance with her."

After a few moments of uninterrupted celebration, number forty seven, who had done such a tremendous job with organizing the Pennsylvania aspect of distribution for the eastern attack plan, approached to offer both his congratulations and heartfelt thanks for the evening. After a kiss of good cheer on the cheek from the hostess, he looked at his host Samuel and offered his hand. Then in the grip of a firm handshake he said, "I await my next assignment from you with great anticipation number two."

"You have done well number forty seven, and another assignment with regard to the defense of Texas will come your way shortly my friend. For now, Victoria and I wish you a happy New Year. Now please continue to enjoy the evening and the birth of our Republic with many of our other good friends."

Ms. Holloway had moved through the mass of people to stand at the side of Samuel and Victoria shortly before they concluded their conversation with number forty seven, and after the man moved away, she was offered champagne by Samuel. Then Victoria leaned closer to her husband's ear so that only he and Ms. Holloway could hear, and quietly asked, "Do either of you think that number forty seven, or anyone else for that matter, has put the sequencing together yet?"

Samuel responded quickly, "That's difficult to know with any certainty, but I haven't heard any conversation about it. I don't personally think anyone has, as most of the numbered operatives and those beneath them probably assume that they just haven't been introduced to each of the other numbered players as of yet. For security purposes that remains a good and useful thing, and it would be beneficial if that belief were maintained within the ranks for as long as possible."

Then after reaching for her glass, Ms. Holloway added, "I suppose that's true Samuel, but someone is bound to figure it out eventually. Now let's toast again to our new nation?"

With a clink of their collective glasses, Samuel and Victoria leaned in close to kiss the opposite cheeks of their longtime confidant. Then Victoria softly whispered into her ear, "We would be honored to toast to our new nation with you my dear friend."

Samuel was once again quick to follow suit by stating, "And if I may be so bold as to say so, I promised you that with concentrated effort we could achieve our desired goal."

Looking up at the man she had known for nearly fifty years since he was a brash teenager in possession of an unwavering ambitious thirst, Ms. Holloway replied, "Yes Samuel, you were right. And thank you for everything."

With an even closer lean for security sake, Samuel added, "You deserve many thanks as well number one. It was you who devised the foundation of this intricate and brazen plan years ago. Because of that early vision along with strong effort and conviction, all of our collective dreams have now become reality."

KEEP READING FOR
AN EXCLUSIVE SNEAK PEEK OF

LONESTAR RISING

TO THE REPUBLIC: BOOK TWO

BY
KURT WINANS

COMING SOON

CHAPTER ONE

NEW YEAR`S MORNING

President Jordan Harwell had briefly taken part in the obligatory New Year's Eve celebration at the White House with family members and a few close friends, but he needed to paste a false smile on his face while doing so. The attempt to showcase his more relaxed and festive side for those around him was a nice gesture, even if it lacked sincerity. Most within the room understood that the heavy weight on the Presidents heart and mind exceeded what any of his predecessors may have experienced during the first thirty minutes of a new calendar year. A somber mood was justifiably in order for the man, but was in no way a reflection upon the action of those currently in his presence. Instead the focus of his troublesome state was centered on an event that would take place very shortly, and there was nothing that he, or anyone else, could do to stop it.

After being gently reminded by a staff member when the time reached twelve thirty, President Harwell excused himself from the State Dining Room and made his way toward the oval office. Faithful as always, his longtime personal secretary Mrs. Dawson was waiting for him in the outer office. In spite of the late hour, she had insisted on being present to assist in any way possible when the hour of inconceivable change would occur, and neither the President nor his Chief of Staff Christopher Westin could change her mind.

At that same instant, the countdown of minutes as opposed to hours, days, months or years of waiting for 2027 neared its completion within the Tillman mansion and the surrounding grounds. That grand party to usher in the new Republic of Texas was in full swing, but before Samuel Tillman could relax and revel in the current moment, he had first addressed the pressing business of the night. During a conversation a few hours earlier with two of his guests, numbers three and seven, Samuel had been assured that the necessary personnel were in route from the various staging areas to what would become their duty stations. In anticipation of what an easily predictable President Harwell and his Washington D.C. brain trust would attempt during the transitional moment of midnight central standard time, Texas would be prepared with a counter move.

Having moved into the oval office with Mrs. Dawson mere strides behind, President Harwell was soon joined by Christopher Westin and the Director of Homeland Security. When the latter of the two arrived at twelve fifty, the President asked, "Is everything ready to go director?"

"Yes Mr. President. I should receive a call of verification within five minutes after midnight in Texas."

Via the global media, the internet, or by the time honored traditional form of face to face human communication, the separation of Texas was not even close to being secretive information. Therefore a simple plan was developed in Washington D.C., and if Texas really wanted to go through with their declaration of independence from the United States, then they would begin by dealing with a potentially huge challenge in the very first moments of their existence as a new Republic. By decree from President Harwell, as delivered through the Director currently in the oval office with him, all personnel from the

United States Customs and Border Patrol were to abandon their posts along the various crossing points of the Rio Grande River that defined the border between Mexico and the United States. It was believed that with no authoritative presence along the border to halt it, a flood of illegal immigrants would enter Texas during the upcoming hours and days before the new government could respond to the action. Any problems that might develop as a result of that supposed onslaught were of no concern to the United States.

On paper the plan seemed like a good idea, and those in Washington felt that they could catch Texas napping while in a celebratory mood. Unfortunately that wasn't the case. With the necessary funding to thwart such a plan having been assured weeks before from Samuel and number three, the commanding general of the Texas National Guard had his subordinate officers move superior numbers of troops to within fifty yards of all the established border crossings. In a choreographed maneuver from Brownsville and McAllen at the southern tip, to Laredo, Eagle Pass, and Del Rio further to the northwest, the troops arrived at said positions less than five minutes before midnight. Much further to the west, beyond the region of Big Bend National Park, the same was true at the more remote crossing in Presidio. The only portion of the state where the troops wouldn't achieve that last minute element of surprise would be in the extreme western tip near El Paso, as the synchronized arrival would be early. With that small chunk of Texas being within the Mountain Time zone, the first of what was hoped would be many treaties between the Republic of Texas and the United States was agreed upon. The terms of that quickly drawn up treaty were that no portion of Texas would separate from the United States until the year of 2027 began, so the transition wouldn't take place for another hour. Nevertheless, the troops in that region would be ready to assume their new posts when the time came. There were no illusions within the ranks of stopping those who would use desolate locations for illegal entry throughout the coming hours and days, but then again, it wasn't a major concern. In that regard, the border patrol that was in the process of abandoning their posts hadn't always been effective either. No, the point of this maneuver was larger in scope. Texas wanted to show the United States that it was prepared to defend her borders, southern or otherwise.

As the clock struck midnight and the male and female border agents moved away from their posts, superior numbers took their place. Then when the time reached five minutes after one in the oval office, the Director of Homeland Security received the first of many calls. What he heard was not good news, and he braced himself before delivering it to President Harwell. After turning toward his boss, he said, "Sir, I'm afraid the results are not as we would have hoped."

"What do you mean director?"

"They must have seen our plan coming, because Texas National Guard troops were ready to step into position as our agents abandoned their posts."

"What? Did they do that at all of the crossings?"

"I have no confirmation of that yet sir, but it would seem logical that if Texas was prepared for our plan at one crossing, then they were prepared at all the others as well."

At the Tillman mansion north of Crockett Texas, the commanding general of the Texas National Guard was in the quietest place he could find. With use of the latest burn phone given to him by number twenty three, he dialed the number for the officer in charge of the Brownsville crossing. After hearing the good news from him and conferring with several other officers at the other locations, he rejoined the party to locate Samuel. Then he said, "You were right number two. Harwell had the customs and border patrol agents abandon their posts. It's good that we were ready for that."

Looking at his old friend with a wry smile, he replied, "Well, up to this point Harwell has been predictable with his actions, but things may not be as easy in the future. Now is everything secure?"

"Yes it is. None of my officers reported having any trouble with the outgoing agents, and we have successfully assumed control of all border crossings with the exception of those near El Paso. If the events of a short time ago are any indication, we will have those secured as well in less than an hour."

"That's good news. As usual, you have done exceptionally well number seven. I don't know how the organization would have been able to accomplish some of our objectives throughout the past year without your efforts."

"That's kind of you to say number two."

"Not at all number seven, you deserve thanks. Now please let me refill your glass so you can rejoin the celebration."

ABOUT THE AUTHOR

Kurt possesses a spirit of adventure, which drives his thirst for experiencing new places and activities. He maintains a love for the great outdoors, and enjoys traveling whenever his schedule permits. One of his favorite activities is hiking in the clean mountain air, where the tranquil locations provide him with an opportunity to develop characters and storylines for his books. Kurt currently resides in Northern Nevada, where he and his wife have lived for more than a decade.

ALSO AVAILABLE FROM
KURT WINANS

THE NEW WORLD SERIES

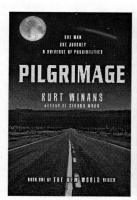

ALL TITLES AVAILABLE IN
TRADE SOFTCOVER & EBOOK

CPSIA information can be obtained
at www.ICGtesting.com
Printed in the USA
FSOW01n0615040817
37099FS